THE TRUTH ACCORDING TO EMBER

BERKLEY TITLES BY DANICA NAVA

The Truth According to Ember
Love Is a War Song

LOVE IS A WAR SONG

DANICA NAVA

BERKLEY ROMANCE
NEW YORK

BERKLEY ROMANCE
Published by Berkley
An imprint of Penguin Random House LLC
1745 Broadway, New York, NY 10019
penguinrandomhouse.com

Book design by Jenni Surasky
Title page art: Guitar © DinosArt / Shutterstock

Library of Congress Cataloging-in-Publication Data

Names: Nava, Danica, author.
Title: Love is a war song / Danica Nava.
Description: First edition. | New York: Berkley Romance, 2025.
Identifiers: LCCN 2024047268 (print) | LCCN 2024047269 (ebook) |
ISBN 9780593642627 (trade paperback) | ISBN 9780593815434 (ebook)
Subjects: LCGFT: Romance fiction. | Novels.
Classification: LCC PS3614.A923 L68 2025 (print) |
LCC PS3614.A923 (ebook) | DDC 813/.6—dc23/eng/20241004
LC record available at https://lccn.loc.gov/2024047268
LC ebook record available at https://lccn.loc.gov/2024047269

First Edition: July 2025

Printed in the United States of America
1st Printing

The authorized representative in the EU for product safety and compliance
is Penguin Random House Ireland, Morrison Chambers, 32 Nassau Street,
Dublin D02 YH68, Ireland, https://eu-contact.penguin.ie.

For my mother, who raised me on country music

AUTHOR'S NOTE

This book deals with emotionally difficult topics, including loss of family members, addiction, and reference to the term *savage*. Any readers who believe that such content may upset them or trigger traumatic memories are encouraged to consider their emotional well-being when deciding whether to continue reading this book.

LOVE IS A WAR SONG

THREE NEARLY NAKED MEN DRENCHED IN OIL GYRATED around me, their *things* barely covered in short tan-hide loincloths that dangled between their thighs. When I was a little girl dreaming of being a singer like Norah Jones, this was not what I had pictured.

I pictured myself onstage wearing a flowing gown draped over the bench of a gorgeous grand piano as I slammed the keys and crooned into the microphone. I could hear the crowd in my mind singing along to the songs I poured my soul into, cheering as I hit the bridge and shook my hair all over the place.

Instead of all that, I was filming my first solo music video off my debut album, dressed in next to nothing, stumbling through choreography with male dancers wearing even less, lip-synching the words to a song where I have zero writing credit. Not that I really wanted credit for the majority of the chorus being just "oh oh oh" approximately three billion times, but writing was what I thought I did best. When I was finally given this record deal, I had thought some of the songs I wrote and demoed for my label would make it onto my album. None of them did. With autotune, anyone could be a pop singer, but I was a songwriter first. Sadly, that was not what the executives who controlled my career believed.

The only reason the powers that be were investing so heavily in this music video *now* was because of the success of my leading single, "I Need a Warrior Tonight." They weren't sure a Native American pop star could enter the charts. I not only debuted my single in the *Billboard* Hot 100, but the song has stayed there for nine weeks. Now we were all scrambling to get this music video shot and released to capitalize on the success. Afraid the market attention would turn, and this would all be a waste. It couldn't be. I wouldn't let it.

There was one thing I never called myself—a dancer. Yet here I was trying to remember the intricate choreography while wearing five-inch stilettos to get one flawless take. My concentrated face looked too "angry," and we had been filming this sequence for what felt like hours. A slippery, toned butt cheek of one of the dancers whacked my hand, causing hysterical laughter to bubble out of me. I missed my cue mouthing the words to the next line of this absurd song and I knew I was about to get in trouble.

"Cut!" Fabian, the most coveted music video director in the world, threw his headset as he stormed over to me. My song cut off and was replaced with silence.

I tried to stop laughing, I really did. But then one of the dancers, I think he said his name was Justin in rehearsal, wiggled his eyebrows at me from under his bad wig and headband. It was so ridiculous, that—paired with his super white teeth contrasted with the orangey-bronze spray tan—it was too much. I hadn't come across a whole lot of Native Americans in Hollywood, but I knew this was too over the top to be thought of as authentic.

This was bad. Fabian's forehead vein was throbbing under his flowing locks with bleach-blond highlights.

I snorted, which sent me into another fit of giggles and then I started hiccupping.

"Avery! This shoot is already three days over budget, and you laugh and refuse to take me and my vision seriously," he whined with his French accent.

"I'm...I..." My laughter was so unhinged I couldn't even form an apology.

"You mock me!" He threw his clipboard onto the floor and charged out of the studio warehouse where we built the forest set for my music video.

I should've run after him and apologized to smooth things over. My label pulled many strings to get him to direct this video last minute for *me*—a "gamble." Everything needed to be perfect. But I couldn't catch my breath and my eyes started to water. When was the last time I laughed so hard? That deep-belly, feel-it-in-your-toes laughter? I needed it. It had been guest performances on late-night talk shows, meet and greets with radio stations across the nation, and grinding in the studio to make sure each track hit like this single, for the past month.

It was all hard work and no sleep—many creative differences and debates on my sound and look—and it all culminated in this music video. And I looked like I belonged in a western created by Adam Sandler. My skimpy tan-hide two-piece bikini had feathers and beads hanging down like a flapper's fringe. This shit was funny, and it wasn't supposed to be. In my delirious, lack-of-sleep state, it all seemed to be in bad taste. But everyone who held the purse strings loved it. I just wanted my own music video, and this was how I could get it. This was the launchpad for my solo career; I needed to pay my dues before I could take more creative control with my music.

Before I could extract myself from the group of barely covered male dancers, I heard a noise that could raise the dead.

My mother.

"Avery!" The shrill was accented with the echoing clicks of her Jimmy Choo stilettos on the concrete floor of the downtown Los Angeles warehouse where we were filming. My mom was a yard away from me and on reflex, my shoulders hunched over in anticipation of the earful my momager was going to unleash on me.

"Why did I just see Fabian run out of here yelling that he quit?" she asked me.

"Because I'm so tired—" *Hiccup.* I took a deep breath to try to banish the hiccups away, holding it in trying to get to ten.

"Entirely unprofessional," she hissed under her breath, and turned her cold eyes to the dancers. They dispersed faster than I could blink.

Hiccup. I giggled. Mistake. I gulped down air again.

"All my sacrifice to get you here, near the pinnacle of success, and you would throw it away because you are *tired*? With your *Rolling Stone* cover dropping so soon, one would think you'd be working extra hard to get this music video perfect. Laugh on your own time, but not on production's."

I expelled my breath. The mention of my magazine cover ruffled my feathers a little bit. She dropped it as if I didn't do all the hard work to even get that opportunity, that I haven't been working around the clock for years. "Mom, lighten up. We've been filming all week and have to have all the shots by now. Fabian even said we're over budget."

"Do you want this music video to flop?" She crossed her arms and her face looked unamused, but still perfect from her spa treatments and Botox.

I hated when she asked me rhetorical questions. Obviously, I did not want my song or accompanying music video to flop. But I also did not want to create a reputation for being expensive *this* early in my career.

"No, Mom."

"Right. So, why don't you let everyone do their jobs and make the best damn music video this genre has ever seen."

"That's stretching it," I mumbled. She caught it and did not think it was funny. She attempted to glare, but with all the Botox in her forehead and around her eyes, the effect was less than intimidating since her eyelids were the only things that could move. Still, I could interpret the subtle sign of her displeasure. A common occurrence for me, but I really did try to make her proud. She sacrificed so much for me over the years, what was a few more hours dancing?

"Sorry," I squeaked as I looked down and got back into place.

"Places!" she yelled. "Run through rehearsal, I'll bring the director back. Let's wrap this shoot strong!"

Hiccup. "Let's take it from the top one more time." I clapped to my dancers. I cocked my hip in my starting pose and counted in. "Five! Six! Seven! Eight!" We got back to work.

When filming finally wrapped, it was at 11:02 p.m. and Fabian and I were back on good terms. I mean, I wasn't thrilled the last shot filmed was of me crawling on the fake forest floor toward the camera looking as sexually suggestive as possible, but as everyone liked to tell me—sex sells.

The only crawling I wanted to do was into bed, which I couldn't do because I had to catch a flight to Dallas for rehearsal for a show in a few nights. A sold-out show opening for the hottest rapper on the planet—My$teriou$ Money. Another incredible opportunity I had earned from my time being featured (creditless) on tracks since I was nineteen.

A legendary and award-winning director for my music video and a sold-out show opening for one of the most popular artists of the century was great and all for exposure, but *Rolling Stone* was career-making and they had chosen me to be on the cover—alone.

My idols have appeared on the cover and some multiple times, like our lord and savior, Britney freaking Spears. If I had a quarter of the success with even one song to define a generation like she had, then I could die thinking that I really "made it." Even if I wasn't quite the dancer Britney is, she is the Queen of Pop.

I smiled to myself and ripped the stilettos off my feet and waddled to my robe that was waiting in my chair. Los Angeles as a city was really cool; however, filming in Los Angeles was not. The warehouse wasn't exactly a private place. It was right in the middle of downtown near the garment district and someone leaked that I was here. There was a group of fans clutching headshots of me waiting outside the warehouse with a few paps, most likely hoping to get my signature so they could turn around and sell them online.

This wasn't the worst part about my job or public status, but it wasn't the best either. Not after a grueling shooting schedule, no sleep, and a charley horse cramp in my right arch, but most of those people had been waiting out there since early this morning and the least I could do was say hi to them. I always tried my best to treat my fans right.

My trailer was located in the parking lot adjacent to the warehouse, so encountering the crowd was inevitable. I stepped into the cool night air to cheers and yelling.

"Is that Avery Fox?" a young girl asked her dad.

"Oh my gosh, it *is* Avery Fox! Deuxmoi was right! She's here filming!" a man in basketball shorts and Beats headphones wrapped around his neck said to his much shorter companion who was rocking an oversized flannel buttoned up to his neck.

"Avery! Avery!" Two teenage girls rushed toward me.

I spread my arms out to give them each a hug. My mom, who was power walking behind me, glued to her phone and oblivious to her surroundings, crashed into my back.

"Watch it!" Her voice was stern, but once she noticed the small group of people with their phones out, she plastered her phony smile on. "Well, hello!" she cooed.

"Hey, everyone!" I waved.

"Can we get a photo with you?" the teen girls asked so fast the words bled together. Their excitement was contagious.

"Of course!" I bent my knees a little, so my head was closer to theirs, and smiled for the million selfies they took in succession.

"I think you got a good one in there," I said as I straightened.

"We loved you in the Disney Channel's *A Midsummer Night's Dream: The Musical*! Your song as Helena, 'Blind Cupid,' is our favorite! It's like our 'Hopelessly Devoted to You' but for young people."

Ouch. Kids say the darndest things.

"You girls are so sweet, but nothing comes close to beating *Grease*!" I laughed. Out of all the shows and films I did as a kid, that last made-for-TV musical movie from seven years ago was my calling card. I didn't even want to do that project back then. I wanted to give up acting and focus on my music. Now my mom was going to gloat and rub it in *again* that she "told me so" and that her career strategy for me was all "falling into place." When, really, the actress they had originally cast had gotten arrested for a DUI and Disney dumped her faster than these girls asked me for a photograph.

They needed an actress with a spotless reputation, and as a dorky sixteen-year-old whose mother never let her out of her sight, I fit the bill.

It also helped that as a descendant of the Muscogee Nation of Oklahoma, I was a great "diversity" hire for the shareholders, as my agent liked to phrase it. My mother preferred to say that Hollywood "owed" us.

"Is it true you are going to be in *Rolling Stone* tomorrow?" the preteen girl with glasses and braces asked. They had to have been pushing thirteen with their awkward, gangly limbs.

"How could you have heard about that?" I put my hands on my hips in mock outrage. It was my mother who sent a tip to Deuxmoi after the photo shoot six weeks ago, trying to make sure there was public discourse about it in case *Rolling Stone* found a better option for the cover and tried to bump me.

"We can never be too careful," she had said.

No one likes to think their mother capable of extortion or blackmail, but not everyone had a mother like Harriett Fox. I'd once watched her rip a disposable camera out of an old lady's hands when I was sixteen, because she thought there might have been a photo of me on it. My mother was a control freak and my public image had to be curated and spotless. When my mother got the film developed, we discovered the poor woman had taken a photo of some sign over my head. I wasn't in any shot.

"Can I get a photo with you? You were my high school celebrity crush," the basketball shorts–wearing man mentioned unnecessarily.

"Of course!" I smiled and pretended that hearing about being crushes or "fantasies" of young men didn't gross me out. He didn't look much older than me. Less creepy than the old men who said they were introduced to my work through their daughters. He at least kept it very vague with "crush" and I appreciated it. Until he wrapped his arm around my shoulder and pretended to lick my cheek.

"This is awesome! No one would have believed me otherwise. I'm gonna throw this on IG!" He didn't so much as look up from his phone or throw me a parting glance. He got his weird photo and left.

I wish I could say that people didn't try to lick me in photos on a regular basis. I did one music video in what I would call my Miley Cyrus Era. My label wanted me to be a little edgier on the tracks I was featured on to gauge audience interest, and I licked the wannabe rock star one-hit wonder in the music video for our song together. That was an artistic choice, but for some reason, strange people thought it was permission to get their tongues up in my face.

I forced myself to smile unaffectedly and posed for more photos, even signing a notebook and a water bottle.

"Okay, that's all the time she has. We've got a plane to catch. Thank you, everyone." My mother ushered me away from the crowd, wrapping her arm around me as she directed me to my trailer. "Honestly, I don't know how you can stand hugging so many of these people. This is how we catch colds, and you cannot afford to get sick right now." She lightly scolded me, but I tuned her out. As long as my fans were happy, that was all that mattered to me.

YOUR FANS ARE NOT HAPPY." NILES, MY DESIGNATED
A&R rep from my label, said on speakerphone. His uppity
British accent sounded more nasally than usual. Frankly, I'd never
heard him this upset in my four years working with him.

My *Rolling Stone* cover story was released two days ago, and
since then, I've had the worst two days of my life. It was not the
crowning accomplishment we all dreamed it would be. It was quite
literally the worst thing the internet had ever seen. Perez Hilton
came out of celebrity-bashing retirement to drag my ass across the
For You pages of elder millennials and I was "cringe" to the entirety
of Gen Z. Those kids were terrifying with their specific cruelty.
They did one Google search and saw I didn't have a dad. There were
hundreds of comments, all iterations of *No wonder your dad never
wanted you.*

I had to turn off comments to everything, which was an even
bigger mistake because now in the court of public opinion, I was
worse than guilty. I was canceled.

One video with over one million views would be seared in my
brain forever. The content creator said "Miss Fake Pocahontas

turned off her comments, ignoring her fans and those she harmed. She's damaged her career for good. Just wait, I bet in forty-eight hours she's going to release a video apology filmed in front of a random nondescript wall. No, girl, it didn't work for Mila Kunis and Ashton Kutcher, it won't work for you. RIP, Avery. You need a brain tonight, not a warrior." She filmed it on the floor of her dorm room and burned me at the stake with that one.

Every costar and so-called friend I had made throughout my entire life and career had been releasing Notes app–screenshotted statements to their social media feeds distancing themselves from me and condemning my cover. There was a mass unfollowing. Even Logan Wilson, who played my brother in a Costner western a decade ago, blocked me. He hit me up just last week asking for tickets to my show. Now I didn't exist.

I was moving through the stages of grief. I tried to deny it was happening yesterday. My delusional and optimistic self believed it would blow over and that it was just a few loud naysayers and not a chorus of thousands of angry fans. But it went even further— several tribal chiefs were featured on rotating morning news shows from Zoom to condemn me and the headdress.

I was public enemy number one. My publicity team worked in overdrive to run a report this morning on my approval ratings compared to recent scandals and mine were lower than Hilaria Baldwin's when it broke that she really was a white girl from Boston and not from Spain. She grew up speaking English and there was no way she actually forgot the word *cucumber*. So, I had that going for me. Yay.

I was lying on the floor of my hotel room trying to focus on my breathing. I had a show in two hours to open for My$teriou$ Money. Everything was supposed to be aligning for my ascension into pop stardom, not crashing and burning.

My best friend, Chelsea, was supposed to be doing my hair and makeup before the show, but she could barely be extracted from My$teriou$'s side. They had been hooking up on and off for a couple months. This only added more stress, because if I was late, I'd get an earful from everyone, especially my mother.

I doomscrolled social media on my phone. It was once my dream to be on the Trending pane—but never like this.

#averyfoxisfake 1.2m posts
#elonmusk 730.4k posts
#bringsnackwrapsback 27.8k posts

How was my post volume higher than whatever new nonsense Elon Musk was up to? How was that fair? Certainly, the conversation and public demand to bring back McDonald's Snack Wraps was a much more interesting topic. Real change could happen there. I was pro Snack Wrap. I was spiraling, desperately looking for anything I could do to change the tide.

I switched over to TikTok and it was worse.

So.

Much.

Worse.

Someone made a filter using the *Rolling Stone* cover and a cutout hole where my face was supposed to be with the title "Pretendian Pop Princess."

Men, women, and children were using the filter to make fun of me and lip-synch my song. I was the laughingstock of the music industry and I also discovered there was a subset on Twitter called NDN Twitter—which stood for Indian—where all the Native Americans on the site came together to share memes, jokes, and discuss Native issues like enrollment, land rights, and current events affecting Indian Country . . . like me. They all hated me there too.

Being a child actor, I was used to weird rumors and conspiracy theories about me, but this was a war zone. Completely untrue assumptions and fake facts were headline-breaking news. People I had barely encountered in my life were giving interviews on how I duped them all into believing I was Native American.

An "expert" on the evening news last night even said my duplicitous nature would leave scars of trauma on all the children who looked up to me.

"This was all one large misunderstanding—" my mother said, trying to smooth things over, but Niles immediately cut her off.

"You said you were Native American," he said.

"Of course we're Indian!" my mother screamed.

I threw my arm over my eyes, using the plush hotel terry cloth robe to block out the world and the new creepy fan mail that littered the hotel room floor around me. I couldn't bring myself to open any from this latest batch. Someone in the hotel lobby posted a photo online of me checking in so everyone knew we were staying at the Four Seasons in Dallas. I'd received more hate mail in twenty-four hours than in all my years performing on Disney. This was all hand-delivered to the hotel.

"My assistant printed out a few articles and they say it's disrespectful and inaccurate to use the word 'Indian.' I'm told it's politically correct to say Native American or Indigenous," Niles continued. "We need major damage control. Can you get the chief or whatever to vouch for you?"

"I grew up in Broken Arrow, Oklahoma. I think I know what

we call ourselves, and you honestly believe I have the principal chief of our nation on speed dial?"

"Well, how do you suggest we fix this?" Niles's demand came out like a whine.

"I emailed five suggestions, but I think the best and quickest way to turn this around is to send Avery to Oklahoma to my mother."

"And are you and your mother enrolled? The discourse seems to be pretty divided online on if you have to be enrolled or not."

"I am." My mother sighed.

"Then why isn't Avery? I have no idea what that entails, but it would appease the critics if that were the case. Perhaps send Avery on an apology tour, because I have to admit, the loud arguments online don't look good, and their position is compelling."

"It's a lot of paperwork and it takes months to hear back. I just never took the time. I'm used to people taking me at my word." Her voice was quiet, full of warning.

Niles continued on as if he wasn't listening. "There are over half a million comments on Instagram calling to boycott Carl's Jr. if they don't remove her song from their new "All American" ad. Look, I'm in London on holiday visiting my mum, no one expected this, but we have to fix it immediately. Avery is a liability for Grand Records right now." Niles's voice was solemn, and the tone said more than his words.

Goose bumps flared across my skin, and I had a sinking feeling in my stomach as I sat up, inching closer to my mother and the phone perched on the small table in the suite.

"What do you mean?" my mother asked, her voice cold and quiet.

"Figure it out or we are canning the album and washing our hands of this whole thing."

The line went dead, and my mom screamed her outrage at the

phone. I had nothing in me left to cry. I'd spent the last forty-eight hours sobbing. I had received plenty of criticism in my career, but this was pure, unadulterated hatred and the most devastating part was, the criticism was justified.

I wasn't put in a feathered crown, but a warbonnet. A feathered and rhinestoned warbonnet, to be more accurate, and a matching crystal bikini as an homage to Cher's "Half-Breed" costume. My big hit "I Need a Warrior Tonight" was a hype dance track up there with Britney and J.Lo. Cher's sexy look was "all the rage," they told me. My mom had lusted over the set and didn't think anything was wrong with it. We all thought it was beautiful and clearly just a costume. We giggled, excited with the hair and makeup team about how amazing this idea was. It was edgy and not serious. Never in a million years did we think anyone would be offended. We were in on the joke. Taking back this Native maiden stereo-type. Reclaiming it.

But it backfired, because of my ignorance. It wasn't powerful. It was problematic.

I didn't know men, chiefs really, were the only ones allowed to wear warbonnets as high distinctions of honor. Nor did I know only certain Plains tribes wore these things. Things that I now knew were called *regalia*. It felt like a sad excuse, but I wasn't raised any-where near this. The only exposure I had to it growing up was the movie *Peter Pan*. I remembered seeing Peter wearing one and the lost boys and Darling kids in the feather headbands. Which, thanks to this huge mistake, I now knew was also extremely problematic and racist. So racist.

The public was in an uproar now, but my music video hadn't even dropped. That would be the final nail in my coffin. Though I was sure the music video and the album would be scrapped by my record company to save face with the public.

This company was a machine and the rich old white men at the top were never subtle about letting me know just how small and inconsequential I was within it. I never wanted "I Need a Warrior Tonight" to be on my album, period, let alone my lead single. I had brought recordings of my own songs. I wanted songs heavy on piano like Alicia Keys's. Not that I had her vocal range, but I wanted lyrics that flowed like poetry. I had walked into the meeting with Grand Records with rose-colored glasses. They offered a ten-album deal with real money on the table.

My heart sank when they laughed off my ideas. They wanted a sexy Native pop star on their roster. The people demanded diversity, and this was their plan to expand. It was clear if I said no, then they would just find someone else. I wanted to sing more than anything in this world. I couldn't let this opportunity I had worked for since I was a child go to someone else. So, I agreed to do the album their way, in hopes that if I showed up and didn't ruffle any feathers then they would let me include my own songs. If I kept paying my dues, then the next album would be all me—my vision.

I threw myself back on the floor, arms over my eyes, and wanted to sink into the carpet forever. We all fucked up, but I was the one posing wearing a feather headdress. I never stopped to ask if it was okay, or what image of myself I wanted out in the world. I blindly followed orders doing what I was told like a lamb to slaughter. Where was the public outrage for the men who controlled my future as a new artist?

"Get up," my mother ordered.

"No," I sniffled. What I wanted and needed was a hug and I couldn't even remember the last time she gave me one—at least one that was genuine. When did our relationship change to all business? My life was never normal, but this was something I needed to work on in therapy. How could I get my mother back to being my mom? I was in a crisis. I didn't need to be coddled all the time, but at this particularly distressing time, it would be nice to just have a mom, not a manager.

"Dry your eyes and get ready. Where's Chelsea? What are we paying her for?" My mother started pacing the room. "You just need to get through this performance and then tomorrow, we'll go on the offense on social media and all the daytime shows. I haven't spoken to my mother in years, but to save you I'll do it. Don't ever say I've never done anything for you."

I sat up from the floor. "What? You were serious about that? You never talk about grandma or Oklahoma."

My mother sat down on the edge of the bed and rubbed her temples.

All my life when I asked if we had family, all she said was they were dead to her. As a five-year-old, I thought that meant they were all actually dead. Then, when I was thirteen, I understood the nuance. My mother *hated* her family. When I tried to ask why, she would snap at me to mind my business and go back to studying my lines.

I never received Christmas gifts or birthday cards from this family. I did remember one phone call my mother had when I was little. I couldn't hear what was said on the other end of the line, but I heard my mother say clear as day, "Never contact us again."

That was the first and only hint I had that the family tried to connect with us. But it was just me and my mother, who was always younger than all the other moms at my auditions and worked twice as hard as everyone I knew. All I wanted was to make her life easy and to sing.

Singing was my refuge. I auditioned and acted in whatever Mom asked me to. But singing is what I did for just me. When I couldn't sleep, I'd hum melodies, riffing off my favorite songs until they became something new. When I was nervous, I'd quietly sing to myself. Right now, the music in me was dead. What if I could never sing again?

I jumped when there was a knock on the door. Texas was an open carry state, and thanks to all the creepy hate mail—thirty percent were vague death threats, and the other almost seventy were overt and explicit ones, a small portion was bizarre and gross love letters—I now needed my label to hire a bodyguard for me. And seeing as how the call with Niles ended rather poorly, I doubted they would spring for one.

My mom took one last deep breath, then walked to the door to look in the peephole. I knew whoever was on the other side was friendly, because my mom immediately unlocked the locks and opened the door.

Chelsea solemnly walked in with My$teriou$ Money on her heels. My usually chipper friend was looking at the ground, and My$teriou$ was wearing dark sunglasses inside, so I couldn't tell where he was looking, but I had a feeling it was not at me.

"Good, you're here. Let's get Avery ready." My mother's cool tone left no room for conversation as she closed the door and the security lock.

"Well, um . . ." Chelsea lowered herself onto the floor next to me as My$teriou$ dropped into the wingback chair, his diamond-encrusted chains jingling like wind chimes.

I sat up and looked at my friend. She had been my best friend for the last four years, since we hired her to go on the road with me as my hair and makeup artist. She was my ride-or-die bitch, but right now her spunk was gone. Her blond hair was twisted back into a claw clip, and she was rocking the "clean girl" clear glossy makeup, looking like she could rival one of the Hadid sisters. But her expression was bleak.

This wasn't going to be good. I turned to My$teriou$.

"You're cutting me out of the lineup." It was not a question, because I knew there was only one reason he was here.

"Avery, baby, you know I love you. These threats have my team worried, and I have to look out for the safety of everyone I employ. I was told a naked man wearing war paint broke into the venue shouting that he is your warrior, and he was going to take you."

"A man did *what?*" I've had my fair share of adoring fans who had crossed boundaries, but nothing to this extreme.

My$teriou$ waved off my concern. "The police got him and I hope he gets some professional help. We just can't have this around a show that's supposed to be about celebrating creativity. No one can guarantee your safety while you're onstage. What if they start throwing things at you?"

I hadn't thought anyone would try to actually hurt me while I was performing. What if they hurt the band or dancers? I couldn't have anyone come to harm because of me. "Yeah, I get it. My$teriou$, I appreciate you telling me in person."

"It's Sean in private." He jumped up from his seat with a speed I didn't think possible while wearing all that gold and diamonds. I stood from the floor to give him a hug.

"I'll see you after the show, babe?" he asked Chelsea.

She still sat on the floor and nodded. My$teriou$ bent to give her a kiss and then was out the door.

"Unbelievable!" my mother shrieked as I sat back down next to Chelsea. The sound popped the tension in the room.

This was just another blow to my mother and all her plans.

"Enough, Mom! There is nothing you or I can do. Everyone hates me and my song. I'm not performing tonight or any night." My voice cracked, and I had to take a deep breath to stop the tears from starting up again.

"Don't say that! This could totally blow over as soon as the internet has something else to talk about," Chelsea tried to reassure me.

"I'm reviewing the contract. They can't just cut you and let you fall into obscurity. Surely with a ten-album contract we could try something new with the next one." My mother was already at the desk and opening her laptop. "I'm not letting the mob bully us. People are all talk, honey. No one is going to try to harm you for a cover on a magazine." She put on her readers and focused on her screen.

I couldn't stay in this hotel suite with my angry mother. All I had ever wanted to do was sing and perform my songs and now that was off the table all because of a photo. My career was over and the melodies that always danced around my brain were gone. That hurt the most. My penance for being so stupid and always going along with everything.

"What am I going to do?" I whispered so that my mother wouldn't hear me. Not that it really mattered—once she was in contract land reading all the legalese she wouldn't notice if my hair caught fire.

"Maybe you can post an apology on YouTube?" Chelsea offered.

"What, like a disgraced YouTuber?" She opened her mouth to speak. "If you suggest I sing the apology, then I'm throwing you out."

Chelsea immediately shut her mouth and crossed her arms. "It was just a suggestion," she muttered.

I let out another sigh since that appeared to be all I could do at this point.

"I need to get out of here." It felt like the walls of the suite were closing in. I needed fresh air.

"I don't know, Avery. People really hate you right now. Maybe we should just get room service and watch a movie."

"Aha! They can't just drop you. I'm calling our lawyer!" my mother exclaimed, practically giddy, and picked up her cell phone.

"Nope, I'm not staying in here for that call. Let's go." I jumped up off the floor and tugged Chelsea up, dragging her to the bathroom. I shed the robe and kicked it aside. I was wearing leggings and a T-shirt.

"I think if I go with no makeup and a sweatshirt with a hood no one will be able to tell it's me."

Chelsea didn't look convinced.

I sank to my knees and dug through my suitcase that was on the bathroom floor until I found my old baby-blue sweatshirt that zipped all the way up. I've had it since I was fifteen and it was so soft from all the washes that it was like a security blanket. I zipped it up then threw Chelsea a smile over my shoulder, pretending everything in my life wasn't burning down in flames.

"Maybe take your hair down from the bun, so you can hide your face behind your hair."

"Good idea." I ripped the elastic out of my hair, shaking it loose. "Let's go!"

I snatched my black Gucci quilted crossbody bag and threw open the door to freedom.

The elevator was full of old businessmen who probably had absolutely no idea who I was, but I kept my head down and hid behind Chelsea until we made it to the lobby. It was swarming with people, young people. Shit. I grabbed Chelsea's hand and hunched over as I ran to a huge potted tree.

"This isn't looking good," Chelsea whispered.

A group of young girls wearing My$teriou$ Money tour shirts walked in front of the tree. Definitely not good. The likelihood that someone here would recognize me was huge.

"I think if we just power walk with our heads down we can make it out."

"Avery, this is a terrible—"

"Avery? Are you Avery Fox?" a loud young voice sounded from behind us.

I turned around and discovered we were hiding behind a tree that was in front of the lobby bathrooms. A young woman who looked close to my age stood in front of the bathroom door in shock.

"What? Who? Me? Avery is such a common name."

"Let's go," Chelsea whispered.

"No way, you *are* Avery Fox. Hey, girls! It's Avery Fox!" she yelled. It suddenly felt like one of those scenes in movies where people are at a dance or a club and someone says something embarrassing and the record scratches and everything goes silent before all the attention is directed at them.

Every single head turned toward the oversized pot we were still crouched behind.

Then chaos descended. People rushed over to try to get photos of me. Flashes were going off.

"Make a break for it!" I yelled to Chelsea as I ran back toward the elevator. Thankfully the concierge stopped the mob from following us to the elevator hall. The moments we waited for an elevator car to arrive were excruciating. And there in the trash can in between the elevators were several copies of my magazine. Covered in grime and spilled coffee. A real-life metaphor for my career.

Chelsea made to speak, and I cut her off.

"Don't even think about saying 'I told you so.'"

"Well, I did." She crossed her arms over her chest.

I felt hopeless and like a feral animal resisting going back in its cage. The suite, while luxurious, was just that—a cage.

This was fucking bad. I couldn't go anywhere. I didn't want to go to bumfuck Oklahoma and do whatever it was that people in Oklahoma did. If I was going to have to go into hiding, I'd rather just go to Costa Rica and ride out this debacle on the beach. A dollar stretched pretty far out there. I could make a quiet life for myself and maybe, in a year or two, resurface.

When we got back in our room, my mother was pacing in front of the blaring TV.

"There you are! Look at this!" She pointed to the screen.

It was a video playing on repeat on TMZ of me on set of the music video in the leather bikini with the male dancers in wigs and headbands. This was not going to help matters. Out of context, that footage, along with the cover, was damning.

"Who leaked the footage?" I asked, feeling nauseated. There was no way I'd ever recover from this.

"It doesn't matter. You are the biggest story on the news right now, and people are paying top dollar for paparazzi photos of you and any other newsworthy tidbits to keep the ravenous media cycle fed."

"Ugh!" I stormed past her and launched myself onto the bed. "I'm an idiot."

"Should you maybe make a statement?" Chelsea asked.

"No, our PR team said silence is the best course of action right now. You have to go to Oklahoma, Avery. I called my mother."

I looked up at the sound of my mom's resigned voice. She looked drawn and exhausted like she had gone to battle. She leaned against the dresser that housed the TV.

"What did she say?" I whispered.

My mother made a sound between a scoff and a sardonic laugh. "She said we are embarrassing the family."

"Oh." I didn't know what I had hoped for, but that made me feel more deflated.

"She agreed to let you go stay with her, so you're going."

"You won't go with me?" I squeaked. This was my family, but I didn't know them. She knew them.

"No, I'm not coming with you. Our lawyer said the label is well within their rights to cancel the album and potential tour. If they do, you will never get another record deal. The contract we signed prohibits it. This is it. We have to fix this."

"I'm not going." Now this woman wants to swoop in as some savior when my mother and I struggled alone for years? It didn't feel right, as much as I longed to have family. I didn't want it like this.

"You have to go. Just listen to me. Broken Arrow is a small town. It's a place where you can lie low and let all of this blow over without paparazzi everywhere. Your grandmother is well-connected in the community. I think this is a great opportunity to go and win over the hearts of everyone there. Then these lies that you aren't really Native can just go away," my mother said. Her tone was soft and as she crossed her arms and stared at the carpet I got a glimpse of my old mom, the one who I knew loved me and didn't think of me as some product to push and monetize.

This was the whole problem. I could lie low in a town no one knew my connection to because no one believed I was Muscogee to begin with. Was she even sending me because she feared for my safety, or was this all about my public image? I wanted her to want me safe first, my album be damned. "What, you just expect me to show up at my estranged grandmother's house? Someone I have never met, someone who has never bothered to get to know me? All while avoiding paparazzi and trying to win over the tribe?"

"Yes. It wouldn't be for long and you can take some photos and I can see about arranging an interview where you can talk about your heritage. Oprah is a long shot, but we could definitely get Hoda from *The Today Show* interested."

I watched as my mother's gears started turning in her head, devising some scheme.

"What heritage, Mom?"

She rolled her eyes. "Really, Avery? This again?"

"Yeah, this again." I mocked her tone and didn't care if she didn't appreciate my sass. I listened to her always and this time, I was burned and had become a social pariah. "All I know is what you have told me, which is next to nothing. We are Muscogee Creek, and our family is in Oklahoma. The only problem is you have never told me anything else! My DMs are full of people asking me if I'm enrolled and what my blood quantum is. I don't even know what any of that means. Now I have to go force myself on some old woman to save our lifestyle and you don't even want to go with me to help me!"

I stopped to take a breath, and Chelsea patted my back.

"You just are Native American, Avery. That's how it works." The way she growled those words out made my hackles rise. "No one had to prove shit when I was your age or younger. I don't get how it is now, but I left Oklahoma and that way of life behind me. I wanted more for me and you. But if we have to send you there to snap a few photos to get your record deal out of jeopardy, then you will do it. That is how I'm helping you. I vowed to never go back there, and my mother knows why."

"Maybe I should leave," Chelsea said, and got up to go, her arms raised like my mother was a spooked horse.

"No, stay," my mother ordered. "We're going to pack and get Avery ready for her trip tomorrow."

"I'm flying to Oklahoma tomorrow?" It was happening so suddenly, all of it, and I could barely wrap my head around it.

"No, not flying."

THE SUN BEAT DOWN ON ME AS WE WAITED FOR THE all clear from the driver to load onto the Greyhound bus. There was a queue, but I didn't care to be at the front of the line. I was trying not to draw attention to myself, which was difficult considering I stuck out like a sore thumb.

"Here, I got you a muffin to snack on and put a little something in there to keep you entertained. Maybe help in your research." Chelsea handed me a white paper bag. Intrigued, I spread out the handles and saw the tiny mass-market paperback book.

"What's this?" I pulled it out. "*Savage Chief* by Edie McNight. What the fuck is this, Chelsea?"

"Shhh! I don't want your mom to hear." She pushed the book back into the bag while my mother purchased my ticket. "It's one of my guilty little pleasures. I stole this from my mom's bathroom stack when I was fourteen and I love to read it when I need to feel a little swoony."

"You read your mom's western romance when you want to feel swoony? I don't know how I feel about that . . . or that I am only just now learning about it."

"Just trust me, this lady has a million of them and they are all about Native American men."

"And you think this is how I'll learn more about my heritage?" I gave her a sardonic look. How would an old-ass bodice ripper do that? This was the twenty-first century. These characters had never even heard of a phone before.

"I'm just trying to help. You have a long bus ride ahead of you. Beats scrolling online and seeing your face everywhere."

"Touché."

"All right, here is your ticket. You all set?" my mother asked, all business, counting my many bags.

"I guess."

"Now boarding bus sixteen to Tulsa, Oklahoma." The voice of a bored Greyhound employee boomed through the speakers of the station.

"You better get lined up."

After they helped me load all my luggage, I hugged both my mother and Chelsea and said goodbye. Their sendoff was rather unceremonious. I get that my mother decided it was safer to ride a bus than risk being seen at an airport and having someone catch wind of this wild plan to go to Oklahoma and win over the tribe. But I felt like we could have done a little more planning to have me avoid sitting on a bus that smelled like stinky feet and old cheese.

I looked down at my bus ticket stub.

FROM: DALLAS, TX
TO: TULSA, OK
CONNECTION: OKLAHOMA CITY, OK

That line made my heart stop. A connection? That couldn't be right. I shot up to ask the driver just as the bus started rolling, the momentum pushing me back in my seat.

"Um, excuse me! Sir?" I shouted to the bus driver.

Everyone was looking at me and not happily. I guess I broke some unwritten rule of silence. But I had to get off this thing. I had four suitcases under the bus. I couldn't move all those by myself.

"Sir!" I called again, rushing to the front of the bus as the driver cruised down the street. He stopped at a red light.

"What?" he asked.

"I was unaware that this bus has a connection. I thought this was a straight shot to Tulsa."

"Nope, only one nonstop and you missed it."

The light turned green, and I grabbed the back of his seat to steady myself.

"Are there attendants to help transfer bags to the next bus?"

"Attendants?" He cackled. "Ma'am, this is the Greyhound. Attendants . . ." He laughed again. "G'won back and sit down now. Next stop, Oklahoma City."

Using the tops of the headrests of the aisle seats to stabilize myself, I walked back to my seat, keeping my head down to avoid the snickers from the fellow passengers. My mother was right about one thing. No one recognized me or cared who I was here.

I wasn't a famous pop singer and child star to them—I was just a nobody.

The poor excuse for a pocket barely fit my ticket as I shoved it in and took my satchel bag off over my head, putting it on the seat next to me along with the snack bag and book.

I took in everyone around me: a young mother with a baby, two old ladies traveling together, and a young guy who looked like he walked straight out of a Fall Out Boy music video circa 2006—flat-ironed bangs and all. He flashed me a grin and I gave him the smallest smile I could muster back. I didn't want to be rude, but I also did not want to encourage conversation just in case I was recognized easily again like last night.

Closing my eyes, I counted my breaths to center myself. The last few nights had been an emotional roller coaster where I got next to no sleep. And last night I just kept thinking about my grandmother. She was like this phantom presence in my life. I'd never seen even a photo of her. As a kid I imagined she looked like Mrs. Claus, a jolly old lady who baked cookies. But as I've gotten older, I understood that my mother would never have run away from a sweet old lady. There was a lot of hurt in the past that my mother refused to tell me about. What would this long-awaited reception be like? The bus bumped along the highway as we went north.

Something smelled foul and I heard laughing from one of the older ladies and then the baby started screaming and crying.

This was *so* not first class.

I pulled my hood farther down my face and tried to meditate and block out my surroundings. In my mind's eye, I pictured myself in a cabana in Costa Rica, drinking a margarita and pushing all thoughts about my family away. Before long, I'd convinced myself to relax and was startled awake when the bus stopped. I wiped drool from my mouth and looked out the window. The bus station sign read OKLAHOMA CITY.

I had slept for hours.

Great. Now I had to get all my stuff to the next bus. I filed in line to get out and stopped next to the driver, feeling my side for my purse to tip him, and my hand brushed air. I rubbed both hands all over my sides and looked for my purse, spinning in a circle.

Where. Was. My. Bag?!

I pushed past the people behind me to get back to my seat. It wasn't there. I dropped to my knees and felt around the grimy floor to see if it had fallen.

My hands finally found something—it was the white paper bag. I ripped it open, and the muffin was gone but the lousy book remained. Someone swiped my purse and snack! Who would do that?

No, no, no. My money and my phone were in there. What would I do in a world without a phone? It was definitely an example of first-world problems, but I couldn't help it. I cried. And it wasn't the pretty dainty cry I learned to do at Disney. No, this was the full-on snotty hyperventilating cry.

Three pieces of my matched luggage were lined up outside the bus and the driver was wheeling the fourth to join the group. Shit. I sprinted to get them before someone else tried to take my possessions away from me. All that was in there were clothes, shoes, and makeup, but they were mine.

"Sleeping Beauty finally wakes up," the bus driver said. His look was one of pure judgment as he crossed his arms and shook his head at me.

"Sorry."

"Attendant," he said under his breath, and walked away, without looking at me again.

One by one I wheeled my suitcases to bus eleven, where the new driver helped me load them under that bus. At least I had my ticket stub in my pocket. That was the only smart thing I did.

I chose a seat right in front this time, hoping being close to the driver would mean I was safer and less susceptible to theft, granted all I had on me was my sweater and this dumb book.

My stomach rumbled. I had no money for food and no phone to update my mother or Chelsea. I stared out the window and Fall Out Boy walked into the bus station with a black quilted Gucci crossbody bag. He had nice taste. I had a bag just like that.

"Wait!" I yelled. The driver, a friendly-looking older lady, clutched her chest.

"What, child?"

"That guy stole my purse!" I pointed out the window.

"What guy?" she asked.

I looked at her and said, "The one in super skinny plaid jeans." I looked back out the window and he was gone.

No!

I cried for the first fifteen minutes of the drive. Then I sat in self-pity for the remainder of the journey to Tulsa, watching the flat scenery with dead, tired eyes, thinking to myself that I deserved this. This was my hell. I did that stupid photo shoot and now I was paying dearly.

Tulsa was a big city. So was Oklahoma City, but I hadn't bothered to pay attention since it was a mad dash to load my stuff onto the next bus. Now, sitting on my largest white Rimowa trunk by the curb waiting for my grandmother, I took it in. There were lots of buses and cars. Some trees. Hundreds of strangers.

Where was my grandmother? I had no phone or watch, but I guessed I'd been sitting here for twenty minutes.

I started kicking a pebble between my feet like a super low-stakes foosball to pass the time. I needed food and water so bad, when I used the station bathroom—not an easy feat with all my luggage stacked in a stall—I cupped my hands and gulped down as much water from the faucet as I could.

As the day wore on, I was reduced lower and lower. Now to add insult to injury, I was stood up. I fished the book out of the paper bag and started reading. What the hell was this? I turned back to the copyright page and it had been published in 2001. How did Chelsea read this once, let alone dozens of times, and then proceed to read an entire series like this? I was questioning her judgment big time.

With nothing else to do, I kept reading. Then the leading lady's wagon got attacked by Native Americans and they stole her son. Wait, weren't they the good people she was supposed to fall in love with?

I kept turning the pages. Oh, wait, a new Native warrior came to save the day. I needed a break. This plot was more complicated than my life and that was saying something.

I looked up to the parking lot again as the clouds parted and the setting sun's rays shone down on a cute little old lady wearing cowboy boots and decked out in silver-and-turquoise jewelry. I jumped up, dropping the terrible book on the ground, and ran to her, wrapping my arms around her neck.

"Grandma!"

The lady froze, her arms did not wrap around me. I pulled back to look at her face to see if I could find a family resemblance.

I found none.

"Grandma?" I asked with less confidence.

"Get off me, you crazy bum!" She pushed me away. "I got a gun in my purse."

"It's me, Avery?"

"I don't care if you're Mother Teresa, you don't just grab people. This generation." The lady grumbled as she stalked away and into the bus station.

I hated today. I picked up the book, brushing off the dirt and pebbles that stuck to the old, discolored pages.

A thick and throaty laugh hummed around me.

Great. I had an audience. That was the final straw. I whipped around to meet the owner of the laugh and my breath left me. The man laughing at my misfortune was tall, dark, and handsome.

Just what I needed.

I rolled my eyes and focused on the book. I was covered in

grime from the floor of the bus and running on empty. Flirty Avery was dead.

"You doin' all right there?" he asked in a voice as rich as leather.

"Yeah, great." I raised my voice but didn't bother to look at him again. I just threw a thumbs-up over my shoulder and continued to wallow in my misery.

At least when I did meet my grandma, it couldn't be worse than getting threatened with an armed weapon. So, there was that for silver linings. I sat back down on my trunk and stared at my feet. I was wearing Golden Goose sneakers and was disgusted with myself. I had spent $600 for a pair of artificially distressed shoes to make it look like used street wear. Now they were indeed dirty with real dirt and grime and a piece of an old gummy bear stuck to the bottom of one.

The tabloids were right. I was a fake. Everything about me was curated, even down to my fake-dirty now real-dirty shoes.

A pair of dusty cowboy boots entered the space below the pages I was attempting to read. I lowered my book, looking at those boots. Covering the tops were a pair of light-wash boot-cut jeans also covered in dust. My eyes followed the toned line up, to an equally dust-speckled black T-shirt, then up to the tanned face of a god.

It was the handsome man who laughed at me.

"What can I do for you?" I asked.

"You Avery Fox?" he asked, his voice gruff with a slight twang.

Oh shit. He recognized me. I'd been found out.

"Who's asking?"

"Lottie Fox sent me." At my blank stare he added, "Your grandmother."

"Oh, right. Yes, Lottie." I said her name like I said it all the time, letting it roll off my tongue. I knew her name was Loretta. I had no idea Lottie was short for Loretta, though I couldn't say I knew anyone with either of those names.

"Is she in the car waiting?" I got up from the curb, looking over his shoulder, trying to guess which car was his.

"Nope, just me. Gotta get going if you want to make it back for food. With our luck, Red and Davey won't save nothin'."

I watched in stunned silence as this man took the handle of my biggest suitcase and one of the smaller ones and began wheeling them to an old white pickup truck.

"Unless you want to keep *reading*," he said, not even bothering to turn around.

Ugh. I *so* did not want anyone knowing I read any part of that trash, let alone a hot guy. At least I had been found and I would not be stuck alone in this random city with no phone or money.

"Could you be careful with my bags, please? They're new," I said as I grabbed my remaining two smaller suitcases to quickly follow him. He walked with such authority; it was like I was on autopilot doing as he said. I really tried not to look at his ass, but the denim fit him perfectly. Then I had a very worried thought. "Are we . . . related?" I asked.

He huffed a laugh and threw over his shoulder, "No," and kept walking.

Phew. I did not want to be having any of those types of thoughts about a potential cousin or something. Now I could say as an impartial party that this guy had a fine ass.

He pushed the handle down into the suitcase, then his tan, corded muscles flexed as he lifted the hefty thing and threw it into the bed of his filthy truck.

"Hey! Don't do that!"

He stopped to give me a strange look. "I have rope to tie them down."

"Okay, but don't throw them. These are really nice and you're gonna scuff them all up and get them dirty."

"It's luggage." He said it simply and gave me a blank stare.

"So?"

"Luggage is meant to get chucked around. Will they crack open and ruin your clothes if they're tossed around?"

"No, these are, like, top of the line, really high quality."

"All right then," he said with a grunt as he chucked the other one in.

"They're Rimowa!" I gripped the edge of the truck bed, looking in, and could see scuffs already. I hadn't even taken the brand-deal photos with them yet. Now I was going to have to pay for these.

"You!" I turned on him. "I don't know who you think you are, but today is not the day to try me. I've been on buses for nine hours, have had no food, had to drink water from the faucet in the disgusting bus station bathroom, been threatened with a gun by an old lady, my purse and phone were stolen, and this has gone too far! My own grandmother couldn't even be bothered to pick me up herself! Instead, she sends some . . . some . . . dirty cowboy in her stead and you're ruining all I have left even when I asked you nicely to be careful!"

Tears started falling down my face again, and honestly, I was a little impressed. If I still wanted to act, I now knew I could literally cry for hours on end with no problem. All I had to do was be pushed past my limits, humiliated on a global scale, have nothing left to my name, and be at the mercy of an Oklahoma cowboy.

"Lucas," he said. He just stood there weathering all I unleashed on him and barely batted an eye. "I work for your grandmother."

"And how can I verify that? You could be some obsessed fan."

This got a reaction out of him. He snickered and said, "Not a fan, trust me."

"What's that supposed to mean?" I crossed my arms.

"I live on a ranch, not under a rock, lady." He brushed past me and got the other bags and threw them in. "You're welcome to stay here. But if you want to come to the ranch then get in."

He walked to the driver's door, disappearing inside.

I ran to the passenger window that was rolled down. "You said you had rope!"

"That was before you called me a dirty cowboy." He turned the key in the ignition and nodded with his chin to the passenger seat. "Get in."

I threw open the door and plopped down with a huff.

"How far away is the ranch?"

"'Bout twenty minutes or so."

"Great."

"There's a PowerBar in the glove compartment." All I could do was stare at him, which was a mistake, because I noticed his dark thick brows and his nose hooked a little in a hot, hawkish way. "You said you were hungry."

Our eyes were stuck in a standoff. I didn't want to accept anything from this asshole. My stomach grumbled and it broke the moment.

"Fine. I'm sorry I threw your bags," he mumbled.

"Thank you, and I'll ignore the eye roll that went with the apology." I crossed my arms, looking out my window.

He chuckled. "Eat the PowerBar. I don't want to have to carry you into the house if you pass out."

Then he shifted his truck into drive and drove out of the city. I'm ashamed to say I ate that PowerBar in three bites.

4

WHO ARE RED AND DAVEY?" I ASKED TO BREAK THE silence, staring at the feathers hanging from the rearview mirror. I had no idea what kind of feathers they were, but they were black-and-white striped. There were three in total wrapped together in a piece of dark brown leather that looked aged and worn with four different-colored beads, black, white, yellow, and red, all stacked on top of one another. It had been only a few minutes, but I was so far out of my comfort zone, and after eating the PowerBar I did feel a little bad for calling my non-cousin and certainly-not-a-fan ride a "dirty cowboy."

"Your grandma's other workers," he said, looking straight at the road. I guess I really offended him.

"Thanks for the PowerBar," I said as I started picking at a hangnail on my pinky finger.

He grunted in response, again not looking at me.

I tried to plow on. "I'm sorry I called you a dirty cowboy, it's just that I had such a hard day—"

"As you screamed in the parking lot," he said, cutting me off. We were stopped at a red light waiting to turn left.

I opened my mouth, taking a breath to start a conversation when he turned on the radio. An old country song filled the cab. The baritone of the man was low and mellow as his voice crooned in my ear until he reached for a high note in the chorus. It was nice. I'd never heard the song before.

"Who's this?" I asked.

"You don't know Garth Brooks?" Lucas asked me, finally turning to look at me, bewildered.

"Umm no, not this song. What is it?" I spent plenty of time at karaoke bars. I knew "Friends in Low Places" thanks to many drunken people screaming out that song over the years, but that was the extent of my Garth Brooks knowledge.

"'The Dance.'" Lucas stared at me and all I had in response was my blank expression. "It's his most famous song. You really have never heard it before?"

"No."

"Unbelievable," he muttered to himself, and started driving along the street heading to the highway.

"We are heading east on the 64? What is the 64, is that like a freeway?"

"*The* 64? It's a highway. Is that how you Californians talk? We don't say 'the' before any highway, interstate, freeway, or road for that matter."

"Oh, like the Facebook movie! 'Drop the "the," it's cleaner.'" I laughed at my joke.

Lucas turned to look at me like I was weird.

"Twenty minutes made it seem like the ranch was really close and in the city. And we just say 'the 101' or 'the 10.' I never thought it was weird," I added to defend my original question before I went back to picking my hangnail.

"Broken Arrow is close, just outside of Tulsa. It's more rural." That was all Lucas said before he turned up the volume on the radio and I got the hint that the conversation was over.

Driving on *highway* 64 in Oklahoma was a lot different than in Los Angeles. There was no traffic and the houses and churches in the city started to spread out farther apart from each other until we drove past many open fields of land. Everything was so green, and some places had grass that looked almost as tall as me as we zipped by.

The song on the radio faded into a commercial and Lucas quickly turned the tuner to another station. I heard the hand drums first, then my voice and the million harmonies I recorded starting to blare through the speakers.

I was shocked. Truthfully, I have never had my own car and never listened to the radio. I would listen to my iPod back in the day and now I stream everything on my phone. So, hearing myself play on the radio was extremely rare. I had only ever heard myself on the radio once when I was first told the song I was featured on would be premiering on the Ryan Seacrest show years ago.

We turned and looked at each other at the same time. His expression could be described only as a cringe, like he was experiencing secondhand embarrassment listening to my song. A chart-topping song. He was feral.

Lucas punched the volume knob, and the radio was silenced. He turned me off!

"How rude!"

"Listening to that is rude. It's an assault to my ears."

"An assault to your ears? I can't believe you just said that to my face."

"It's better than behind your back. Haven't you had enough of *that* lately?"

How did this cowboy who lived on a ranch in the outskirts of Tulsa, Oklahoma, know so much?

"You seem to know a lot about me for someone who isn't a fan. Are you an obsessed hater? Is that what this is? You know I have come across a lot of you over the years and to look me up that much to keep track of what I'm doing to hate or make fun of me makes you a fan. In the words of Cardi B, 'It benefits me.'" I huffed a breath, threw myself back into the seat, and crossed my arms. I couldn't believe I had to share air with this arrogant man.

"Let's get one thing straight, lady. I am not obsessed. This damn song has been playing everywhere for weeks—gas stations, the supermarket, Dollar Tree, even Walmart! I can't avoid this dumb song, and I have tried, trust me. This isn't music."

"Oh, and some cowboy in bumfuck Oklahoma is an expert on what is music? There are instruments, melodies, chords, harmonies, a sick beat, and a hook that people love to sing at the top of their lungs. It's music."

"Just because it can be defined as music doesn't make it *music*," Lucas said as he tapped his fist to his heart. "You can't feel what you are singing in here. You're singing nonsense, pandering to white people." He punched the volume button again and my chorus blasted through the cab. "What does this part even mean?!" He threw one hand to the speaker as if he could motion to the individual music notes coming out.

This guy was nuts. I have read critical reviews of my work. I get hate comments on my Instagram and Twitter, but I had never had to sit in the small, confined cab of a truck with no means of escape with a handsome stranger who dragged me and my music for filth. Everything online, the hate mail, and then the bus were nothing compared to this. This was the innermost ring of hell, and I could do nothing but wait for my song to end. Still, he looked over at me, expecting an answer.

Two could play this game.

"Well, Mozart, these lyrics are metaphors for sex. I'm shocked by all your ranting about music and feeling it in your heart, that the meaning went over your head."

"Oh, the metaphors are so simple a thirteen-year-old boy could have written them. I asked what does this mean? What is this song about? You have these hand drums, and some pretty vocals, but what does this song mean?"

"Pretty vocals—hah! I knew you were a fan. It's a club track, man. People dance and sing and have fun. Not everything is a sad song about dancing."

"Garth Brooks isn't singing a sad song about dancing!" Lucas was incensed and I laughed in his face. Was Garth Brooks his dad with how protective he was over the man?

"I just listened to half his song, and it was about a dance he was going to miss."

"Okay, Miss Metaphor, the dance means a love that is over and how he wouldn't change a thing and then later he would never choose to change his memories, because if he forgot the pain, he would forget the love too."

"I didn't get to hear the whole song!" Now I was shouting. "I can interpret lyrics as well as write them, jerkface!"

"Can you? I just heard you sing the words 'we out here huntin' and gatherin'.'" He actually took both hands off the wheel to air quote the lyrics back to me. "And did you just call me jerkface?"

"Yeah, I did and I'll do it again. I didn't write *this* song, jerkface."

"Who did?" he asked as he changed lanes, preparing to exit the highway.

"Hans Nilsson and Leif Gunnarsson."

Lucas gave me another bewildered look.

"They wrote three number one singles for Britney and two for Madonna." I looked down at my hands; my pinky was bleeding from where I tugged the hangnail off in anger.

"Two middle-aged Swedish men wrote a song about being a Native American woman in America? What the actual fuck?"

Was it ideal? No. I would have loved the opportunity to pitch a few of the songs I have written to work with these talented songwriters, but the label told me I couldn't. That was just the way this business was.

"You know, Lucas whatever the hell your last name is, I don't like you."

"The feeling is mutual, lady."

"Stop calling me lady!" I turned to look out the window as we drove down a paved road lined with elm trees. It was actually really beautiful. I would have liked it better if I wasn't arguing with someone I met not even a half hour ago.

"Sorry, is 'princess' better?"

"What's your problem? I didn't ask you to pick me up and I've never done anything to you." I threw my hands in the air. If I were a religious person, I would be praying for patience.

"Do you have any idea what your song is doing for the women in our community?"

"I hope it's empowering them to embrace themselves and have fun. Are you a Native American woman, Lucas?"

"Of course not, but I've grown up in the community. I was raised by a Native woman and am close to Lottie, who has done so much for everyone. So, yeah, it's a fun and catchy song, but slithering around in a tan-hide bikini wearing a headdress keeps perpetuating the same overly sexualized image Hollywood keeps force-feeding us."

"Are you slut-shaming me now? I would argue that me allowing myself to feel beautiful and sexy is taking back that narrative. Do you think that maybe we were making fun of that Indian Princess image we always see? How many Native pop singers do you know of?"

"We have a lot of great local singers, princess." He slowed down to make a right onto a dirt road; it was bumpy with a few big puddles from a recent rain.

"I'm sure there are, but how many are known on a national scale? International? We can't change the whole industry by forcing our way in and making demands. We have to give the people the image they are used to and once we are in, then we can start to make changes."

"Did your team feed you that lie? What changes have you made? Everyone hates you."

My puffed-up, self-righteous chest completely deflated, because he was right. I did exactly what my producers and label executives wanted, down to the last feather on the bonnet. And now the internet wanted change, and they wanted to throw me out with the trash too.

"As far as the entire world is concerned, I don't belong here," I said quietly.

"You're Lottie's granddaughter. Of course you belong here—if you want to. That's for you to decide, not the world."

His last comment stunned me. I had only ever had my mother, so this concept of choosing to belong to a family left me feeling as off-kilter as this uneven dirt road. We continued to drive in silence, my body swaying with each dip in the road. There were horses grazing in the fields, and then I saw it. My grandmother's house.

It was an old white colonial-style ranch house. This was what my mother kept from me.

Lucas pulled into the drive next to a black Lincoln Town Car. I looked at the front door and watched in confusion as a disheveled man in a gray suit carrying an old beat-up briefcase ran down the front steps.

"You have thirty days, Lottie!" he shouted as he got to his car.

"You stay off my property and email like a civilized person!" A middle-aged woman wearing denim coveralls, a bright yellow bandanna around her neck, and a mess of graying hair coming out of a scrunchy at the side of her head yelled as she cocked a shotgun and aimed it for Suit Man.

Holy shit.

"Lucas! She has a gun!" I hunched down below the window.

"Don't worry, it's not loaded," he tried to reassure me.

Boom! A shot fired and the small hairs on my arms rose.

"Shit! I told Red to hide the ammo." Lucas crouched down too. We were both too scared to look up, but we heard the Town Car skid on the gravel as it hightailed it out of there.

I was safer back at the bus station. How was this my life now?

"Safe to come out!" The woman started banging on my passenger window. I peeked up through my arms. She had the shotgun resting on her shoulder like a freaking Continental soldier. No way in hell was I getting out of this truck.

"Lucas, take me back to the train station."

"Uh, you got money?" he asked while sitting up from his crouched position, straightening his dusty T-shirt.

"No, do you? I'll pay you back plus five hundred dollars for the inconvenience."

He whistled. "I don't have money, but you should get out and meet your grandma. She isn't a patient woman."

I stole another look and she was standing right there, in the same spot, watching me with an arched eyebrow. She was testing me.

I took a deep breath and opened the truck door.

WELCOME TO RED FOX RANCH," THIS WOMAN—MY biological grandmother—said. I looked at her face and saw my mother. They had the same mouth and chin, but what I focused on were *my* eyes on her face. We shared the same golden almond eyes, a little slanted, framed by thin dark brows. This gave us a hard-edged look. On my face, they gave the impression of mystery, on hers . . . this woman had seen some shit. Her eyes pierced through me in a look of disappointment, like I was lacking in whatever she expected me to be. Disappointed or not, there was no denying that we were related.

I was family with this complete stranger holding a gun that was fired into the roof of the porch only minutes ago. I looked past her head back at said porch where debris was falling from the ceiling.

"Do you shoot at visitors often?" I asked.

"It was a warning shot. I didn't aim it at him. Which is what you will say to the sheriff if they come poking their noses here. Got it?"

I didn't know my grandmother for more than a minute and already I was directed to corroborate a story to the authorities? It was looking clearer why my mother cut off contact. This was not normal.

"Yeow!" A shout sounded to my left. I squinted toward the barn at the bottom of the little hill and saw a tall man missing his left arm followed by a scruffy-looking shorter man. Both were wearing black cowboy hats and dusty boots.

"Shit, Lottie! How'd you find the ammo?" the tall man shouted.

"I always have spare lying around for emergencies, and I ain't telling you where my hiding spot is," Lottie shouted back.

I eyed the vile thing in her arms. I had never been this close to a live weapon before. It made me uncomfortable, and even being in the vicinity of such a thing went against all my pacifist principles.

I stole a glance at Lucas and he gave me a strange look of pity. That really made my blood boil. I had listened to him rant about how terribly he thought of me and my music and now, because I was—rightfully—scared of a gun, he pitied me. Now I was human. I was just about to tell him off again when he walked over to my grandmother.

"How about I take that and put it away in the safe," Lucas said, reaching for the gun in Lottie's arms. She acquiesced gladly.

"Sure, take it inside," she told him. He started walking away and she halted his steps. "Wait till the guys catch up, there's something I want to say to everyone."

"All right." Lucas clicked the safety lock into place on the shotgun, then started looking everywhere but at me.

Lottie turned her gaze to me and I couldn't take more of her disappointing appraisal. I would just have to kill her with kindness.

"Thank you for letting me stay until things cool down and it's safer for me to go home . . . er . . . Grandma?" My voice hitched up in question saying the unfamiliar word aloud.

She visibly cringed.

"Lottie is fine," she corrected me, turning to motion to the men to hurry up the hill. "We don't have all day, Davey. Red, I know you can walk faster than that."

The men grumbled and started jogging up the hill.

"Great, thank you for joining us. Boys, this is my granddaughter, Avery. Avery, these are my hired help, though not much help *lately*."

The men all rolled their eyes and smiled.

"Nice to meet you," I said.

"This big fellow is Davey, he's in charge of the horses. Red has been here since before your momma left, he's a jack-of-all-trades. And Lucas you already met. He has been here eleven years and manages the day-to-day for me. Boys, you will all behave like gentlemen around Avery. No dirty jokes and no one better come on to her while she's here. Got it?"

"Yes, ma'am," they all mumbled in unison.

"Red is too old to be flirting with you and Davey is engaged to our farrier, Mary Beth, who comes and trims the hooves and shoes the horses every six weeks or so. Lucas has made it clear to everyone he hates your guts, so there should be no issues, but if I catch a whiff of any funny business y'all will be dismissed with no pay. Now back to work." Lottie jutted her chin out the same way Lucas did, as if the gesture encompassed a directional order and authority all in one.

I couldn't even look at that shit-talker Lucas. He hated me? Well, that went both ways, buddy. I regretted apologizing to him for calling him a dirty cowboy.

"We are glad to have you here, Miss Avery," Red said as he tipped his hat. Up close, I could see his hat had an intricately beaded band. The pattern looked like arrows in the colors of the sunset. I'd seen some people wearing similar "Southwestern"-style accessories at Coachella before. I always liked it. Not sure why he was called Red though, was that his given name or a nickname for the fading red hair peppered with gray?

"You can just call me Avery." I waved him off.

"Welcome to the chaos," Davey said, and snickered to himself before following Red back down to the barn.

Lucas took the gun inside.

I watched them all go, wishing someone was still here to act as a buffer between me and my grandmother . . . Lottie. Now it felt weird to even think of the word *grandmother* in my head.

"How's your mother?" she asked me point-blank with no emotion. I felt like I was talking to a drill sergeant.

"She's good," I answered, staring down at my feet.

"Haven't spoken to her in twenty years, we lost my mom and dad in that time. Glad she is good." By the tone of her voice, she was not glad at all. She sounded downright pissed.

"Get your bags and I'll show you where you'll stay." Lottie turned on her heel, the gravel crunching as she marched into the house.

One by one I tried to heft my luggage out of Lucas's dirty truck. I had no leverage and they were too heavy to pull out on my own. I hopped into the bed and pushed each one over the edge and out onto the ground. I jumped from the truck and the impact sent shocks through my shins and I cursed and kicked the closest trunk.

The once-beautiful matching set of luggage was scuffed and filthy with no place on a ranch in the middle of nowhere. Just like me.

I let myself feel anger and despair for ten more seconds, taking a deep breath in. On my exhale, I picked up the biggest trunk and started wheeling it toward the house. It got stuck, and I just kept tugging and dragged it up the three steps onto the porch.

I'll be honest, when I pictured my grandmother in my head at the bus station, I had envisioned a little old lady wearing a sunny yellow dress with an apron, maybe some freshly baked cookies. Instead, what I had was this scary gun-totin' woman. This was like *The Beverly Hillbillies* but less friendly. Inside, clutter littered every surface within the foyer, as if everyone had been too busy to put things away. To my left was a pile of boots by the door and a dozen different jackets hung on the coat pegs along the wall. On my right, piles of mail were haphazardly stacked on the little sideboard. A few were stamped with FINAL NOTICE or LATE. I looked away, afraid to be caught snooping, even though these were out for all to see.

The house was a home. Lived in. There was evidence of so much history that immediately hit me as soon as I crossed the threshold. Despite the size of the property, it was unpretentious. The walls had a few pieces of artwork—if one could call an old tin rooster nailed to the wall art. The place wasn't as large as the mansions in Los Angeles where I've gone to parties or stayed with friends, but it was better. It was a home that generations of my family had lived in. Family I had never known. I felt a crack form in my heart. A large mahogany grandfather clock stood proudly next to the stairs, and it made me wonder, if Lottie was my grandmother, then who was my grandfather?

I'd seen no photos growing up, and my mother never spoke of them. All my life when I asked about them, she just said, "It's complicated."

Something happened to cause this chasm and I was determined to find out what. It wasn't like I had anything else to do, with my career being flushed down the toilet.

I couldn't see Lottie anywhere, so I tentatively started wheeling my suitcase farther inside. Off the foyer to the right was an impressive living room of sorts. It was clean and mostly free of clutter, so likely the more formal sitting room. The couches were an old blue plaid but looked like the perfect stuffing level to sink into and never want to leave. The hall to the left housed a dining room and another door that I assumed led to the kitchen. Everything was painted in shades of tan. More plaid in the colors red and navy accented the rest of the beige house from what I could see. Honestly, it was like if I Googled "country living," these were the images that would come up.

"Up here." Lottie's voice above me made me jump.

I followed her voice up to the banister on the second floor where Lottie was standing impatiently waiting for me to join her. I did my best getting the trunk up the full flight of stairs; the landing break in the middle was a helpful reprieve.

"My room is straight down this hall at the end." She pointed to the left of the stairs. "Your room is this way." Lottie walked right and straight down to the complete opposite end of the hall. As far away as possible under one roof.

I followed in silence.

Lottie opened the door to the guest room and ushered me in. All my eyes could focus on were the chickens.

Embroidered chickens were framed and hung on the wall. There were watercolor chickens. A stuffed pillow in the shape of a chicken sat on the chair by the window. There was a pair of carved wooden chickens on the vanity. Chickens. Chickens. Chickens. The quilted bedspread was in a soft, aged shade of buttercream and thankfully didn't have any chickens on it.

I knew absolutely nothing about this woman apart from that she was comfortable shooting guns to scare away bankers. But now I knew two new things: she loved chickens and possibly the color yellow.

The four-poster bed was made of a dark, rich wood that was

polished to shine in the soft fading light coming through the windows. There was an antique dresser that matched the bed and vanity. It was a nice room, apart from the extreme poultry theme.

"It's lovely, thank you," I said with a smile. It was genuinely a nice room, even if I had to wake up to a million chickens staring at me.

"Well, I'm sure it's not like the fancy things you're used to, but it does have an attached bathroom. It's a shared bathroom, but as it's only you and me in the house, no one else will be using it."

"It's perfect."

"Y'all were a little late getting back and with the uninvited visitor showing up, I pushed dinner back a little to give you time to clean up. So, I'll let you get the rest of your things and settle in. Come downstairs for dinner in thirty minutes, sound good?"

"Yes, thanks," I said. I lost count of the number of thank-yous I'd given in these short minutes. What else could I say? What could I ask? What was allowed? I wanted to ask if she could show me which room had been my mother's, but Lottie's demeanor did not inspire any warmth. In fact, her cold, hard exterior scared me. Perhaps she preferred it that way. And maybe this room was my mother's. Though she never acquired any artwork or decor of the poultry variety in my whole life. It was hard to imagine my mother here in the country, but I could see where my mother got her strict, businesslike manner. I wondered if that was how Lottie was when raising her.

I settled all my luggage in the room with a few minutes to spare. I got out a change of clothes and raced to the bathroom to quickly wash my face, but I caught a whiff of my underarms after a full day of traveling and stress—I smelled worse than the bus. I pumped the lemon verbena liquid hand soap into my hands and scrubbed my pits with a fervor.

There. Now I felt more human. More like me.

I came down the stairs slowly, taking my time to see what else I could discover. There wasn't a single family photo on the wall, which was a bummer. Every house I'd visited always had family photos in hallways by the bedrooms or along the wall leading up the stairs.

My hand brushed the empty space and I noticed discoloration in a few different places in the shape of ninety-degree angles. It looked like there had been photos here, but they'd been removed. I felt my heart constrict. Had Lottie removed those photos after my mother left? Or when her parents passed away? Or right before I arrived?

The sound of the front door closing broke me from the spell of trying to decipher how many photos had been removed.

It was Lucas. He had cleaned up since I saw him last. Gone were the dusty boots and clothes and this time he wore no hat. Instead, his hair looked freshly washed and combed back from his face. The bastard was more handsome than any actors, models, or musicians I had ever encountered in all my time in the entertainment industry. What. The. Hell.

He noticed me gawking at him while I stood on the stairs. He openly stared back. Even from the length of a room and halfway up the stairs I could track the movement of his eyes, the way they perused my body. No doubt judging me some more.

I rolled my eyes and continued my descent.

Lucas planted himself in the same spot in the foyer, his legs spread out, hands behind his back, and waited for me.

That was unexpected.

I *knew* he had to be an obsessed fan.

"Can I help you?" I asked.

"Nah, just waiting for you. Figured you wouldn't know where to go."

"My nose works, I can follow the smell of food." I arched a brow at him.

Lucas scoffed, looking down with a small smile. "Let's eat then." He took off in the direction of the dining room.

When I made it into the dining room, I noticed Lottie had changed into a clean brown velour tracksuit, her hair tied in a severe knot at the top of her head. The men were already seated. Lottie sat at the head of the table with one seat empty to her right. Unfortunately, Lucas sat next to the empty chair, and I wondered if it was too late to ask to take some food up to my room to eat in private. Lottie looked at me and then to the seat, and I got the hint. I quickly made it to the chair, trying to draw as little attention to myself as I could, which was impossible as I was a stranger to everyone and stuck out like a sore thumb.

Once seated, I gave the group a weak smile and pathetic wave. Who did I think I was? Miss America? Waving as if saying, *Hello, thank you for allowing me to crash-land into your lives and disrupt all your routines, please do dig into your food.*

"Great, she's here. Let's dive in," Davey said.

Yeah, let's. The food smelled amazing. There was a platter of fried chicken, biscuits, a bowl of corn, and another bowl of green beans.

"Not before grace," Lottie said, leveling Davey with a look that felt like it had more weight and meaning behind it than I could comprehend.

I took my cues from Lottie and put my hands together and bowed my head. I'd watched a few seasons of *7th Heaven* back in the day, so I got the gist of it.

As I listened to Lottie thank our Lord and Creator for the meal, I wished I didn't have such a heightened awareness of Lucas sitting next to me. I could feel the heat from his muscular thigh.

Once we all said "Amen," Lottie served herself a drumstick and handed the platter to me. I chose the biggest piece I could see, already planning on seconds or thirds. That PowerBar did very little to quash my hunger.

I ate in silence, listening to the flow of conversation about the goings-on of the ranch and the horses. I choked on a spoonful of the buttery corn when Davey casually mentioned masturbating a horse. As if that was a normal, everyday occurrence.

What in the actual fuck? Was that legal? Did the horse consent? I looked around, bewildered, and everyone kept talking without even batting an eye. Lucas smirked at my reaction. No doubt relishing my ignorance of horse affairs. I didn't think horse semen was the subject to be all hoity-toity about, but that was just me. If I were an expert on horses, spouting knowledge about horse peen would not be something I'd do at the dinner table to prove my point.

"I think we need to put poor Avery out of her misery and explain a little about what we do. I can see her head is about to explode," Red said with a laugh. The crinkles around his eyes made him look friendly and he looked at me with eyes full of mirth. I think I liked Red best of all at this table. He wiped his wiry beard with a napkin. His dusty clothes were also gone and he wore no hat. He tied his long, fading hair in a ponytail and wore a clean paisley button-up shirt. It looked well loved and well worn with the blue color faded in spots on the sleeves.

Red had history here and I genuinely wanted to hear about it. So long as he kept the topic of masturbating horses to a minimum. I looked to Lottie to see if it was all right. From the look of the empty wall of missing pictures, I wasn't sure how much she wanted me to know about this place. But all she did was grab her glass of water and nodded for Red to continue.

"Since 1930, Red Fox Ranch has been a prominent horse-breeding ranch. We bred some winning stallions and sold coveted brood mares, and also bred horses and ponies for families and such. To breed, we have to keep the male horses away from the females to make sure we don't get any undesirable sires. In our prime, we had ten racehorse studs that people would pay thousands of dollars for their semen to breed their own horses. It's common. You get it?" Red asked, folding his cloth napkin.

"Umm, I think so? It's like a sperm bank but for horses?"

"Exactly," Davey answered, laughing to himself. He had cleaned up his appearance too. He wore a clean T-shirt and no hat. His hair was short, buzzed close to his scalp. With the heat I experienced, I didn't blame him. I nearly wanted to cut all my hair off too after hauling my luggage from the truck.

"And all that pays for this whole ranch?" I asked.

"It used to," Lottie answered.

"Is that why the man in the suit was here today? Is the business in trouble?" I knew as soon as the question left my mouth it was the wrong thing to ask. My grandmother's face shuttered.

"That's none of your concern. If everyone is done, take your dishes to the sink and load the dishwasher." She got up, taking her plate and the remaining pieces of fried chicken with her. I wanted to cry. Maybe tonight after she went to sleep, I could come and swipe another piece.

The men stayed seated, finishing the food on their plates. I followed their lead, because I was hungry and the food was delicious. I'd never had such flavorful and moist fried chicken. Granted, all I had to compare it to was KFC, and I thought KFC was bomb.

I'd never been the biggest fan of green beans, but these were so soft and almost soupy with little bits of bacon. I wanted seconds and thirds of this meal.

A door slammed somewhere in the house and the sound made me jump. My question must have really pissed off Lottie.

"I'm sorry," I said to the men. I'd ruined their dinner.

"Don't worry about it. It's always like this. Miss Lottie has a short fuse, but she always cools off and comes back," Red said to reassure me. He was the kindest one and therefore I liked him the best.

Davey was hard to read, and Lucas I wished would go ride off on a horse somewhere and never come back.

"Why do you stay?" I blurted out my question. If Lottie was so mercurial, and my mom even left, then why did these men stay? Was it just for their jobs? It looked like they wouldn't have them for much longer.

"That's what family does—you stay, even when it's hard." Red wiped his mouth on his napkin and stood up with his plate and left for the kitchen.

"Does he mean real blood family, or like this job feels like everyone is a family?" I asked Davey, continuing to ignore Lucas right next to me.

"Red's your cousin twice removed, I think," Davey answered. Once I had access to the internet again, I was going to have to Google what *twice removed* means.

"What about you?"

"Nah, my family is from Tahlequah. I'm Cherokee, but we probably share some cousins from way back in the day."

"So Red is my family too." I smiled. Yesterday I had no one and today I met two family members. One was a little deranged. I hoped Lucas hid that gun somewhere Lottie would never be able to find it. "So, you guys just found yourselves here?" I waved my hand in Lucas's general vicinity but refused to personally acknowledge him.

"Basically." Lucas stood up from his seat. "You done?" he asked Davey.

Davey nodded and Lucas grabbed both their plates and went to the kitchen. I scooped my last few bites into my mouth, stopping myself from licking the plate, and went to help put the food away. The men washed the dishes and when they weren't looking, I swiped another biscuit, shoving it into my mouth.

"You don't have to smuggle food like a squirrel. If you're still hungry you can eat more," Lucas said from directly behind me, his lips close to my ear.

It startled me and I accidentally swallowed the partially chewed biscuit. It got stuck in my throat and I was gasping for air. A piece of biscuit flew out of my mouth before I could cover it. I'll be damned if I let these people see food spittle as I die.

"Easy now," Lucas said as his large hand slapped my back. The motion dislodged the stuck biscuit, and it went soaring out of my mouth and hit Davey right on the back of his neck.

Red howled in laughter. Davey grunted and wiped at his neck with the dish towel.

Hoarse coughs persisted as I tried to catch my breath. Lucas's hand was still on my back and his patting had eased to soft circles. I could feel his calluses through my thin shirt. His rubbing left gooseflesh in its wake.

"Sorry," I wheezed out to Davey as Red handed me a glass of water. I drained the glass in one gulp and stepped away from Lucas, avoiding his face in my embarrassment at having nearly choked to death within my first couple hours here and my body's reaction to him touching me. I was determined to keep him at arm's length since he was my number one hater.

What was it about being a woman? When a handsome man was mean we still found him attractive? More so, often? I was going to need so much therapy once I left this place.

"I wasn't smuggling food." I turned around on my heel and

crossed my arms. The sounds of ceramic plates being stacked on top of one another faded away as I met Lucas's gray stare.

He smirked, seeing through my lie. This motherfucker. I had been confronted with nothing but hostility—my fans turning on me, my label on the verge of dumping me, and my friends abandoning me. I had had enough. To add insult to injury, I had this random employee of my mother's mother judging me every spare second he had. All I wanted was more food and some sleep.

"Some thank people when they have been helped, you know." He had the audacity to wink at me. But he was right.

"Thank you," I said on a breath. "Listen, Lucas, we have to share space. You don't want me here and I don't want to be here, but neither of us has control in this situation. How about you stay the hell away from me and once I can leave, we just forget about each other and go about our merry way. Sound good?"

"Whatever you say, princess." He took a step toward me and leaned forward, pressing me back into the granite counter. His arm reached behind me and my eyes zeroed in on his corded muscle.

"What are you doing?" I asked, my voice nothing more than a raspy whisper.

"Watch your head."

"My head?" I turned and he opened the upper cabinet behind me, putting the clean glasses away.

Then he winked again and turned around to continue putting dishes away. My cheeks were inflamed, as was my rage. I stormed out of the kitchen and up the stairs, leaving the three of them to finish cleaning. I needed as much space as the house provided from Lucas the Devil.

I stopped at the landing, catching sight of Lottie as she started turning out all the lights on the first floor. I felt like I should have a moment with her alone, away from everyone, to thank her and apologize for my invasive question. She headed up the stairs slowly, as if the day weighed heavy on her shoulders and her only refuge was sleep. She looked surprised to see me waiting for her.

"Lost already?" she asked.

"No, I just . . . well . . . we haven't really had the opportunity to talk or anything."

"There is time for all that later. Get some rest, we start early in the morning." Lottie walked down the hallway and shut her door.

Her tone wasn't unkind, but it wasn't warm either. She was the most impossible person to get a read on. Did she like me? Did she hate me? Why did she agree to let me come here? I couldn't ponder on these thoughts for long. A cordless phone was charging on the counter outside my bathroom and I took it with me to the chicken room, pressing the speaker to my ear while it rang.

"Yes?" My mother's tone was icy.

"Hi, Mom, it's me."

"Oh, Avery? Honey, I thought it was my mother. Why are you calling on the landline?" She already sounded annoyed.

"I just wanted to let you know that I made it here."

"You couldn't text me back? I've sent you six messages. I've been worried sick, Avery."

"I could've, if my phone hadn't been stolen from me while on the bus."

"What?"

"And my purse."

"Avery . . ." She tsked.

"I know, but it wasn't my fault—"

"Nothing is ever your fault. I'm sure you weren't aware of your surroundings like I taught you to be. All book smarts but no street smarts or sense."

I wanted to let her know I was safe and she wanted to go on a criticizing rant—as if she hadn't given me enough of those.

"So glad to hear your relief that I am fine."

"Of course I'm relieved, but you just added more to my plate. Now not only do I have to try to save your record deal and album, I have to freeze your credit cards and turn off your phone so no Greyhound weirdo tries to steal your identity or all your money. I just love doing thankless task after thankless task."

The exhaustion was hitting me and her remarks stung, making my eyes water.

"Can you please have a new card sent to me here and new phone?"

"I'll get to it when I get to it. If I'm being honest with you, unplugging during this media circus is the best thing you can do. And the least my mother can do is pay for your upkeep for a week or two."

"No, Mom, I really don't want to impose on everyone here."

"Then you email our financial adviser and fix it yourself. I'm busy saving your career."

She hung up. No *I love you, chin up, it will get better* pep talk before saying good night.

My mother didn't have the easiest job in the world, but she wasn't exactly an on-call emergency room doctor, literally saving lives. We struggled so much for years and right now I needed my mom. I needed a hug and for someone to care enough to tell me that it would be okay in the end. That I wouldn't forever be defined by one bad mistake.

I was stuck here around more people than I ever thought I could claim as family and had never felt so alone.

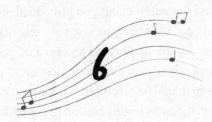

I HAD NO IDEA "WE START EARLY" INCLUDED *ME*.

It was still dark outside when I was ripped from my sleep with the overhead light glaring into my eyes and a stern "Get up" from Lottie.

"What time is it?" I asked, barely able to hide my irritation at the rude awakening.

"Five thirty. Dress in something you don't care about getting dirty and meet me downstairs."

"Why?"

"This is a working ranch, no one stays here for free. C'mon, get movin'. You have ten minutes." She swooped out of the room as fast as she had entered, slamming the door after her.

Ten minutes? I knew I should have showered last night, but I was so tired and wrung out from the levels of anxiety and sadness I just passed out. I barely managed to take my pants off before crawling into bed.

I got up, put on the same jeans I had worn to dinner last night, shoved my feet into the Golden Goose sneakers, and yawned my way downstairs, stomach growling.

The house was dark, but I followed the dim light coming from the kitchen. Coffee was brewing and there was a pot of oatmeal on the stove. Lottie was fixing herself a bowl when she noticed me.

"Eat up and make sure you're good and full. Lunch is a ways away and we got a lot to do until then."

There was a stack of bowls next to the stove and I ladled myself a big helping. There was sugar and cinnamon on the counter, and I sprinkled a little bit in. Back home, I limited my sugar intake and counted my calories. I had to. Any unflattering image of me slouching would result in people posting zoomed-in photos all over the internet and calling me a pig. When I switched up birth controls to the shot and I first gained some weight as a result, it became public discourse. The digital footprint of my life would take up pages and pages on Google, but the physical space I was allowed to occupy could be no bigger than a size two. It never stopped hurting to see that said about yourself. Even though these offensive comments always trickled in, there were many who defended me, but it was hard to focus on those when the internet trolls were the loudest. Weight loss and fitness brands capitalized on all the tabloid stories and reached out to me and my mom for partnerships. It wasn't ideal, but the money was nice. That extra income paid my mortgage, but I resented all the gummy sugar-free vitamins and detox powders. They were all means to an end and that end was freedom.

Just remembering the nasty aftertaste of stevia in my coffee made me add another spoonful of the white sugarcane granules. After the last twenty-four hours I had, I thought I deserved it.

Lottie took her coffee and oatmeal into the dining room. I had no choice but to follow, sitting in the same seat as the night before.

Lottie put on a pair of reading glasses and shook out a magazine and started reading. I didn't want to interrupt her morning routine, but I very much wanted to know what the hell she expected me to do. I wasn't exactly used to manual labor.

I blew on my oatmeal and took a bite. It was heaven, warm and creamy, rich with butter, and so sweet. I loved it. I didn't think I could go back to date sugar again.

"'Avery Fox, twenty-three, pictured below in stills from her latest music video, has shocked the internet and the world with her latest stunt on the cover of *Rolling Stone.*'" Lottie's voice broke the silence, reading aloud from her tabloid. I dropped my spoon into the dish, my mouth hung open, shocked that she would own a tabloid and read it out loud in front of me.

She continued, "'Once she charmed children and their parents starring in hit Disney movies like *A Midsummer Night's Dream: The Musical*, but recently she has followed the path of Miley Cyrus and many other child stars. "She is breaking the good-girl image with overly sexualized outfits and music. I don't want my kids seeing her and thinking that growing up means dressing provocatively," said one concerned parent who spoke to us. It is making some lawmakers debate whether there should be legislation in place to protect children from acting in Hollywood—'"

"Okay, I got it." I cut her off. I couldn't bear listening to this same trash coming out of the mouth of a woman who was supposed to love me. Maybe there was no inherent love on the primal, DNA level, but maybe she could grow to like me. Or at least try to get to know the *real* me and not what these tabloids projected me to be.

"It should be comforting to know your embarrassing stunt is inspiring real change within that depraved industry. Hopefully no other children are forced to do what you did and then turn out like you, parading around in a loincloth." She angrily spooned oatmeal into her mouth.

This experience of public disgrace had taught me the many levels of hurt and embarrassment I could feel. But nothing could prepare me for the condemnation from my grandmother. My eyes turned glassy, but the hurt gave way to anger. She didn't know me and I sure as hell didn't know her.

"I have never worn a 'loincloth.' If my career is so disgusting to you, then why did you agree to let me stay here?"

"Because we're family. Despite what your mother thinks or says, we take care of our own. I think you could use some structure with a positive influence so you don't feel the need to shake your bare ass on television." Lottie threw the tabloid down onto the table in disgust.

Family? Now we were family? The woman had said like five sentences to me in our entire acquaintance and now we were "family" and she felt she could judge, condemn, and lecture me? Or provide me "structure" as if I were a toddler with some minor behavior issues and I just needed more control? Control was how I got into this mess. No one could possibly understand that. Not when it was far easier to judge from a distance.

"Lottie, respectfully, you're wrong. I have never shaken my bare ass on television. I have worked hard all my life. You may not agree with how I was raised or what I do for work, but I will not sit here and subject myself to ridicule and scorn from a woman who never so much as sent me a birthday card."

"I see you have your mother's bite to you. I would suggest you don't speak on things you know nothing about."

I pushed my oatmeal away, my appetite lost to anger. "I know nothing because neither you nor my mother tells me anything. All I knew growing up was that my mother's family was far away and we didn't talk to them. It has been me and my mom my whole life. I don't even know who my father is. My mom did the best she could, and I am happy I could provide a steady income for us."

It was steady while I had work. During the dry seasons where I wouldn't get cast in anything or a pilot I filmed was never picked up, it was really hard. But there was no way the woman sitting next to me could wrap her brain around it. Not now at least, if ever.

I was starting to see why my mother never talked about her.

"You were a baby, a child, a teenager. You were never allowed to be that. You should never have had to work to provide for you and your mother in the most expensive state to live in. That is too much to put on a kid." Lottie's voice was softer than I had heard it before. She sat back in her dining chair, bringing her finger to her temple and rubbing it in a circle. Her eyes had a faraway look to them and it was like her finger was a drill to the side of her head, almost as if she was trying to rub away the headache and the memories. It was exactly what my mother did when she thought no one was looking.

"Look, I don't know what happened between you and my mom. I don't know anything about this place or family. Do I have a grandfather? I was hoping I could learn about all of it, connect, and be a family. If it's too much, then I'll just go."

"Where?" She dropped her hand and looked at me. "The first phone call I received from your mother in twenty years, she says your life is in danger and you need to stay away from the public eye. This was the first time since she left that she ever asked me for help. So, as hard as it is for me to wrap my head around all that you do, I am not going to turn you out."

"Thank you," I said for the millionth time. She offended me greatly, but I was still in her debt.

"Stop thanking me. The boys are gonna roll up in here in a few minutes to eat and then we are going to put you to work."

"I don't know anything about horses. I don't even know if I like horses!" I said.

"Of course you like horses. It's in your blood."

"In my blood? Is that the Native part of my blood that the public is convinced I don't have?"

She rolled her eyes. "Outsiders don't know anything. You want to get enrolled, we can get you enrolled, but it won't be today. You want a roof over your head and food in your belly? Then you gotta work."

I perked up. I could get enrolled? This entire public cancellation could get resolved and I could go back to LA. Maybe I could even help Lottie in return. My mind started spinning, dreaming up all the possibilities to solve all our problems. "I saw the guy from the bank leaving yesterday and the notices by the door. If you need help, I'll gladly pay off the mortgage or whatever else you need. My purse was stolen yesterday, but I can call my mom and we can get it handled in a day."

Again, I had said the wrong thing.

Storm clouds gathered in her golden eyes. "I will not touch your money, and I don't want you telling your mother about what you saw yesterday. Got it?"

"Sorry, I just wanted to help." I looked down at my hands. I couldn't say or do anything right in this woman's company. I felt like a stranger in my own skin sitting next to her, questioning everything about myself.

"You'll help by mucking the paddock and then helping prepare the meals. Got it?"

"Yes."

"Yes, what?" Lottie arched her brow at me in a pointed look.

"Ma'am?" My voice hitched up in a question.

She nodded. "Now eat your food."

Her attention was thankfully taken away from me and the tabloid by the men coming in for breakfast. I barely even noticed

Lucas, who was holding his cowboy hat in his hand and wearing a navy T-shirt and black jeans. If he looked at me, I didn't notice as I forced myself to finish every last bite of the now cold and congealed sweet porridge, because it couldn't be worse than learning to muck a paddock. What even was that?

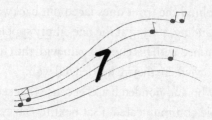

7

THE HEAT AND HUMIDITY HIT ME LIKE A TIDAL WAVE AS I walked outside. It had to be at least eighty degrees. I could already feel sweat forming along my back. Lottie led everyone to a golf cart at the side of the house next to the cellar. A real cellar. I didn't know why that was cool to me. Probably because it looked just like the old cellar Dorothy couldn't get open during the tornado in *The Wizard of Oz*. I was a theater kid, what could I say? But now I was thinking about tornadoes in Oklahoma.

"How do you know when to prepare for a tornado?" I asked.

"We check the weather reports. We're nearing the end of the season, but it's June so we do gotta be alert," Red answered with his slow Okie drawl. There were many reasons that I wished I still had my phone. I was dying to text Chelsea about all of this and check my Instagram and Twitter follower numbers (I wanted to keep my sponsorship deals). And now I wanted to constantly check the weather report. I did *not* want to be caught up in a tornado. We didn't have those in Los Angeles. What did you even do if you were outside in a field and a tornado manifested out of nowhere? This was a lot to consider and think about before it was even seven in the morning.

Lottie sat in the driver's seat next to Red. Davey sat in the back, the seats behind the front ones faced out backward. Lucas and I were left standing, staring at the one empty spot left.

He motioned with his chin—again with the chin pointing. "Go ahead, I know where they're headed. I'll walk."

I bit my lip and nodded back, because that seemed to be how these people communicated. I sat next to Davey, my butt barely hitting the seat before Lottie backed up, accelerating like a bat out of hell. Davey grabbed me to keep me in the seat. It felt like she shifted into drive without even braking from reverse. We zipped past Lucas and down the small slope of a hill toward the barn.

"You ever been around animals, Miss Holly*wood*?" Davey teased me. *Hollywood* contained too many *o*'s the way he said it, extending the "wood" for an extra couple of seconds.

"I once worked with the monkey who was in the second *Pirates of the Caribbean* movie," I offered. I had to let her sit on my shoulder and it was cute and all, but seeing a monkey that close to my face was unnerving—her eyes and expressions were a little too human for me. That monkey was never meant to perform to the whims of people. She should have been free in a jungle somewhere. She loved her trainer, clutching him during breaks on set like a little baby, but there were moments doing take after take where she looked so sad and tired. Not all that different from me and the other kids on that shoot. But I had the ability to say no, not that it would have mattered anyway.

"No shit! You know Jack the monkey?" Davey used the end of his left arm to bump my shoulder. His playfulness made me smile; it felt like I had a friend in Davey, because he was actually nice to me. It made me feel less of an outsider.

"No, I know Chiquita the actor monkey." I used my shoulder to nudge Davey back.

The golf cart came to an abrupt stop and once again Davey had to keep me from falling out.

"Inside we have fifteen stalls, but since it's summer and breeding season, all our horses sleep in the eastern paddock. We board a few horses as well and those are in the western paddock, both geldings and mares," Lottie said while getting out of the cart.

I needed a notepad. What was a gelding? Were those the babies?

I hopped off the golf cart and could feel my breakfast start to come up. Next time I was going to walk. Once I got my bearings, I started to follow everyone into the barn. But then I noticed the horses.

Big horses, huge, nibbling on the grass next to the fence.

I was skeptical about loving horses just because it was "in my blood." That gene must have skipped my generation, because I was frozen in place, terrified to get any closer. The closest horse to me chuffed and I took another step back, worried that it was horse speak for *Get out of my territory*.

Red came through the open door of the barn carrying a pitchfork—an actual pitchfork. I'd only ever seen those in movies. Behind him, an out-of-breath Lucas pushed a wheelbarrow full of hay. He must have jogged down the hill.

"Come over here, Miss Avery." Red waved me over, walking to the horse-with-an-attitude. He used the pitchfork to hitch the hay over the fence. All the other horses came over for the fresh food.

I shook my head. "I'm good here."

"Feeding the horses is the best part. Well, apart from actually riding them." Red smiled at me encouragingly.

"Forget it, Red. Princess here is too scared to get her hands dirty," Lucas said, dumping the remainder of the contents of the wheelbarrow on the ground. Then he started pushing the barrow back toward the barn, not even sparing me a glance.

I had enough of preconceived notions about me and my character. I marched up to Red, yanking the pitchfork out of his hand. How hard could it be?

"So what do I do with this? I just scoop it up like an oversized fork?"

Red lifted his hat and scratched his forehead. "Yeah, but you gotta make sure you aim right or—"

The hay didn't make it anywhere close to the other side of the fence. Instead, the flakes of hay rained over my head as I lost my balance from the awkward weight and length of the pitchfork. I slipped and fell back into the gate. Red had the decency to stifle his laugh.

"How about I show you my technique?" Red reached for the pitchfork and I gladly handed it over. I blamed Lucas.

Red placed both hands on the pitchfork, gripping one closer to the fork-end and the other farther up the handle, and flung the scoop of hay over in a beautiful arc, where it landed softly on the dirt on the other side. Four horses already started nibbling. I pantomimed the motion with my own hands, confident my next try wouldn't be as bad as my first. Then I felt a tug at the back of my head, as if someone was pulling my hair.

On impulse, I swatted my hand back and felt slobber and a hot mouth. I yelped. A horse was eating my hair! I tried to yank my ponytail out of its mouth, but it held on tight and then my head snapped back. This was how I was going to die. I was going to be eaten by a big Shamu of a horse chewing on my ponytail. There would be nothing left of me, this is what the tabloids would remember.

The headlines flashed before my eyes:

DISGRACED FORMER CHILD ACTOR TURNED POP STAR DIED IN A FREAK HORSE ACCIDENT. THIS IS THE MOST RECENT CASE IN MODERN HISTORY OF A PERSON BEING EATEN ALIVE BY A HORSE.

"Whoa there, Peso, spit it out. That's it." Red coaxed my hair from the demon's mouth. "There you go, all free."

I snatched my hair back, trying to feel through the saliva and chewed-up hay just how much of it was gone. The end of my ponytail was inches shorter and jagged. It was hard to imagine a day worse than yesterday, but now I could add being nearly eaten to death to my long list of Shit Avery Has Experienced, and today was looking like it would top the bus ride from hell.

"Oh shiiit! What happened to you?" Davey laughed, pushing another wheelbarrow full of hay with his one hand out of the barn.

"Be nice, Davey. Peso tried to eat her hair." Red was scooping more hay and throwing it over.

"Not tried, he was successful," I sobbed, though no tears came. It appeared I'd cried everything out on the bus. Which was for the better, as I didn't want Know-It-All-Lucas seeing me cry. Again.

"Horses love hay, you shouldn't put it in your hair like that," Davey offered, unhelpfully. Some new friend.

"I didn't— You know what, no. I'm not even going to acknowledge that. There has to be something I can do that doesn't involve these beasts." I swatted at the loose hay that was falling down my face and sticking to the thin layer of sweat that coated all my exposed skin.

"This is it." Davey spread his arms out wide to show that the horse ranch was in fact all about horses.

"Run on into the barn, there's a hat you can borrow to tuck in the rest of your hair," Red said with a smile as he leaned on the handle of the pitchfork.

I nodded my thanks and headed for the barn, deciding that Red was the only person on this godforsaken property I liked.

I was about to step through the door but paused. Five feet away, Lottie was brushing a horse and cooing sweet nothings to it, calling it "beauty" and "lovey." Straight up, I thought the horse was kind of weird-looking. I could see its big ugly chompers as it munched on the long grass in exaggerated circles. It looked friendly enough as it nudged Lottie's face with its snout, but those teeth looked like they could take off my whole hand. And since Peso out there made a meal out of five inches of my hair, I would take no chances.

There had to be something I could do that didn't involve me getting close to these animals. Staying inside and cooking meals was sounding better and better.

"Avery, step in from the door." Lottie waved me over without looking at me, as if she could feel my presence. "You'll freak out the horses hovering like that."

I'd scare the horses? That was rich. These things outnumbered us all and I didn't trust a single one.

To make Lottie happy, I stepped through the open door and was hit with that animal-and-hay smell. It wasn't bad. It wasn't great either. Maybe I just wasn't used to it. I glanced at the walls, seeing if there was a coatrack or something with this promised spare hat.

Lucas walked out of a room from the far end of the barn carrying a full white plastic five-gallon bucket, his biceps flexed and strained holding it by the thin wire handle. There was really nowhere else to look, so I wasn't checking him out. I was stuck next to the horse and Lottie, and it wasn't fair that this judgy man was so handsome. He rolled his eyes as he passed me through the door.

Handsome and mean. I hated him.

I rolled my eyes back at him, but it was too late. He was already out the door and had the last "word." He may have won this particular battle, but I was going to win the war. Before I left this hellhole, he was going to become my biggest fan, humming and singing all my songs to himself as he went about his work here at the ranch.

This new mission gave me some confidence—enough to deal with the Lucas problem—but not enough to want to be near a horse. I slowly inched my way to Lottie.

Lottie finally looked at me. "What in the Sam Hill happened to you?"

"One of your demon horses ate my hair." I crossed my arms protectively across my chest.

Her lips wobbled and I braced myself for the sting of humiliation.

I went my entire life never knowing her and now that I knew she existed, a piece of my soft, hopeful heart really wanted her to like me. I wanted them all to like me.

Her mouth spread into a wide smile and she laughed a full-belly cackle, sounding like a witch from an old cartoon movie.

"Ha-ha. It's funny, I know. Can I do something that doesn't involve me being near these things?" I nodded to the big horse nuzzling her face. The beast smiled, as if it too thought my humiliation was the best thing to happen to this ranch.

Lottie dabbed her eyes with the back of her hand and nodded her head toward the horse. "Come here."

I shook my head, feet planted in my spot. I wasn't going to move any closer, this right here was close enough.

"Now, now, come on. Rakko won't bite." Lottie grabbed my wrist, gently, and pulled me closer to the horse, depositing the brush into my shaking hand.

"Thlock-go?" I tried to replicate the name, but my tongue tripped over the first part. "What does it mean?" I asked as I warily eyed the horse, making sure it wasn't enticed to take a bite of me.

"Horse," Lottie answered simply.

"You named your horse *Horse*?"

"No, I named him the Mvskoke word for horse, Rakko."

"It's beautiful." I gave the thing a timid smile.

"A beautiful name for a beautiful horse."

Rakko could tell he was getting praise, because his black tail started swinging and he made a pleased chuffing sound.

"His black fur and tail are pretty, I guess," I conceded.

"Horses don't have fur, they have a hair coat. Hair that needs to be brushed—so go on then." Lottie placed her aged hand over mine and brought the brush to Rakko's huge torso and started brushing from the top of his back and down toward the floor. "Like that, keep going."

She released my hand and I stood awkwardly, a little too far with my arm outstretched, brushing the same spot a few times. Rakko brought his big head around and nudged me in the gut, pushing me closer.

I shrieked a nervous laugh being so close to a beast of this size, but Rakko just stood there, contentedly flicking his tail, so I continued to brush.

"There you go, you're getting it."

"Do we have to brush all the horses' hair? This could be my job, as long as they don't try to eat me."

"Yes, we brush down all the horses every day, but as I told you,

you need to be pulling your weight. I can't have you playing hair-dresser."

Even though my mother kept me from our family, she did raise me to respect my elders, so it took everything within me to not huff and roll my eyes. After a beat I said, "I don't want to play hair-dresser. I want to not be afraid of the horses so I can work as you said." I stepped away from Rakko, handing the brush back to Lottie. "Red mentioned a spare hat I could use and I'll take it and head back out to help the guys."

Lottie tsked, ignoring the brush, and moved to the wall lined with horse equipment—lots of leather dangly things, blanket-looking things, and saddles. I was sure before I left here I'd know exactly what each item was. She picked up one of the small blankets and walked back to me and Rakko.

"You want to get comfortable around the horses then we will start with the basics. This is a saddle pad, it keeps the saddle from chafing. Rakko is my personal horse—he is a stud, but I ride him."

"Heck yeah you are, buddy." I tentatively tapped the only horse who had been nice to me so far.

"Stud means we use him for breeding and impregnating the mares."

"Oh, Rakko gets around." I giggled at my joke, but Lottie was back to that unimpressed stank face.

She returned to the wall and grabbed an aged saddle, the buff leather showing the patina of years of use and care. I loved a good leather conditioner as much as the next leather goods enthusiast. I took care of all my boots and bags, so they would last forever and keep their resale value in case of a rainy day. Looks like that rainy day came a lot sooner than I thought, what with my career tanking.

I had to take a steadying breath to bring me back to here and now. There were lessons I could learn here, about who I was and where I came from. If I had to suffer being around horses, then I would make it worth it and learn as much as I could.

I watched, mesmerized as Lottie tossed the saddle onto Rakko's back and began securing the buckles, pulling the straps tight.

"Grab me the bridle," she ordered without looking at me.

"Okay . . ." I went to the wall and assumed the dangly leather things were reins, but I was lost with what a bridle was. "What am I looking for exactly? Could you describe it?"

An arm brushed past me.

"This," Lucas said, holding the requested bridle. I would never have guessed it in a million years.

"Thanks." I took the leather-and-metal contraption from his weather-tanned hand and gave it to Lottie.

"I'm going out for my ride. Lucas, you're in charge till I get back. Give Avery your old hat and show her how to change the water in the troughs."

Lottie made quick work getting Rakko ready for their ride. Lucas and I awkwardly stood next to each other, watching. I was new, but I wasn't sure what Lucas's excuse was.

She made a clicking sound with her tongue and kicked Rakko with her heels and took off out of the barn.

"So where is this hat?" I turned and asked my new *manager*. Seriously, what the fuck?

"Back here." I followed Lucas to that same room on the far end of the barn. It was a boring stockroom full of bags of feed and shelves lined with boxes and canisters. Lucas took an old cowboy hat off the top shelf and dusted it off.

"Here," he said as he handed the hat to me. His fingers brushed mine as he plopped the hat in my hands. I decided to ignore the static from his touch and instead examined the old hat—the straw loosely woven together, the light tan color that was aged to a dark brown around the edges. I balled up my hay-encrusted ponytail, twirling the ends around into a bun, and plopped the hat onto my head.

He didn't watch me; instead he reached up and grabbed a small bucket full of cleaning supplies.

"How do I look?" I beamed my most winning smile at him, mustering up a cheerful tone.

"Who cares when we're surrounded by horse shit?" He brushed off my attempt at levity, turning on the heel of his boot, and walked past me and out of the barn.

What was with this guy?

"Hey!" I called after him.

He refused to stop, just kept walking to the paddock with the fewer horses, opened the gate, and let it slam shut as he walked in.

"I said hey!" I shouted, running now to catch up to him, throwing the gate open.

Lucas was at the big tub of water, squatting as he reached down with the bucket and then pushed the tub over. Scummy water full of debris flowed out and onto the dry red dirt.

I maneuvered to avoid piles of horse poop and the flood of nasty water and planted myself right in front of the judgmental asshat.

"What is your problem? At this point it has to be about more than just my song. You have a vendetta against me, and I can't work under these conditions."

"What work? All you have been doing is making a mess and complaining." He frowned and looked over my head.

"You can at least look me in the eyes."

"Where are the horses?" He was looking frantically now around the paddock. "Fuck!" He took off running.

I turned around and saw the gate wide open with four horses galloping away in the distance.

Lucas whistled to Red and Davey. They stopped their chores and came out to meet Lucas. On unhurried feet I went over to see what the commotion was all about.

"Tack up Peso and Tiny and get the horses. I'll deal with the liability."

"Excuse me?" I just knew he was referring to me.

"Why the hell would you leave the gate open?"

"Umm, first time on a ranch, remember?" Were there rules? Why wouldn't they tell me the rules first? This was one hundred percent on them.

Davey snickered, his hand covering his mouth. He looked like he was ready for some live entertainment.

"C'mon," Red said, tugging Davey away.

"Hell no, I gotta stay for this." Davey laughed.

"Get the horses, man," Lucas ordered, his tone brooking no room for rebuttal.

The men left to wrangle the horses, and once Lucas was sure they had it handled, his head whipped to me. His flinty eyes were on me like a hawk and I was his prey. He stepped closer, taking a breath to steady himself, but he clenched his fists, like he was using all of his willpower to contain his anger.

"Never leave a gate open. That's rule number one. Now I'm going to show you the basics so you don't cost me or my guys our jobs, but you better pay attention because I ain't repeating shit."

"That never would have happened if you didn't insult me, storm off, and then ignore me."

"My job isn't to be your friend. Hell, I'm not even your babysitter. We all have jobs to do and limited hours in the day to do it. It's not my fault you lack basic common sense."

"Lack common sense? Do you hear yourself? I'm not an idiot, Lucas. I was thrown into this new environment having never been around a horse in my life. The least you can do is walk me through the basics to make both our lives a little easier."

Lucas closed his eyes, breathing in through his nose, then slowly released through his mouth.

"Fair enough. The guys are getting the horses, but the next time that happens it will be you tracking down each and every horse, roping them, and bringing them all back in. Got it?"

"Peachy." I gave him a saccharine smile and hoped the *Fuck you* I was thinking was clearly communicated through my eyes.

He narrowed his eyes like he got the message.

"I dumped the first trough for you. You saw how I did it, you can do the rest. We have three in the western paddock and four in the eastern . . . What's that look?"

"I don't have a look?"

"You most certainly do. As soon as I said 'western paddock' you no longer had two eyebrows, they converged to one. You do know what directions are, right? North, south, east, west?"

"Yes, Lucas. Never Eat Soggy Waffles." I rolled my eyes.

"Then ask your question."

"I don't want to, you're mean."

Lucas settled his weight onto his right leg and crossed his arms, as if he were making himself comfortable. "Ask your question."

"Not now."

"Avery."

"Lucas." I settled my weight onto my right leg and crossed my arms to mimic his stance.

"Fine . . . I promise I won't be mean."

"No, promise you won't judge me."

"I don't judge you." Now he rolled *his* eyes, clearly exasperated.

"That's all you've been doing since I met you, bucko."

"Did you just call me bucko? What is this, 1997?"

"See right there. You are a judger."

He took another breath. "I promise I won't be mean and I won't judge you based on your question. I want you to understand what you have to do to limit any more disasters that follow you wherever you go."

"Well, the last part of that sentence was unnecessary."

"Just ask your question." Lucas lifted his hands in resignation.

"You and Lottie keep saying eastern and western paddocks. How do you know which one is east and which one is west?"

"Easy." He moved behind me, placing his hands on my shoulders firmly but not roughly, and physically pivoted me left and right.

"Facing the barn this way toward the front doors is north. To our left is west and to our right is east. So that's how you can tell them apart and if you get lost on the property you can find your way. The house is south." He leaned his head close, lips nearly brushing my ear. "Make sense?"

My breath hitched at his proximity and shivers cascaded down my spine. "Yes. Thank you." I cleared my throat to hide the effect he had on me.

"Okay, good." He released me quickly, almost as if he hadn't realized he was touching me. "Now get to scrubbing. We need all these troughs scrubbed and later I'll take you around the property to clean the ones we have out in the pasture."

"How big is the property?"

"Roughly two hundred acres."

"How many troughs cover two hundred acres?"

"We have some of the property fenced off, but there are six out there."

"I have to scrub fourteen troughs? And are they all that big?"

"No, the ones along the fence in the pasture are bigger. Better get scrubbing."

I shook my shoulders, brushing off the negativity, and turned east. Take that, Lucas, I know east now and I am unstoppable. The ranch really was beautiful with the sky so blue.

Squish.

Oh no.

I looked down. My Golden Goose sneaker was ankle-deep in horse poo.

Shit.

CAN YOU COOK OR CLEAN?" LOTTIE ASKED ME.

"I mean ... I'd consider myself an expert in trough cleaning." I looked down at my blistered hand from where I held the scrub brush and vigorously cleaned all fourteen scummy tubs all day. I'd never seen my hands so wrinkled and pruned in my life.

"Congratulations, your first day of honest labor. Doesn't it feel good to work with your hands?"

You know, I was getting sick and tired of hearing her throw shade at me and my work ethic.

"Being awkwardly stooped over a rubber tub scrubbing for hours is nothing compared to doing the same sixteen measures of choreography in five-inch heels for nine hours, hungry and tired. That always seemed pretty honest to me." I lifted my eyebrow, letting my sass show.

She shook her head and sighed. "Peanut butter and jelly sandwiches were an interesting choice for lunch."

"What was wrong with it? You didn't exactly give me a menu."

"It's fine for lunch every now and then, but the men do back-breaking labor and need hearty meals. Can you cook anything else?"

"If you tell me what to do, I could figure it out. Do you have a laptop or something I could borrow, because if you have a dish in mind, I can watch a YouTube video to see how to make it." I wanted to seem more competent than her basic leading question hinted at.

Lottie walked over to the pantry, opened the door, and disappeared. After a moment she came out with an old, thick book with—shocker—red plaid on the cover. She handed it to me.

"What's this?"

"A cookbook."

"*Better Homes and Gardens: New Cook Book, Tenth Edition.* Wow, how old is this?"

"Older than you."

"So, what, I just pick something from here?"

"Basically. For tonight we'll do something easy. You and I can come up with a meal plan to prep and make things easier for the rest of the week while you get the flow of the place."

"I love that idea, thank you, Lottie. I really do want to do well while I'm here."

Lottie's eyes shuttered. Like my genuine gratitude made her uncomfortable. She opened the dishwasher. "Start unloading these and I'll show you where everything goes. After your embarrassing display with the horses and working your hands to the bone scrubbing the troughs—next time ask for some gloves—your primary responsibility will be this kitchen."

I immediately started unloading the plates, stacking them neatly on the counter. Truthfully, I was relieved I didn't have to go back to the horses tomorrow.

She continued, "You'll be cooking three square meals a day for everyone and then cleaning up this kitchen. Since you look like you like shopping, I'll have you go through the attic and the cellar to start cleaning things up to sell."

"Oh, like cataloging and putting things online?" I asked. Lottie nodded her head and pursed her lips in the direction of the upper cabinet behind me. I was starting to understand her unspoken language and put the plates away in their designated place.

"I can do that, easy."

"Before you go thinking it's easier than taking care of the horses—five generations of Foxes have lived on this property. The attic is full of crap."

I nodded, putting the last of the silverware into the proper drawer. After a few moments my stomach rumbled. I guess PB&Js weren't the most filling lunch when doing manual labor.

"So what meal is considered easy?" I asked.

Turned out it was frying catfish, making white rice, and steaming frozen broccoli. It took less than an hour to make it all and left everyone full and satisfied. I was used to high-protein diets with brown rice, usually salmon or a dry chicken breast, and steamed veggies, so I was quite proud of the meal and with how flavorful the catfish was.

"Not bad, Miss Avery," Red said as he tapped my shoulder in the kitchen while we cleaned up. Lottie escaped to do whatever it was she did after dinner.

"Red, I've told you, please call me Avery. We're family."

"It just seems right. Your mom was our Little Miss." Red's smile was sad and his eyes held a distant look. Little Miss was a cute nickname for my mom. While Lottie was harsh and judgmental, nothing seemed so bad that my mom couldn't let me meet these people growing up. This mystery was baffling.

"Comin' through," Davey said as he squeezed past me to grab

the paper towels. "Hollywood, you got any other music besides that one song?"

I didn't need to look at Lucas wiping down the oil splatters on the stove to know his hackles were already raised. Now was the perfect opportunity to launch phase one of Show Lucas His Place.

"I have many songs, Davey. I've been working on a new one too. I saw the piano in the living room, you think it's tuned?"

"Hell yeah it's tuned, Lottie plays it every Sunday," he said as he wiped down the countertop.

My grandmother could play piano? My mother never said music ran in our family, though she never said *anything* about our family. I knew from living with my mom that she was tone-deaf—couldn't match a pitch to save her life. When she was in her feels she would have some wine and sing along off-key to Dido's best CD, *No Angel*. The nostalgic memory made me smile as I towel-dried the glass water cups we used during dinner.

"If you boys want, I could play you a song or two."

"Yes."

"No."

Davey and Lucas answered on top of each other.

"It doesn't have to be one of my songs." I rolled my eyes, putting the final glass away. I didn't need an audience to sing. I hadn't found a TV and there wasn't much reading material apart from a women's Bible I found in the bedside drawer of my room. I wasn't sure if it had always been there, or if Lottie snuck it in there as a big hint for me. I left it where it was.

I left the men in the nearly spotless kitchen to find the piano.

It was a humble instrument; the antique oak was clearly taken care of as I could still smell a hint of the lemon wood polish used to clean it. It was an upright that rested against the wall next to the only window in the living room. The matching wood bench had no cushion, but was inviting nonetheless. I pulled it out and sat down, already feeling more like myself than I had in days.

I let my weary hands rest on the keys. I warmed up with a simple scale, letting my fingers trail up and down the notes to get the feel of the piano.

I may have been a stranger on this ranch surrounded by people who barely tolerated me, but with my hands on the keys I was home. I was Avery Fox, a damn good musician. The notes transported me far, far away and instinct took over. The melody started dancing around me and I sang the first notes of a song I had been desperately trying to get Niles to let me record and put on my album—he refused. He said no one wanted a ballad from me, that my brand was sexy dance music and that was it. Not that it mattered now, since the record was canned.

This wasn't a fun club song people could jump up and down to, but it was the kind that I had hoped couples would gently sway to or little kids would sing to themselves in front of the mirror, pretending the song was for them—because it was. It was for the lovesick, the lonely, the misunderstood. It was a ballad for everyone, letting them know that I saw them and had felt all those things too.

My voice carried as I hit the crescendo and I was really feeling it now. It led into the bridge as I sang for *me*. When finally there were no more lyrics and the notes trailed off, I was back in Lottie's living room.

"Woo!" I turned around to Davey's cheer. Red was smiling and clapping lightly while Lucas stared straight through me as he leaned against the wall. I couldn't tell what he thought from his expressionless face. He looked away first.

"That was a mighty pretty song, Miss Avery." I blushed at Red's compliment.

"It could use some work," Lucas said as he cleared his throat. He pushed himself off the wall, gave the guys a curt nod, and left the room.

"Don't mind anything Lucas says," Red said, getting up off the couch. "I gotta turn in, but I hope you play again soon."

Davey got up too and lightly punched my shoulder with his fist. "I thought it was pretty good. Hey, if you're still around later this summer, maybe you could sing it for my wedding."

"You'd want me to sing at your wedding in front of your friends and family?" I was completely taken aback. Who the hell would want the drama and media circus that has been following me around? I would be a black stain on a day meant to be perfect.

"Shit, no one I know has ever met a celebrity, let alone had one sing at their wedding."

"That might be for the best. The day is meant to celebrate you and your love." Davey's shoulders dropped in disappointment. I quickly added, "But if it's what your fiancée wants too, then maybe we can make it happen."

"I can't wait for you to meet her. She'll be coming to tend to the horses next week, unless you want to head into town with us this weekend?"

"Oh, thank you for the invitation. Can I take a rain check? I'm pretty tired from just one day working here."

"For sure. Well, I'm gonna turn in. Thanks for playing your song."

"Anytime, Davey."

I watched him head out, but he stopped and turned around. "What's it called?"

"'Heartbeats.'"

"It's good." He waved and was off.

With nothing else to do I sat and looked down at my hands. The high feeling I got from playing my music was gone. I flexed my hand and noticed the blister bubble on my palm had popped. Gross. It was as good a time as any to finally take a shower and hopefully fix my hair.

I USED THE embroidered-rooster hand towel to wipe away the steam from my extra-hot shower. The hay was gone, but had been encrusted and caked onto my strands by the horse's saliva. Totally disgusting. I had to shampoo three times before I was sure I had gotten it all out.

After a little digging around in the bathroom I found an old and forgotten pair of cutting shears in the back of one of the vanity drawers. I cut the raggedy ends of my hair in as straight a line as I could manage, then gathered the ends in my fist and started snipping into the bottom as I'd seen so many hair stylists do. I hoped it looked like intentional texture and not what it really was—a poor attempt to mask a butchered mess.

After I was done, I shook my hair out, bringing it around my face and shoulders. It was passable. It was so humid that my usually straight hair in LA was getting a little wave pattern as it air-dried. I liked it. A yawn escaped me and my eyes were red and tired.

Trudging out of the bathroom, I checked the time on the bedside table. It was only eight thirty. I couldn't remember a time that I went to bed earlier than ten, and lately with all the studio time and shoots I was used to getting to sleep by two or three in the morning.

With no phone, laptop, or television, I flopped onto the bed and turned off the light. I laid there for hours. Eternity probably.

It could use some work. Lucas's low voice rumbled through my head. Well, his manners and personality could use some work. What did some cowboy in Broken Arrow, Oklahoma, know of songwriting anyway? I should just ignore him like all the other haters who leave rude comments on my feed. But unlike those strangers hiding behind fake profiles, Lucas was here. Impossible to ignore.

Could use some work. I never said it was a finished product. I said it was something I was working on. The gall!

My fingers lifted in the air and I started playing my imaginary piano in the dark, the notes ringing in my head. My melody was perfect. Every note fit exactly where it needed to go. My lyrics could use some work. Some of the couplets didn't have the emotional punch I'd prefer and the rhymes were sloppy, but it was a work in progress.

It seemed Lucas demanded perfection and I was being judged and measured by some old-fashioned standard he set about what the paragon of a woman should be. Well, it should come as no surprise to him that I was not a paragon of a woman. Shit, according to Google I was about as bad as they got. And truthfully, I couldn't say I disagreed. I could barely take care of myself. I went along with everything my label and team suggested, completely enamored by the attention and the money.

I disgusted myself.

My brain started missing the imaginary notes and I threw my arms down. When sleep still did not come, I had one last resort.

One sheep. Two sheep. Three sheep.

Fuck this. It was too quiet. There were no sounds of cars or sirens or loud people screaming. It was silent and my mind was too loud. I couldn't take it anymore.

I ripped the blankets off my legs and went to the window, throwing it open.

The night was still warm, but more alive than my quiet room suggested. It sounded like a symphony of crickets and cicadas. The stars blanketed the sky, the clearest I had ever seen them. I had never taken the time to stargaze back home. The smog in Los Angeles was pretty bad so I never even thought to try. But this was how the sky was supposed to be. Open. Clean. Bright.

I looked down at the lawn by the giant old oak tree and smiled at what looked like dancing stars. Fireflies.

Never in my life had I seen a real firefly.

Sleep wasn't going to happen, so I shoved my feet into the still-wet Golden Goose sneakers. I winced at the feeling. They got a good hose-down after the horse poo incident, though the right shoelace was beyond salvageable, so I tossed it. My feet squeaked in the soaking shoes as I snuck out of the house and went outside to dance with the stars.

9

THERE WAS SOMETHING MAGICAL AND THRILLING about being on this expanse of a property, alone with nothing but the stars, the crickets, and the fireflies as company. I stood beneath the oak tree I could see from my window and one friendly little lightning bug playfully flew between my fingers.

Under these stars, I wasn't disgraced singer Avery Fox. Right now, I was just a girl (with terrible insomnia) free to do whatever I wanted. I left the fireflies to float through the night air and meandered around the property.

Apart from the cellar and the golf cart out front, there wasn't really much else of note. The porch had wooden rocking chairs, but I didn't feel like sitting. My legs were restless.

Maybe the horses weren't so scary when they were sleeping. The hill sloped down gradually, and it wasn't all that far. I took my time walking, my arms crossed. I couldn't get Lucas's comment out of my head.

Did he really have to go out of his way to shit on my music? I started singing the song to myself. My gut told me the opening verse was right, but the pre-chorus and parts of the chorus didn't feel right yet. The idea was there, and I could keep working on it. So I was proud I had the song in the shape it was in. It was hard-won and I wished Niles and my mother would sit and listen to hear its potential.

Two horses were by the fence of the eastern paddock. Could one of them be Peso? I kept my distance to be sure. It was dark and the air was like a warm hug. I started humming and whistling the melody of "Heartbeats." It just seemed right.

I continued my quiet whistling, walking along the barn. A rough hand covered my mouth, a big arm wrapped around my middle, and I was thrust back and through the door of the barn. My scream was muffled against my attacker's hand.

I bucked my head back and flailed my legs, trying to get purchase and nail my attacker. I would not go down without a fight.

"Calm down! I'm not trying to hurt you," the man whispered in my ear frustratedly. I was incensed. Not trying to hurt me? Just trying to abduct me for nefarious purposes no doubt. I continued to try to scream, then I bit down on his hand.

"Fuck!" He released me and I barely managed to catch my balance before I could fall on my face.

"Stay away from me!" I scrambled for the door, but the rough hand caught mine.

"Avery, calm down. It's me."

I turned around to the man. Lucas.

"What the hell, Lucas!" I extracted my hand from his. "What's your problem?"

"Mine? Why the hell are you skulking around after midnight like some witch here to haunt us? And did no one ever tell you not to whistle at night? You must be deranged!"

"News flash, it's a free country. I can walk around wherever I want and I can sing and whistle and be happy. I don't need your permission."

"News flash, princess, you're in Indian Country. Whistling at night attracts horrors you can't even imagine."

"Well, it summoned you, so I can imagine it."

"I'm just trying to look out for you."

"Really? You call covering my mouth and grabbing me from behind with brute force 'looking out for me'?"

"I had to get you to stop whistling and inside the barn."

"What's the big deal? I wasn't even loud."

"Don't you know anything?"

"I know that before stepping foot in Oklahoma there were only three ways to piss me off. Now there are four. All I have to do is see your face and it will set me straight off."

"You could always go back home, sweetheart."

"Not a chance, *sweetheart*." During this entire exchange our bodies drifted closer together, his nose a hair's breadth away from mine. His gray eyes looked black in the darkness.

His slightly opened mouth was inches from mine; we were sharing space and breath. It was a mistake to look there. I should have looked anywhere other than at his mouth. I had no business admiring his face, or noticing that his bottom lip was fuller than his top. Guilt had me snap my eyes back to his. He tracked everything my eyes did.

Did I just imagine that he got closer to me in half a second? He clenched his jaw. I was affecting him. This was how I could get him back. Lottie didn't tell me I couldn't flirt with the men here. They had to keep their distance from me.

I shook my hair away from my face and my chest. This time it was his eyes that traced my face, trailing from my nose and lingering on my mouth before continuing their descent down my neck and stopping at my exposed collar.

He sucked in a breath.

It was only because it had been almost a year since I broke up with my last boyfriend and I was tired beyond belief that Lucas's proximity was intoxicating in my overtired state. The sound of his breath, and his masculine scent that was sweet, earthy, almost woodsy. It wasn't a scent from a bottle. This was all Lucas, all of what he encountered and surrounded himself with throughout the day. I had to know what it was.

"What the hell are you wearing?" he asked, his voice lethally quiet.

"Huh?" I was still in the Lucas trance.

"Where are your clothes?"

I blinked away my stupor, embarrassed I was so close, leaning into this man. I must have been really desperate to obsess about his fragrance. I stepped away from his body heat.

"I'm wearing my pajamas." I adjusted the spaghetti strap of my nightgown.

"You sleep in this every night?" he asked in a groan.

"It hits right above my knee." I rolled my eyes. It wasn't all that scandalous.

"Creator, give me strength," he pleaded in an agonized whisper. "You can't be wandering around like this."

"Like what? I couldn't sleep so I was taking a walk. Nobody was out here." He was looking at the pitch-black ceiling now.

"You'll catch a chill or something."

"A chill? It's over eighty in the middle of the night."

"This is a working ranch full of horse shit. You'll get chewed up by the bugs."

"I haven't noticed any bugs apart from the fireflies."

He seemed desperate now, taking a step away from me and running his fingers through his hair. "You can't be this obtuse."

"I think you're complimenting me. In a very weird and round-about way."

He gave a flustered laugh, a tight smile on his lips. "C'mon, Avery. Didn't take you for the type of woman to fish for compliments."

"I'm not." I cocked my head, meeting his stare dead-on.

He opened his mouth to speak, when all the horses started whining. The full moon was the only thing that provided any light, so I couldn't be sure if it was a trick of the light, but it looked like all the color drained from Lucas's face.

He moved to the door silently, rolling it closed.

"What are you doing?" I asked.

He shushed me with one hand as he secured the lock into place, before he guided me away from the door with a hand on my back. He brought us to an empty stall.

"What is it? Why did you lock the barn?"

"This is why we never whistle at night. Something heard you and now it's out there and scaring the shit out of the horses."

"What is it? Like a wolf or something?"

"Wolf? In Oklahoma?" He looked flabbergasted. "You really don't know shit," he mumbled as he motioned for me to sit on the ground and left the stall.

"I know a lot of things," I whispered to no one.

"Yeah, is any of it useful?" He came back into the stall with two blankets. He continued, "You have a whole song and persona about being Native and you don't even know the first thing."

"How is that my fault? My mom grew up here, but I never knew all of this existed. I was raised in LA and I went to school on set for the most part. It wasn't like I was around any other Native American students. My mom sure as shit never mentioned anything about her life growing up. I don't know what I don't know." My voice broke and I looked away.

Why was I bothering to justify myself to him?

He paused as he arranged the blankets around us.

"Hey, don't cry." His voice was gentle, how I imagined he spoke to a spooked horse.

"Why am I here, Lucas?" I asked, fed up.

"You tell me, princess. You just showed up out of the blue. Was it really so bad that you couldn't face some online trolls?"

I laughed a soulless, bitter laugh. "It was a lot more than online trolls. I had death threats sent to my hotel and the venue before my show. I meant, why am I locked in this barn, sitting on the floor of this horse stall, with you."

"I ain't going out there. Who knows what you summoned. Could be a Kolowa for all I know."

"A Kolowa? What the heck is that?"

"A bad monster. You don't want to know."

"When do you think it's safe to leave the barn then?"

"When the sun comes up."

"Are you serious? And you think *I'm* ridiculous? I can't sleep on the floor of a barn next to you."

"Who says I wanted to sleep on the floor of the barn next to you?"

I held up the blanket and raised my brow.

"You can have your own stall, there are fourteen others. I'm staying right here, because I plan on livin'."

"It could have been something harmless that spooked the horses. This is ridiculous." I stood up to go.

"Oh no, I'm not sending Lottie's headstrong granddaughter out there when an ogre or something is spooking the horses."

That made me pause. I wasn't convinced there was a Kolowa out there, whatever it was, but what if there was a bear out there? Or worse, a cougar or a pack of coyotes? "Would you walk with me?"

"Hell no. I just said I plan on living. Haven't you seen any horror movies where stupid people make stupid decisions? Nope. Won't be me. I am staying right here."

"Unbelievable."

Bang! Something large hit the wall of the barn and I screamed and threw myself down to the ground on top of Lucas.

"Shh! You want it to know right where we are?" he whispered again in that angry, loud whisper.

I buried my head in his chest, and surprisingly Lucas's toned arms wound around my torso.

"I don't like this." My whine was muffled in his chest.

"We'll be fine in here."

We lay like that for a few moments, until both of our heart rates slowed down and I grew too aware of the fact that I was lying on top of the most handsome man I'd ever seen, feeling all his muscles under my thin silk nightgown. When I pulled away, he let me go. I turned onto my back, but my arm and shoulder were still touching his.

"You really received death threats?" Lucas asked me. His tone was soft, kind.

"Several. My team believed them to be credible, so here I am."

"I'm really sorry. I had no idea."

"No one does, not really. People see me on TV, or on their feeds. People start to think I am not a real person, but a brand or product that they own. It's a weird parasocial relationship and when the people love me, they really love me. But as you saw, at the flip of the switch, it turned very quickly into hate."

"It's not all hate. I have seen quite a few people sticking up for you." He nudged my shoulder with his.

The motion and sentiment made me smile. I really did have some ride-or-die fans and for that I was grateful.

When I didn't say anything, he asked, "Why did you think coming here was the best thing for you?"

"It was my mom. No one knows about this place and we figured if I could learn my roots then it would get this 'Pretendian' label off of me."

I could feel Lucas tense as he listened to my answer. "What? Did you hear the Kolowa again?"

"No." He moved away from me just a fraction, but I could feel the loss of his heat.

"What's the matter?" I turned on my side to look at him.

He didn't turn to face me, he lay there now with his arm under his head, staring up at the pitch-black ceiling.

"It sounds like you and your mom just want to use us."

"What do you mean, *use you*?"

"Exactly that. You only showed up here because your career took a turn for the worse, and you just want to connect with us and take that back to the media as . . . I don't know . . . clout?"

"That's not what this is. I'm sorry it took this whole shitty mess for me to finally come here. I have never had a family. It was always just me and my mom. Now I have a grandmother. Red is my cousin. I want to know these connections. My family. My *heritage*. Am I not allowed to discover what that means for me?"

"Yes." He sighed. "It's just we are a community. We look out for each other, so for us to welcome you into our fold and show you our ways only for you to just up and leave . . . What then? How are you helping your community?"

"I hadn't really thought that far," I admitted. "I am just getting through things as they come. I have barely had a single civil conversation with Lottie." Hearing my predicament and purpose for being here through Lucas's perspective gave me a sinking feeling. He was right. I was just hoping to get my affiliation secured and go back to my life in the city. "I might regret saying this, and will deny it tomorrow, but I think you're right."

With my eyes fully adjusted to the darkness and the little light shining through the window of the barn, I saw Lucas's eyebrow arch in complete surprise.

"Of course I am," he said with a smile.

"I've tried talking to Lottie, but she shut me down. I saw the late notices and heard what the banker said the other day. I think I could easily save this ranch and business, but she wants nothing to do with me or my money." How much could property in Broken Arrow cost, really? I was sure it was a fraction of the price tags for houses in LA.

"Lottie is a proud woman. She has had to run this entire place by herself for the past decade. Don't repeat this, but the business isn't worth saving. It's not profitable and we will be in the same place in a couple years."

"So you think Lottie should sell it?"

"No, I think she should evolve with the times. There are so many horse breeders and land is so cheap, people aren't boarding their horses like they used to. Building a stall isn't hard and horses can be outside all year round."

"It sounds like you've given this a lot of thought."

"This is my life."

"How would you suggest Lottie evolve the business then?"

"Easy—turn this place into a youth horse-rehabilitation center. We have horses and there are so many kids who need help. They could come here and help take care of the horses and ride them as therapy. There are government grants and business loans. Really make Red Fox Ranch into a true legacy that means something."

"Is that your dream?"

"Yeah." Lucas rubbed his eye. I was tired too, but I had a feeling he was being bashful.

"Why haven't you gone off on your own to start this business?"

"I don't have the capital. I've been living here and working for Lottie since I was sixteen. She needs me."

"I'd help you start this ranch."

"What? You'd give me money? Nah. You don't even know me."

"I'm starting to find out you aren't as big of a grumpy jerk as you led me to believe."

"No, I'm an asshole."

We laughed. "Have you ever had someone believe in your dreams before?"

He didn't answer.

"That first yes is magic. I remember when I landed my agent after I did a few nonunion commercials. Having someone say yes opens so many doors and it changed my life."

"I wouldn't take your money, Avery."

"Where will you and Lottie go then if she has to sell and it's all gone?"

"I'd try to find another job on a different ranch." He shrugged.

"It's too bad you can't try to convince her to convert this ranch to a rehabilitation center. I'd be your angel investor or something. She wouldn't even have to know."

"You'd do that?" He turned around to face me now.

"This is my family home. I may not know this family, but I have the means to help. I don't want to see her lose all this history, especially before I can even learn it. My whole childhood I dreamed of having a family like this. I pretended my Kermit the Frog stuffed animal was my uncle for a solid year."

"I don't want her to lose this place either. I know we can get this ranch right side up and help people in the process. What would you want in return? Fifty percent of the profits or something?"

"What? No. This is my grandmother. I wouldn't take money from her pocket."

"Then what do you want? I'd want to make sure you get something out of this too."

What would I want? I had money, but what I lacked were people. All I had was Chelsea and I could barely contact her. She was with My$teriou$ Money now since this scandal screwed her over. She had to earn a living. "It would be nice to have a friend. Someone who can show me the ropes on what it means to be Muscogee, what our culture is all about."

"You want someone to teach you to be Indian?" He sounded dubious.

"Not someone. You."

"You help me save this ranch and I show you the ropes?"

"Yes. You have to genuinely and patiently teach me our ways." I held my breath in hope.

The moment stretched in silence as Lucas considered my proposition. "Ancestors help me, but you got a deal."

"Really?"

"Yes."

"Yay!"

"Shh, keep it down."

"Sorry."

We lay there, inches apart, in silence. Just when I thought he was already asleep, he said, "Kermit the Frog would make the best uncle."

I smiled to myself.

"He was the best."

I could tell he was nodding in the dark. "We should really get some sleep."

"Thank you, Lucas," I whispered.

"Consider this your first lesson. We don't ever whistle at night."

AT SOME POINT IN THE WEE HOURS OF THE MORNING I had fallen asleep, because I was once again rudely awoken before my body was ready.

"Why will no one here let me sleep?" I groaned, sitting up with a crick in my neck and sharp pain on my side. I never wanted to sleep on the hard floor of a horse stall ever again.

"We gotta get you back to the house before anyone sees us and assumes the worst." Lucas's tired voice was throatier, and god dammit, sexier than his normal voice.

Sleep refused to relinquish my sight back to me, so half of the vision in my right eye was blurry, but it looked like Lucas was blushing and adamantly staring at the ground.

"You might want to fix your nightgown," Lucas said, clearing the frog from his throat.

The left strap of my slip had fallen down and while there was no nipple visible, there was quite a lot of flesh hanging out for my liking. "Oops." I tried to laugh it off. It was not like I came out of the house in the middle of the night to seduce anyone here. I hadn't even thought twice about my pajamas. It was hot, this was the best thing in my suitcase to keep me cool, and I threw it on. When I left for my walk I forgot I was even wearing it.

I stood up and shook my right leg; it had fallen asleep and the tingles were painful. I limped around looking for my shoes that I had kicked off before sleeping. It was unbelievable. They were still damp.

"What time is it?" I asked Lucas, who was peeking through the window.

"A little before five."

"You can tell that just by looking at the sky?" This was some Crocodile Dundee shit. I liked it.

"Oh yeah, the ancestors taught us way back when how to tell the hour based on the color of the clouds as they move in the pre-dawn sky."

I scurried to the window. "Wow, how do I do that? You know what, I think I see what you mean. That dark purple means five?" I asked, looking at the still-dark world that was slowly giving in to the day.

"No."

"Not purple?" I squinted. "I don't really see another color."

"I was joking." He nudged me with his shoulder and continued, "I'm wearing a watch. We don't know mumbo jumbo shit. That's lesson two. You need to be less naive when you're around the uncles and elders. They'll razz you to hell."

"Oh." I flushed with embarrassment. "I need to get back inside before Lottie is up and around. I guess I'll see you a little later."

Lucas nodded at me and watched as I snuck out of the barn. By the time I made it back to the house, it was still dark and quiet. On silent, hurried feet I made it safely to my room right before I heard Lottie's bedroom door shut and her pitter-patter as she walked in the hall and past my door.

My chest heaved as I tried to gulp down breaths. I quickly changed into a floral blouse and a pair of jeans to go and make breakfast.

Biscuits and gravy was a favorite breakfast dish of mine that I rarely ordered anymore, but since I was here, I thought—fuck it— I'll eat all the calories I want. I was bound to work it off anyway.

There was no sausage in the fridge, but there was a pound of bacon so I fried that up easily. The *Better Homes and Gardens* cookbook had a biscuit recipe and I did my best to follow along. I popped them in the oven to bake.

I dumped the bacon grease into a bowl and started on the gravy, sprinkling the flour to brown as the recipe said. It turned brown really fast so I quickly poured in the milk. I stirred it around with the bacon bits, and the milk started bubbling and frothing. With the spatula, I tried to stir faster and pop the bigger bubbles, but nothing seemed to help. Then the worst thing happened. Mixed with the bacon bits were now curdled clods of milk. It was a disaster. The clock on the stove read six and the guys would be in at any moment. It was a miracle Lottie hadn't come to check on me.

I got a new pan out and I tried to pick out the pieces of bacon to start a new batch of gravy. I went to the fridge, desperate to see if there was anything I could add to the gravy, and I found some lunch meat. I wasn't proud of it, but these people didn't expect much from me. I grabbed the bologna and started chopping it up to add to the pan.

A foul burning smell came from the stove—the biscuits! I couldn't lose them too. I threw open the oven door and mercifully they were fine. Where was the smell coming from? I stood from my crouched position and looked at the charred pieces of milk-covered bacon on the new pan. I'd forgotten to turn the burner down—they were completely scorched. Fuck!

I turned the burner off and sank to the floor. I needed a You-Tube cooking influencer to show me the ropes.

"Smells like we're eating charcoal for breakfast." Lucas's morning rumble floated to my ears. This was just great.

"Sorry. I'll fix it. Peanut butter and jelly sandwiches." I stood up and headed to the pantry for the peanut butter and bread.

"Nah, wait. We can fix this." Lucas walked to the refrigerator and opened the freezer door and pulled out a frosty gallon Ziploc bag full of green stuff, maybe spinach. He handed it to me.

"What's that for?" I asked.

"We're makin' scrambled eggs with wild onions." He pulled out the whole carton of eggs from the fridge. "Get a bowl and whisk. Consider this lesson three, we love our wild onions."

"They kind of look like normal green onions," I said as I followed his instructions.

Lucas set the eggs down next to me. "Crack all of these and whisk 'em up good." He took the bag of onions, pulled out a huge handful, and threw them in the sink, turning the faucet on and cranked to the hottest setting.

"Did Lottie pick these?"

"Me."

"Do you grow these on the property?" I asked, cracking another egg into the bowl.

"I ain't telling you where I get my wild onions."

"Why is it a secret?" You would think these were a hidden clue from a *National Treasure* movie.

"They are getting harder and harder to find every year. This is a traditional herb. Did you keep the bacon grease?"

"It's in that blue bowl by the sink."

"Perfect." He smiled at the bowl as he lifted it, engulfing the edges of the dish with one hand and taking it back to the stove.

Ding!

The egg timer went off. The biscuits were ready.

"Yay! Move over!" Oven mitts ready, I pulled out the steaming tray of biscuits and they looked perfect.

"Not bad." Lucas looked over my shoulder.

"Was that praise, Lucas? Be careful, a girl could get used to it." I turned around in time to meet the twinkle in his eyes and my stomach flipped.

I set the baking tray precariously on the stove, pushing the pans of ruined gravy and burnt bacon bits to the back burners.

"Here." Lucas brushed past me and set a cooling rack on the counter next to the oven. "We need more space to cook the onions and eggs." He then took the fucked-up pans to the sink. I'd deal with those later.

He brought the now-thawed onions and threw them into the warm bacon grease and started frying them up. He jerked his chin at me and then the pan. I got the message and reached for the spatula.

"Now you can pour in the eggs," he said, his mouth so close to my ear it sent a shiver straight to my toes.

"Ah shit, somethin' smells great!" Davey's loud voice boomed through the house. I felt the lack of Lucas's heat at my back, knowing instantly he stepped away.

The eggs cooked up in no time and it was a good thing they did, because Lottie walked in followed by Davey and Red. Her nostrils flared twice and her eyes tracked the entire kitchen. I saw the mess through her eyes and I shuddered. There was flour on the floor, dirty dishes covered the entire counter surface, the pans were stacked in the sink, and it smelled like burnt milk and bacon.

But I wanted to focus on the positive—the eggs were fluffy and smelled delicious and the biscuits were the most perfect things I had ever seen. Pillsbury commercials were mediocre compared to these.

"Bon appétit!" I spread my arms out like a thrilled magician. We piled our plates with food and sat down to eat.

I waited to take a bite, excitedly watching everyone else. I had always felt proud of my work on the screen and in the studio, but this was different. The men shoveled the eggs in their mouths.

"Nothin' on this planet better than eggs and wild onions," Red mumbled through a full mouth.

"Could use some salt, but otherwise these are good," Lottie said as she forked another dainty bite into her mouth.

Crap. I knew I forgot something. I didn't season them. Oh well. I took a bite and the flavor exploded in my mouth. When Lucas threw the onions into the pan, I was worried the flavor would be too strong and overwhelming, but the taste was very mellow and delicate. I loved it.

Next up were the fluffy biscuits. I pulled the top off and slathered butter on the warm inside and took a bite, ready to savor the moment.

Instead, I spit it out and everyone followed.

"Disgusting." Davey wiped his tongue on his napkin.

"I followed the recipe to a T. I don't know what happened!" This breakfast was a disaster.

"It tastes like you mixed up the measurements for the salt." Lucas coughed and chugged his water.

"I put in a tablespoon like it said," I huffed.

"Teaspoon," Lottie said.

I put my head in my hands. "I'm sorry, it's early and I'm still a little tired. I must have misread it."

"It's okay, the eggs are great," Red said encouragingly.

"Thanks." I didn't have it in me to admit that the only edible part of this meal was because of Lucas. If it had been up to me, everyone would have been eating PB&Js again.

A hand started patting my back. It made me jump in my seat. When I looked up, I saw Lottie pull her hand away.

"It was a good try. Next time you'll get it. I need another cup of coffee and then I believe everyone knows what they're supposed to do? Avery, you'll clean up the kitchen and when I come back, I'll show you the attic and where to start."

I nodded, biting my lip.

Everyone started clearing their plates and taking them to the kitchen, but Lucas lingered in the chair next to mine.

"It really wasn't all that bad. You're getting the hang of it," he said.

"Careful, we still have lunch and dinner."

"I saw a bunch of chicken in the freezer, that's easy to cook."

"Oh yeah? You like yours medium rare?" I asked him, keeping my face neutral.

It had the desired effect. Lucas looked absolutely horrified and dumbfounded.

I laughed, a real good belly laugh.

"I'm kidding! Of course I know you have to cook chicken all the way through. Give me some credit."

We locked eyes and it felt like it was the first time Lucas actually saw me. Beneath the Avery Fox image and the getting off on the wrong foot. His mouth broke out into a slow, crooked smile. He had a slightly hooked tooth that gave him a wolfish air. It was devastating, because I did not need to be any more attracted to this man.

"You comin', man?" Davey poked his head into the dining room.

Lucas shook his head, like he was shaking himself out of a stupor. He took his plate and left.

THE SUN FILTERED into the musty attic; beams of light illuminated dust motes dancing in the air. It wasn't like the tiny attics I'd come in contact with in crappy rentals in California, where you had to push a small rectangle of cottage cheese drywall up from the ceiling to shove Christmas decor out of the way.

This attic was different. It was huge. An unassuming wood door on the second floor that looked like it led to a closet actually hid a narrow set of stairs that went straight up to the unfinished attic. Exposed wood beams crisscrossed above me and stacks of boxes and crates filled the space. There was only a sliver of room to slip between the stacks to try to find anything.

"This is it," Lottie said, squeezing through the tiny aisle ahead of me. I sucked in my stomach and turned sideways to follow.

"I tried to catalog this stuff years ago, but you know how it is, other things take priority and then next thing you know twenty years pass by and this has just been sitting here collecting dust," Lottie continued. She stopped to sneeze, and I felt my nose tickle in commiseration. "If I reckon correctly, this back here is the oldest stuff that is likely worth the most for antique enthusiasts."

I stopped to stand next to her and stood on my tippy-toes to look over the wall of boxes. Behind it was an old-ass spindle like in *Sleeping Beauty*.

"How the hell am I gonna get that out of here?" I asked, bewildered. No wonder this stuff just sat up here forgotten; it was overwhelming to see the amount of work. I was happy to do it, but I was limited with what I could physically carry down the staircase on my own.

"Oh, I wouldn't worry about that. Focus on all the stuff in the boxes and crates first, make a wider pathway. Then you can take photos of these up here and if we get any takers, we can make moving it a requirement."

I nodded and turned around to the other side of the attic. "Any idea what kind of stuff is over here?"

"No idea." Lottie lifted the lid off the closest box and laughed. I craned my neck to see what could bring such delight to Lottie's eyes.

A rainbow clown wig. She reached in and pulled out a single oversized shoe and a horn.

"Do we have a long history of clowns in the Fox family?" I asked, giggling behind my hand.

"I have no idea what secrets this place holds, but I can't remember anyone wearing a clown costume. This looks like something my uncle Chet would have. He was always pulling pranks."

"Which side of your family did Uncle Chet come from?" I asked in my smallest voice possible, afraid I'd spook her into clamming up again. But if he was her uncle, then that made him my great-uncle. It was another tether to this place, this history. I was desperate for any kernel she would give me about where I came from.

"My daddy's younger brother." She smiled to herself, patting the wig down to put the lid back on. "He was a good man. He had some issues, but you'll find that we all do."

"Like health issues?" Did we have hereditary diseases I should be taking preventative measures for, like heart disease or cancer?

"He was an unsettled soul, always in and out of trouble, till trouble got him in the end." Her mouth visibly zipped up and she rolled her shoulders back.

Curiosity got the better of me. "Did he kill someone?"

"What? Why on God's green earth would you assume that?" Lottie put her hands on her hips like an angry teacher.

I huffed a breath and let out a laugh of exasperation. "You don't tell me anything. I'm left to just let my brain fill in the blanks." I shrugged, hands turned out as far as the small aisle could accommodate.

"Your brain went to murder?" She sounded genuinely shocked.

"I guess that is a messed-up assumption. I won't pry if it hurts you to think about." I looked down at the ground. Maybe our family history was full of pain, and she wasn't purposefully hiding things from me but protecting herself from reliving difficult memories.

"Uncle Chet wasn't a murderer, but he was a klepto. He couldn't help himself. He never needed the things he stole, but he swiped a pack of cigarettes for the hell of it and when the shopkeeper caught him, Chet ran out into the road and was hit by a car."

"Oh my goodness! That's so tragic." What a terrible story.

"It devastated my family. This happened back when I was a little girl, but my daddy was never the same. Do you have a compulsive urge to steal things?" She raised her eyebrow at me in question.

"No, though the internet does believe I stole a false identity and culture. People leave 'culture thief' in the comments of my Instagram."

"Your what-a-gram?"

"Nothing." I shook my head, ashamed I had said anything, even if it was a joke after learning about the tragic ending to my great-uncle Chet.

"I don't know about the internet or grams, but you aren't a 'culture thief.' I don't even know what that means."

"You saw the tabloids, Lottie. No one believes I'm Native American, and you mentioned it would be easy to enroll me, but I don't even know if that would be enough to satisfy everyone I pissed off wearing that warbonnet on the cover of *Rolling Stone*." What Lucas said last night about using them for clout played through my mind. That was not what I wanted to do. I wanted to have family, be a part of something. Belong somewhere. But with how contentious the media was, would they warp my attempts at connection? The last thing I wanted was to make things worse for everyone and keep this narrative in the tabloids going. I didn't want any of this vitriol directed at them—especially not as I was trying to get to know them. I wanted them to like me . . . to love me. I wanted to belong to the Fox family by more than just my name. That dream seemed impossible at the moment, but for Lottie to host me—it felt like there was an opening there.

"I don't know what all the fuss is about. For the week it came out all I heard was Lucas yelling and complaining about it. I mean I get why the greater Indian Country would be up in arms, but for the rest of the country? They were fine with it when Cher did it, or when Johnny Depp did it. There are still so many schools with Indians as mascots, and teenagers wear feather bonnets all over Oklahoma. I don't think it's good at all. But death threats? The conversation needs to be had and everyone needs to respect Native imagery, but it was sad to see so much anger directed at you, when so many get away with it."

"If I could go back in time, I never would have agreed to wear it. It looked edgy and the statement was to reclaim the imagery, but it backfired." I looked around in that dusty attic; it was a time capsule full of relics of our past. If only I could just as easily hide my regrets somewhere in an attic, forget, and move on.

"Can't you tell these people on insta-whatever that you acknowledge you made a mistake and the intended message was lost in the inappropriateness of the medium? I heard one of the ladies in my Bible study say that and thought it was smart."

"Your Bible study talked about me?"

"Well, yeah, it was the biggest news to shake Indian Country since the Redskins changed their name to the Washington Commanders. When our collective voice gets heard, it makes waves."

"Do the ladies in your Bible study hate me?"

"No, sweetheart. No one here hates you." Lottie's tone was gentle.

"Not even you?"

Her honey eyes turned hard, and she clenched her jaw. "Especially not me."

I sucked in a breath, unsure of what to say. It was a loaded moment and my eyes watered. She had no idea how much I needed that. She had not made a single moment of my time here easy, but this made it a little better.

Lottie clapped her hands together. "Now you got work to do. I would start by looking for the easiest boxes to move and you can stick them in one of the spare rooms to start cataloging."

She tried to scoot by me, but there was no room for two grown women, so she got stuck.

We both mumbled "Sorry" and I tried to sidestep back toward the attic door so she could get out, but then she stepped on my foot.

"Don't move, I'll get by." Lottie grabbed the tops of the boxes to use as leverage to climb out.

Stubborn woman.

Lottie made it to the door, but I realized I had no idea how I would catalog, take photos, or upload them online.

"Wait!" I called after her.

"What?"

"Do you have a camera and a computer?"

"Lucas has all that. He runs everything technology-related for me. You can ask him for what you need at lunch. Now I reckon you best get started, so you can make some headway before heading down to make food."

"What time is it right now?"

She stepped back into the attic, dug through a crate by the door, and pulled out a round clock. Each hour had a different chicken picture and the twelve was a rooster. How fitting.

"This still works, use this."

The hands were almost to the eight hour. Lottie nodded with a tight smile and left. I looked all around me at the mess and history of generations of Foxes. Then the clock started to cluck.

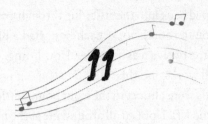

I STACKED FOUR BOXES AT THE BOTTOM OF THE ATTIC
stairway before I ventured to the spare rooms. I chose the one
closest to the attic and it was another time capsule. I had found
what I was sure was my mother's old room. It was the room of a
teenager. The walls were covered in boy band posters and the vanity had Polaroids tucked in between the mirror and the wooden
frame. The photos were of my mother as a young teen with her
friends. She looked so happy and carefree—far from the woman I
had known my whole life. In one photo, she was wearing a costume with a feather boa, clearly in some sort of play. Another was
of her sitting on the floor with a friend, wearing makeup with too
much glitter. It was cute.

One picture stood out, because it had hearts drawn all over it.
It was a photo of her with a boy. He looked maybe a year or two
older than her and she had to have been about sixteen in the photo.
He was wearing a brown cowboy hat and a blue-checkered shirt.
He had light blue eyes and dimples on either side of his smile. My
mother was kissing his cheek. I looked away; it felt like I was invad-
ing her privacy. She had a whole life and family before me. It didn't

look easy, as I'm sure Lottie made my mother do many chores, but it looked a lot easier than how we lived in California for years.

A sinking feeling formed in the pit of my stomach. Her decision to leave must have been due to something truly devastating and horrible. Lottie clearly loved my mom very much—she hadn't changed a single thing in her room; it was exactly how my mother left it. Something happened to sunder this relationship and I had to know what. I'd been here only a few days and I wasn't sure I was really adequately prepared for what it could be.

I moved the boxes into my mother's old room one by one, clearing a large path in the attic to begin the real work once I had the computer and camera from Lucas. The clock clucked again and it was time for me to start getting lunch together.

"FRIED RICE?" LUCAS lifted the glass lid off the ginormous skillet I had used to cook it all up. It was an improvised version of fried rice that I would be embarrassed to serve to anyone in Los Angeles, but out here, what did they care? I used a bag of frozen veggies and some of the frozen chicken. The only Asian seasoning in the house was a bottle of Kikkoman soy sauce that looked older than me—the twist top was crystalized. But I made do.

"Mmm hmm. And it tastes good! I checked." I gave him my most winning smile. After the breakfast fiasco, I was quite impressed with my lunch dish and proud that my skills were improving so quickly.

Lucas set the lid down onto the empty burner and filled his bowl with heaping spoonfuls of the dish. He ducked his head, letting his long hair hide his face, but I saw it—the crooked smile.

I looked down at the ground, trying to hide mine now too, and stepped out of the way so the others could get some. I wanted them all good and full before I served myself. I had been snacking as I cooked.

We settled at the table, all in our appointed seats, and it felt almost like I was a part of the team. I couldn't yet say *family*, but I did feel like the routine was starting to set in. The meals brought us together and while simple fare, it was the best I'd had in a while, maybe ever. I worked hard to make the food that would sustain us, and it was tasty. It was like I gave a little of myself and my love to show that I cared for this place and these people. I couldn't help but wonder if once I was enrolled with the tribe, I would feel more like I belonged.

"Hey, you're doing better already. This was good! You should make it again," Red said with a smile, a piece of rice stuck to the end of his mustache.

"Sure thing, we just gotta go to the store, because I used up everything." Really. After wasting most of the ingredients from breakfast and clearing out the freezer, we had nothing left except for some bread and cheese singles. I guess I could make some grilled cheese for dinner.

"Tomorrow's payday, so we can take you into town to stock up, right, Lottie?" Red asked.

"I need the truck to drive down to Bessie's tomorrow. She's had pneumonia for two weeks and just got back from the hospital. The ladies at the church and I are all taking turns cooking her meals, visiting, and doing some light chores."

"Poor Bessie. I'm glad she's doing better. Maybe you could take the truck this afternoon then to stock up?" Red suggested to me.

"I don't mind going to the store. Who's Bessie?" I asked, because no one ever offered the slightest of explanations or introductions so that I could follow along with anything being said.

"One of our elders and a staple in the community. She makes

handwoven belts for just about everyone. Even after the arthritis gnarled her fingers, she still just kept weaving. Can't keep yarn from her." Davey chuckled as he took another bite of the fried rice.

"I can go with you tomorrow and help. If you want . . . ?" I offered to Lottie.

"That's nice of you. I'd be happy to have the help." With a small smile, Lottie dug into her meal.

"Awesome. This is great, because I found a bin full of yarn in the attic and we can give it to her if she loves yarn that much."

"Excellent idea," Lottie said with a larger smile.

"I can go into town to get groceries. I'll need a ride and some money, since my stuff was stolen . . . and you won't let me ask my mom to send money." I raised my eyebrow, because I still thought it was ridiculous. I had money. Lottie needed money. She was family. It seemed simple.

"I can take you into town after lunch. We don't need your money." Lottie stood with her dish, conversation over. I sighed in defeat.

"Lucas," I said to get his attention. He turned to look at me; again our elbows and knees were only inches apart as we sat next to each other. "Lottie said I need to get the computer and camera from you for the attic project."

"Yeah, you can grab them from me later," he said through a mouthful of food.

After lunch, I waited by the door for Lottie. She was rushing, gathering her things to leave, but then the phone rang.

"Oh drat, I was expecting a call. I need to get that." Lottie disappeared around the corner and I heard her loud *Hello* to whoever was on the other end.

"No, Keith, this place isn't ready for a showing yet."

That piqued my interest and I shuffled closer to the hall to listen more.

"Well, can you push it off another week or two?" She paused, letting Keith speak. "I understand that, but I need all the help I can get."

Her heavy boots started clomping down the hall and toward me. I scuttled back to the door, pretending like I was picking my nails and not eavesdropping.

"Catch." Lottie threw me the keys while she held the phone receiver between her ear and shoulder. She took out a wad of cash from her pocket, licked her fingers, and then counted out several bills before handing them to me. "This is gonna be a while. See if one of the guys can show you where to go."

She turned before I could say anything. I pocketed the money and stared down at the assortment of silver keys, never seeing so many on a single ring before. My palms started to sweat, and it wasn't because I'd stepped outside and was assaulted by the heat and humidity. I hated driving; I had no idea what possessed me to offer to do this. I had a driver's license, got it when I was sixteen, and that was the last time I sat behind the wheel. The traffic in Los Angeles was a nightmare; while driving home from the exam, I got stuck on the 405 because of construction and then—BAM—someone rammed right into me. Since then, I usually had someone driving me places. It worked out so I could put makeup on en route to events or prepare for auditions. Since I retired from acting, I have been using that time to work on my music.

I didn't feel comfortable driving a big truck like Lucas's or even the golf cart. I didn't know a thing about these roads or where the store was. How was I supposed to figure this out without a maps app to help me?

"You okay there, Miss Avery?" Red was walking by, a rake resting over his shoulder.

"Yeah, I'm all good. Just trying to figure out which key is for the golf cart."

"It's not on the ring. Lottie leaves the key in the ignition."

"What? What if bandits come and drive off with it?"

He laughed, a big belly laugh. Maybe I was in the wrong career. With the way I made these folks laugh, I should switch over to comedy. I'd hoped with the success of my single, Lorne Michaels would have invited me to host and perform on *SNL* one day. That wasn't in the cards anymore. I shook off the negative thoughts. They wouldn't help me with the task at hand, which was overcoming my fear of driving.

"This is a stand-your-ground state. Ain't nobody gonna traipse up here with Lottie totin' her guns left and right."

"I thought y'all locked those up."

"Look at you sayin' 'y'all' like a real Okie girl." I beamed at his praise. He took a step forward, leaning conspiratorially, and whispered, "Lottie has more spare guns that even I don't know about."

"That's not reassuring at all. I don't want to happen across any of these wayward guns. What if one goes off?"

"She leaves the safety on, don't worry."

"I'd feel safer without guns lying around."

"You say that now, until one day you need a gun-totin' grandma to scare off a bad boyfriend."

"You must think I have bad taste in men." I rolled my eyes.

"You're a Fox. Of course you have terrible taste in men." Red laughed to himself toward the hill and out of sight. I had no idea what that meant, but after seeing that photo in my mother's room, that sinking feeling grew heavier, as if my stomach was turning into lead.

I opted to take the golf cart only because the size of the truck scared me. How did people see over the dashboard in those things?

The engine purred to life and I shifted into reverse, barely touching the pedal with my toe, and it sent the thing soaring backward. I slammed the brake and the momentum flung my torso into the steering wheel. I groaned.

"You all good here?" Lucas's deep voice came from my right side.

I was winded from the impact but threw a thumbs-up in hopes that he would leave me alone. Just one time on this damn property I'd like to not embarrass myself in front of him.

I heard his feet crunch in the dirt as he approached the passenger side. Rubbing my clavicle, I looked up and wanted to drive away. Lucas had placed his hands on the roof of the cart and was leaning in. It was hot, effortless, like that smolder Flynn Rider does in *Tangled*. He was wearing a white T-shirt today with his black cowboy hat. He cuffed the sleeves of his shirt, which revealed more of his biceps. It was like I was looking at a Native American James Dean. Where did this guy get off looking like that?

"Where are you headed?" he asked.

"To the grocery store."

"In this?" He lifted his eyebrow. His face was full of skepticism.

"Yup! Could you tell me which way it is?"

"The store?"

"Yeah."

"You're not driving this thing into town. Just take the truck."

"I don't know how to drive a big truck."

He rolled his eyes as he pushed himself off the golf cart. "Park the cart back where it was and c'mon." He didn't look behind to make sure I followed his orders. The smug bastard knew that I would.

I met him at the back of the truck.

"You're taking me?"

He nodded. I clapped in delight and skipped toward the passenger door, until my shirt was caught and I was yanked back.

"Whoa, where do you think you're goin'?" Lucas asked me. I twirled around to look at him, but he didn't let go in time and I twisted into him in an accidental embrace.

"To the store." I looked down at his arm. We squirmed to break apart, looking anywhere but at each other.

He cleared his throat before he said, "You're driving."

"I told you I don't know how to drive a truck."

"C'mon, Avery, I know you aren't the helpless girl from days ago. You got a backbone and I'm gonna teach you how to drive this truck. Now are you going to be brave and get behind the wheel to help yourself, or are you gonna be that scared pop princess I met that had everyone making decisions for her?"

Had that only been a few days ago? I could barely remember who that girl was.

I nodded.

"Say it."

"What."

"That you're brave."

"I'm brave." I laughed it off, rolling my eyes.

"I'm not convinced."

"We need to get going, Lucas."

"No, I'm not risking my life in that truck until you sound a little more confident."

"Then you drive."

Lucas crossed his arms and narrowed his eyes at me.

"Fine!" I grunted. "I'm brave!" I threw my arms wide open.

"There we go!"

I hopped in the truck; the seat was so far back my feet couldn't even touch the pedals. Lucas was a big guy. I adjusted the seat and started the engine.

"All right, you know how to drive an automatic?" He looked up at me through his eyebrows, teasing me.

"Ha-ha." I shifted the truck into drive and gently eased the gas. He had parked the truck in the middle of the open space, so there was no need to back out. I maneuvered the truck in a slow arc, cutting back to the dirt path that led down the property to that other street.

I couldn't believe I hadn't left this property in days. I couldn't remember the last time I had stayed in a place this long when I wasn't on a set, in a trailer working. When I had any downtime, I was always going out with friends, hitting up bars and restaurants. It was nice spending this much time with myself. I liked my own company. Without everything that happened, I wasn't sure I was brave enough to face myself in those quiet moments. I certainly never gave myself the time for introspection. Sometimes it was just easier to keep my head down and grind.

"You're doin' great. See what you can do when you put your mind to it?"

"I'm going ten miles an hour." I rolled my eyes.

"We're still goin'." He shrugged. "Now when we come to the road, make a left."

I followed his directions, making our way into town. It was adorable. It looked like a set designer was told to create a cute old Western town and they whipped up Broken Arrow, Oklahoma. The old street was flanked by sidewalks made of brick and antique-looking streetlamps. One huge building had a gorgeous mural. The Native American influence was prevalent. I noticed bronze statues of cowboys on horses and lots of flowers in barrels. I had to make sure my mouth didn't drop open in awe, because while I loved Los Angeles, no neighborhood could come close to replicating this quiet and sleepy town.

He had me keep going straight down the road and we passed a bank with a huge clock—the hour and minute hands were pieces of a broken arrow. I loved it.

"You grew up here?" I asked, because this place was Disney Channel–show perfect. We just needed a laugh track to follow us around on our shenanigans.

"Born and raised." Lucas was leaning back in the passenger seat, his arm hanging out of the rolled-down window.

"Do you like it here?"

"Yeah. I got no desire to leave."

"You've never wanted to leave Broken Arrow? Go travel and see some places?"

He sucked in a breath through his teeth and adjusted his tight pants around his thighs. "I mean, sure, yeah. One day I s'pose."

"Like where?" I was getting exasperated. Was it too much to ask for a little conversation? I stopped at a red light and turned to give him my full, undivided attention. I snapped in his face. "Wake up! What happened to the man that said 'Be brave'?"

"I'm just taking things one day at a time. That's how I live. Sure, one day I'd like to see Machu Picchu."

"Now we're getting somewhere. Why Machu Picchu?"

"'Cause I'd like to see a place built by Indigenous people that's still there. The Inca who built it are gone, but it's a big fuck-you to the myth that Brown and Black people needed the help of aliens to build massive civilizations and structures."

"Okay, that's really cool! You gotta go!"

"One day."

"Maybe that's sooner than you think."

"Oh yeah?" He turned with his crooked smile and my heart sputtered. I looked away to focus on the traffic light.

"Yeah, with the ranch saved and settled, you'll have more free time."

He laughed. "It's gonna be a year or more before the ranch is running smoothly and generating profit. I'm stuck in Oklahoma till then."

"Well, it's a nice dream to have."

"I guess it is."

I drummed my thumbs on the steering wheel until the light finally turned green.

"What about you?" he asked. "You seem like you've been to some cool places."

"Oh yeah, I've been to London to film at the Pinewood Studios lot and did some press in Paris. But lately I've been working and performing gigs in the States. I did get an email about possibly performing at a festival in Ibiza, but that was before . . ." I trailed off. I didn't want to bring all that up with him and risk getting another lecture about how shitty my music was.

"It will all blow over."

"Sure, once I get enrolled and prove myself with everyone here."

"Or even without that. You know how many people do real fucked-up stuff and then a year later they are promoting new projects making people a lot of money. That could be you." He indicated for me to turn right onto a street, and I could see the grocery store a few blocks away.

"I don't want to be that kind of person. This is something that will linger and keep coming back up. I want to do right and make it right, not sweep it under the rug and pretend like it never happened."

"I can respect that."

"And you're gonna respect my music." I turned my nose up. It wouldn't be easy, but I was determined to make everything right.

I was too scared to park close to the store, in a spot between two sedans. I drove to the far end of the parking lot where there were four empty spots in a row and attempted to park. I was crooked, so I cranked the truck into reverse to attempt it again.

I tried four more times to straighten out and didn't get any better.

"All right, enough," Lucas said through laughter.

Our eyes met across the truck cab, an armrest separating us. I could feel my face heat in my attempt not to laugh with him. I really tried my best. I hopped down out of the truck. Despite our newfound truce, I was still determined to make him pay dearly for those insults about my music.

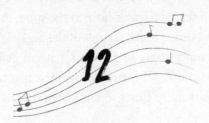

12

THE AIR CONDITIONING WAS BLASTING IN THE STORE and goose bumps covered my arms and legs. Now I wished I hadn't worn denim booty shorts, but the heat here was almost too much to bear.

I pushed the cart around with Lucas following along. These people liked their meat, so I followed the signs for the meat section. Chicken tenders were always easy to pop in the air fryer back home, so I went in search of some.

The prices were a lot cheaper than I'd seen at Gelson's. I snatched an armful of packages of chicken tenders.

"Whoa, what are you doin' there?"

"These are only six bucks apiece, I'm stocking up." I placed them in the cart, but Lucas started putting them back immediately.

"We don't need this much chicken and this cut is expensive. How much money did Lottie give you?"

"I haven't counted it yet."

"Maybe start there."

I dug into my tiny shorts pocket and pulled out the wad. It was $110. He was right. I couldn't get so many packs of these.

"This doesn't seem like enough to feed everyone."

"It's plenty, you just have to shop smart. C'mon, I'll show you how to stretch a dollar. Consider it Indian lesson number four."

"Should we really be saying 'Indian'?" I asked.

"I'm allowed to joke, but I wouldn't let a white person call me Indian. Do you see the difference?" I followed him as I pushed the cart.

"Yes, but I just never grew up saying 'Indian.'"

"What did you say?"

"'Native American,' if we were ever brought up. You'd be surprised by how little Native Americans come up in Los Angeles."

"That doesn't surprise me at all." He looked at tubes of ground meat and focused on reading the packages. I let the conversation die so I could watch him. I shouldn't be ogling, but this man was simply gorgeous. I was a little dazed as I continued to follow him around the store.

Bulk frozen chicken, ground beef, and vegetables on sale took up almost half our budget. Then we stocked up on flour, rice, and beans. After we got butter and milk, the money was gone. Why was dairy so expensive?

It was a lot of food. Frankly, I was used to spending this entire weekly budget on a single lunch for myself. It wasn't always like that growing up, but since I started getting paid more, my mom and I treated ourselves to everything we were denied for years.

"We should check out now and head back," I said as I placed the second gallon of milk into the cart.

"Lucas?" a woman's voice sounded behind us.

I turned to see who it was. The woman looked a little younger than Lottie. She was wearing a black skirt suit with little slingback kitten heels. She looked like a congresswoman or something.

I looked back at Lucas, who was frozen and tense. His shoulders were near his ears and he looked panicked.

The woman's heels clicked wildly as she approached us on hurried feet.

"Lucas, I've been calling you. Why haven't you returned my calls?" She wrapped her arms around him, oblivious to his discomfort.

"Been busy," he mumbled.

"Too busy to call your mama?"

His mother? Plot twist. I looked at her face and then Lucas's. The resemblance was there. She had shoulder-length black hair, slanted eyebrows, and a pointed chin. I could see her in Lucas. But where his eyes were gray like smoke, hers were chocolate brown.

"You know it's your dad's birthday soon. I'm making his favorite roast and want to make sure you'll be there."

"I don't know, Mom. I'm busy. Can I call you later?"

She brushed him off and focused on me. "Now, who is this? Luke, you never said you had a girlfriend. I'm Cat Iron Eyes, Lucas's mother. And you are?" She reached her hand out to me. I had no choice but to take it. Lucas was subtly shaking his head no. No what? Don't take her hand? It was too late—the woman wouldn't let go.

"I'm Avery."

"She's gorgeous, honey. Tell me, are you local?" To the point. How to answer that?

"Mom, can you cool it? We have to go." Lucas started pushing the full cart to the checkout line.

"What? Can't I ask? Is it wrong that a mother would want her only son to be with a local woman? We're Muscogee, you know."

"I'm Muscogee too, ma'am." I paused. Clearly, she thought we were together. Maybe talking him up to his mom would help. "Lucas has been the best thing to ever happen to me."

"Muscogee too! Who's your family?"

"Mom, really, we have to go. I'll go to dinner, but please just drop it."

"I'm Lottie Fox's granddaughter." Lottie never mentioned if she would introduce me around to everyone. I hope I wasn't supposed to be a big secret.

"Is that so?" Cat's smile looked strained, almost fake. Like mentioning Lottie dropped a big bucket of water on her. "All right, honey, I have to head back to the office, but you have to bring your girlfriend. Your father is going to love her."

"I'll happily join you all for dinner. I'll even bake Mr. Iron Eyes a cake."

"What?" Lucas bit out.

"Marvelous, see you in a couple weeks then, honey." Cat kissed Lucas on the cheek before she clickety-clacked in those heels away to the wine section.

"Why would you say that?" Lucas rubbed his eyes with the heels of his palms.

"I was trying to help. You seem distressed. What's the big deal?"

"The big deal is she thinks you're my girlfriend."

"So?"

"So! You aren't my girlfriend."

I rolled my eyes, piling the groceries onto the conveyor belt. "Who cares. Who is she going to tell?"

"The entire town."

"Congratulations, you got yourself a fake celebrity girlfriend. Relax, it's just a dinner. I wonder what kind of recipes there are in that cookbook. Does your dad like chocolate? Also, your last name is Iron Eyes? Why does that sound familiar? Is that a common last name?"

"What? No. It doesn't matter."

"You're right, I'll see what ingredients we have the most of and go from there."

"No, I mean it doesn't matter because you aren't going."

"Of course I am. Your mother invited me specifically." I patted his cheek and added, "Darling." Then I scooted past him to start bagging the groceries.

Not only would Lucas learn to love my music, but I was going to make sure that every single person around him loved me too.

Lucas huffed and shoved food into paper bags. He was sulking. I made him very, very mad.

LUCAS HELPED ME unload the groceries from the truck and put them away in the kitchen. It was all done in complete silence. He didn't look at me or give me more than a grunt when I tried to ask him any questions. He was seething. Maybe I'd overstepped by accepting that dinner invitation. Oops. But it wasn't like he really tried to correct her assumption that we were together. It was extremely awkward, and I didn't want to be rude to the woman by declining her thoughtful invitation. She very clearly had been trying to get ahold of Lucas for a while. Was it also a bonus that I could endear them to me as the ultimate payback to Lucas? Yes, but more important, I didn't want to be impolite.

Once the last bag of dried beans was placed in the pantry, Lucas left the house. I stood in the empty kitchen, knowing I'd have to start cooking dinner, but I didn't want to yet.

My legs had minds of their own and I ran out the door and down the porch.

"Lucas! Wait!" He hadn't made it that far.

He turned around. "What?"

"I still need the computer and camera."

"Can it wait?"

"No." Yes, but I wanted to fix this. He was too quiet.

He closed his eyes and took a deep breath in through his nostrils and held it there for a few seconds before he slowly exhaled and looked me in the eye. "Come on then."

The sun was high, and I had sweat pooling in areas I didn't think were scientifically possible, but I silently trudged along behind him, waiting for the opportunity to apologize.

He led me past the horses in the paddocks—I swear those fuckers were laughing at me. We went around the barn and the land opened up to three single-wide trailers. They weren't terribly old and looked like the kind I had used on countless sets. I didn't know the guys slept in trailers. For some reason I assumed—and I recognize it was fucked up—that they slept in the barn with the horses. In my defense, Lucas did come out of nowhere the other night. This setup made much more sense.

Lucas walked to the farthest one, to my left, or west as Lucas had taught me before. He pulled open the door and stood there. From the outside, it looked like he was mustering up his courage to invite me in.

With his hand he motioned me inside first and I tried to run up the stairs to get in and out as quickly as possible. It was clear I was intruding on his space and he was having major issues with it.

My filthy Golden Goose sneaker, the one missing the lace, came off my foot and caught on the step that was just a little too high, and I couldn't clear it. I started falling forward, but Lucas's toned arm snaked around my waist and stopped me from falling on my face. We stood there, in the doorway of his trailer, his arm holding me pressed against his side, while he was slightly hunched over.

"Steady now," he said. His voice rumbled in my ear and his

proximity was doing things to me. Terrible, sinful, dirty things. Things that I should not be feeling for a man who disdained my very existence. When I got back to Los Angeles I was going to need so much therapy to unpack these deep-rooted issues of wanting everyone's approval, because this could not be healthy.

I hate your music. Oh, let me bone him into loving it and me. I can change him, Your Honor. My head wasn't screwed on straight.

He let go of me and I carefully stepped up into his domain, clearing my throat and warning my inner validation-seeking hussy that she needed to calm the fuck down. I needed to get the camera and computer and go.

Lucas walking in made the trailer shift as it settled with our weight. He avoided looking at me too. Unsure of what to do with my eyes, I scanned his living situation. It was lived-in, years of history and personalization. A small bookcase had a shelf full of books two rows deep. Below it was a shelf full of vinyl records. On top of the bookcase was an old record player. On the counter by the stove was an old stereo with a cassette player. Hanging on the wall was a long, vertical shelf full of CDs and cassette tapes.

It was evident that Lucas loved music.

I looked to the other side of the trailer and there was a little eat-in table and seats—having been in trailers all my life, the seats no doubt turned into a bed. But what made me focus on them was the old acoustic guitar on the seat, its arm resting against the window. Not only did Lucas love music, he played music. His pointed criticism made more sense now coming from a passionate musician and not just some random cowboy who couldn't tell the difference between an F chord and an A.

On the table were stacks of papers, several legal pads full of notes, and old coffee mugs. It looked like Lucas had been burning the midnight oil. If I had to guess, I would think these were the plans for the horse rehabilitation business.

Since Lucas walked to the back bedroom, I stepped closer to the table to catch a glimpse. Many of the sheets were tables full of numbers. Financial plans. *Revenue target* was circled several times.

I wasn't great with numbers, but the math looked good to me. I had no doubt Lucas could work to turn this business around and help kids while doing it. I left his work alone, instead focusing my attention on his music collection. I started with the vinyls.

I crouched down to get eye level, pulling out each one. Old-school country, bluegrass, Motown, classics. I looked to the now-closed door of Lucas's bedroom. Not sure what was keeping him so long, but I kept snooping.

I stood up to look at his CDs and cassette tapes. So many '90s country albums mixed with hip-hop, rap, some U2, which was a surprise, until I saw the eight salsa music albums. Lucas's taste ranged as wide as these two hundred acres of land.

"Sorry, I had to change my shirt, I'd sweated through that one." Lucas was still avoiding my eyes.

He approached me holding out the laptop with the small digital camera on top and a black string—no, shoelace. He had taken the time to unlace one of his shoes to give me a lace. I took his offering.

"Lucas—"

"The charger is here," he continued, cutting me off. He leaned across the table and unplugged the black cord. "So that's that. I really need to finish up some things before it gets dark."

"I'm sorry, Lucas. I didn't know accepting an invitation from your mother would upset you so much."

"Our deal is just for me to show you the ropes around here and you help me save this ranch. That's it. I don't owe you anything else. I don't know you and you don't know me. That was not an invitation to get to know me and my personal life. Okay?"

"Of course. I won't go to the dinner. I didn't want to upset you."

He was quiet for a moment and then his mouth turned up into a small smile. "Oh, you're going and you need to do whatever you can to make that cake taste as bad as you can. Knowing your skills in the kitchen, that shouldn't be too hard."

"Hey! I'm getting better. Why would you want that for your dad on his birthday?" One moment he was mad and the next he was giving me a shoelace as if he cared. One second I can't go to the dinner and now I have to go and ruin it. And yet women have the stereotype of being up and down changing our minds. This man was giving me whiplash.

"It will be a prank. He'll think it's funny."

"You really think so?" I wasn't convinced. His mother looked really prim and proper. A prank over a nice dinner didn't sound like the best way to mend bridges. But I didn't understand his family dynamic.

"Yeah." Lucas's smile was sinister. There was no way in hell his dad would find it funny. Either Lucas was setting me up to make a bad impression in front of his parents, or he wanted to get one over on his dad as a punishment of some sort. I was no one to judge given that I didn't even know who my father was, and I didn't know I had any family until a few days ago, but this seemed fucked up.

"When did you start working here?" My question confused him. It wasn't a non sequitur; something wasn't right.

"When I was sixteen, why?"

"You started working here, what ten, eleven years ago?"

"'Bout eleven, yeah."

"When did you start living here?"

"Same time."

"Oh, Lucas," I whispered. I hugged the laptop to my chest to stop myself from reaching out to hug this man I had barely come to know. Something in my gut told me he would hate a hug from me right now and would think I was pitying him.

A loud knock sounded on the door.

"Yeah?" Lucas shouted.

"I need your help, man." The voice belonged to Davey.

"Comin'," Lucas called back. He looked at me. "I need to go. We good here?"

"Yeah, we're good."

He brushed past me to open the door and I quickly followed.

"Hey, Avery! What's for dinner?"

"I don't know yet, but something good."

"You comin' out with us tomorrow night?" Davey asked.

Lucas was a storm cloud, a bundle of energy as he shoved his hands in his jeans and paced. He obviously did not want me to say yes.

"What's tomorrow night?" I asked.

"We're goin' to the honky-tonk. Gonna drink, line dance. I gotta see my lady."

"Oh, Mary Beth will be there?"

"You remembered her name?" He looked surprised.

"Of course, you see any other women around here? I'm craving friends. I'm going."

"She's gonna love that. I'm not supposed to tell you this, but she loves that Disney movie you did. We all thought the headdress photo shoot was fucked up, but the song is a bop. MB will tell you, I'm sure. Shit, get a drink or two in her and she will blab and tell you all her secrets." He laughed.

"She sounds wonderful."

"You needed my help?" Lucas interrupted our jovial chat.

"Yeah, man. Sorry. I'll catch you later, Avery. Tomorrow, wear your dancing shoes." Davey clicked a finger gun at me and headed to the back barn door with Lucas.

Laptop in tow, I headed to the hen room, aka my bedroom, to get to work on this junk catalog for Lottie, but I had access to the internet again and my fingers were burning to check my email and . . . Google myself.

It wasn't normal, but I was here for a reason—to hide from the public outrage—and call it sadistic, but I wanted to know how bad it had gotten.

I flipped open the laptop and signed onto my email and immediately closed the window.

One thousand unread emails.

I never left my email unread unless there was something my mom or I needed to address in a meeting, but it was my pet peeve to have any unread emails. One thousand? Since I was a glutton for punishment, I opened the web browser and Googled "Avery Fox."

The results were bad. So bad.

It looked like I would be stuck here forever.

I pulled my email back up and started a new draft.

To: Chelsea Brown
Subject: someone stole my phone

Hey, just wanted to let you know someone stole my phone on the bus. I just got access to the internet. I miss you. That book was kind of fucked up. Lol hope you and MM are doing good.

XO, Avery

I hit send and then slammed the laptop shut.

13

"**H**OW LONG HAVE YOU KNOWN BESSIE?" I ASKED AS Lottie drove the truck. The bin of yarn rested between my feet as we bumped along the dirt road to get to Bessie's house.

"Since I was born. Bessie is a pillar of our community. All my life she has been making food for anyone in need, visiting those who get sick, and is just about the best person in our Nation."

"The whole country? That's high praise."

Lottie let out a big, disappointed breath. "The Muscogee Nation," Lottie said as she took her eyes off the bumpy dirt road and leveled me a pointed glance.

"Right, sorry."

"Don't be sorry, just keep up."

"Got it. So how are we helping Bessie today?"

We came up to a small robin's-egg blue single-story house. It was cheerful with dozens of wind chimes and bird feeders hanging from the porch. Squirrels and birds took off as soon as the loud truck came to a stop.

"When you get in there, please refer to her as Grandmother."

"Is she my grandmother too?" I was confused.

"No." Lottie turned off the truck and shifted to me to give me her full attention. "How I was raised in our culture, we refer to our elders as Grandmother and Grandfather. Uncle and Auntie for younger elders, but for Bessie she is Grandmother or Púse."

"Poozee?" I repeated the unfamiliar word. It sounded a little like another word I didn't want to say.

"Pretty close. Maybe just stick to Grandmother until you are feeling more confident with the Mvskoke."

"I just need more practice, but I'll have you know that I played the part of Eliza Doolittle back in the day and the dialect coach told me my pronunciation was the best out of all of us on set."

"I don't know what in the Sam Hill you just said, but sure. Keep practicing. Now, come on. Grab the cooler from the back."

I happily hopped out of Lucas's truck that Lottie borrowed for errands. I decided that when I bought the ranch, I was going to gift them all another truck too. The thought made me smile.

I pulled out the faded blue cooler that I had packed full of chicken and dumpling soup Lottie showed me how to make last night and the slow cooker we left on all night to cook collard greens and bacon. Bessie was going to eat good for a week with this food. I had made extra biscuits (with the correct amount of salt), which were packed in a plastic bag that I had slung over my shoulder.

Lottie stood at the front door waiting for me. When I made it next to her, Lottie opened the door without knocking. Never in my life had I seen a person enter someone else's home without knocking. I never even did this with my friends back home. I guess the likelihood of catching Bessie doing something indecent was extremely low, but it was another culture shock that the door was unlocked.

Where Mom and I lived for most of my life, you had to immediately lock the door behind you as soon as you walked in. Couldn't trust anybody.

Broken Arrow continued to surprise me.

As we entered the cheerful house, I expected Lottie to do the thing that everyone does, saying *Knock, knock* without actually knocking on anything. But Lottie did not do that.

"Hensci, Bessie," Lottie's voice filled the house.

"Estonko?" a raspy voice called from the back of the house, followed by an intense coughing fit.

"She sounds worse than I thought," Lottie mumbled. "Take these through there and heat a serving of everything up."

"You sure this is okay for her to eat for breakfast?" I asked. It was barely after nine in the morning.

"Yes!" Bessie's raspy voice boomed from the back. That answered that. The poor woman was hungry.

I nodded and took the tote bag from Lottie and carried the cooler into the cozy kitchen. Thankfully, all the time I'd spent in Lottie's kitchen had really paid off. I could intuitively infer where the dishes were kept (in the upper cabinet above the dishwasher) and the microwave mounted above the stove made everything really easy.

Hot food in hand, I went in search of Lottie and Bessie. Passing through the dining room I noticed a cute little upright piano against the wall. My fingers twitched to tickle the keys and see if the instrument was in tune, but Bessie needed her food first.

I heard loud cackling followed by a concerning coughing fit. I let the sound guide me to the right room and I popped my head in. Lottie sat on the side of the bed, patting the back of an older woman who was tucked into the bed, with a knitted shawl around her shuddering shoulders.

"Easy, breathe slowly," Lottie murmured. Finally, the coughing stopped. "That's it." Lottie helped settle Bessie against her pillows.

"Smells like bacon," Bessie said in a raspy voice.

"We brought your favorite." Lottie reached her arm out to me, waving me in.

I set the plate of food onto the bedside table.

"This Hattie's girl?" Bessie asked, wordlessly asking for the plate with her gnarled hands. It looked like arthritis made it difficult for her to open them fully.

"Hmm hmm. Bessie, meet Avery. Avery, meet Bessie."

Lottie took the plate into her hands and loaded a spoon with a small bite of chicken and dumplings and raised it to Bessie's mouth like she was a little toddler trying solids for the first time. Bessie swatted her hand away.

"I can feed myself. The hell you doin'?" She took the plate and spoon from Lottie, using one hand to rest the plate against her chest and tucking the spoon between her thumb and palm.

I had to cover my mouth to hide my laughter, but it was too late, they heard. Lottie looked over her shoulder at me with such disapproval, but Bessie was chewing on her food in amusement.

"Sorry . . . Grandmother. I didn't mean to laugh at you." I didn't want to trip over the unfamiliar word *púse* and embarrass myself.

"Hah!" She wiped her hand across her mouth. "You were laughing with me," she said through a mouthful of mushed green beans. "There's a difference."

"Fair point," I said through a smile, moving into the room and settling into the chair next to the bed. It was an old wooden farmhouse dining chair with a faded blue cushion.

"You're the actress?" she asked before shoving another big bite of food into her mouth.

"I'm a musician."

"You play the piano?"

"Yes."

Bessie nodded, scraping the last of the broth into her spoon. I really thought she was considering licking the plate clean.

"Lottie." Bessie handed her the empty plate. "Let's heat up some more while Avery plays me a song."

Bessie threw her covers back and Lottie placed her hand on her shoulder to still her movements. "I don't know if that's such a good idea. The doctor said you need rest."

"The doctor is a hack. I need to eat. They practically starve you in the hospital."

"They feed you three nutritious meals a day."

"Paste without a pinch of salt."

"Bessie."

"Really, Lottie, I'm hungry." Bessie batted her eyelashes and pursed her lips.

"Fine. Avery, come help me get her up."

"Quit babying me. I can get up and walk to the bathroom just fine. I can go a few more feet to the living room. Muttering around like a worried hen."

"We just don't want you falling before you can get seconds of your lunch," I said, trying to be helpful. It appeared it worked since Bessie nodded and wrapped her arm around Lottie's waist and they hobbled out with me on their tails.

Lottie sat Bessie down in the rocking recliner with a direct view of the piano. I sat on the bench, looking for some sheet music.

"What do you like to play?" I asked. "I don't see any practice books."

"I never learned to read sheet music. I learned to play by ear." That made me smile and I spun around on the wooden piano bench.

"I learned to play by ear too! I had to learn to read sheet music though, especially for musical auditions. So you like to play popular songs?" I turned back to the piano. Most popular songs were fairly simple to improvise; generally the same four chords could make up a million songs.

"I haven't played that piano in well over a decade."

I spun back around to look at Bessie. She was staring at her hands. "I'm so sorry. Do your hands cause you pain?"

"My hands, but mostly my heart. My daughter always asked me to play. She's been gone for a long time now."

"What was her favorite song that you would play?"

"Oh, she loved Elton John, but you're too young to know any of his stuff."

"I think I can come up with something." I turned back to the keys, cracked my fingers, then let my hands move up and down the piano to get a feel for the sound. It was a little out of tune, but truthfully, I had practiced on worse. I was no Elton John, but I was a theater kid who did a lot of karaoke parties. There was one song that everyone could sing along to and was fun to play.

I slammed the keys in the telltale *BUM BUM BUM DO DO DO* opening notes and started playing and singing Elton John's "Bennie and the Jets." It had been so long since I let myself go with a piece of music, it was like I was possessed with Sir Elton's mojo. I gave my all, and any notes I couldn't quite remember were easy to ad-lib and put my own Avery spin on. I didn't play the full five minutes, but a condensed version with more repeats of the chorus than verses. I let the notes trail off to end the song and turned around expecting to see happy faces.

What I saw was Bessie quietly sobbing in her chair and Lottie rushing to her with her new plate of food.

"What happened, Púse? Are you all right?" Lottie set the plate down on the floor.

Maybe I should have played something a lot more simple and mellow.

"I'm so sorry, Bessie. I just played the only Elton song I knew."

Bessie looked up, wiping her tears on her shoulder. "It was wonderful. That was my Marie's favorite song. I never played it quite so lively, but she would have loved it. I can feel her here. Thank you." The sobbing and talking elicited another round of coughing.

"I think you had enough excitement for today. Let's get you back into bed." Lottie helped Bessie get up.

"What." *Hack.* "About." *Hack.* "My food?" she barely managed to squeeze out before the coughing took over once more.

"Don't worry, you'll get your food. Once your coughing calms down. Avery, grab the plate."

Not needing to be told twice, I gathered up the plate and set it down on the bedside table while Lottie got Bessie settled back into bed. She finally got her breathing back in order to eat her second helping of her lunch and was soon struggling to keep her eyes open.

"We are going to go and let you sleep. Shauna and Pam will be by later to help with dinner and your evening medication." Lottie leaned over to kiss Bessie's forehead. Bessie lifted her arm and patted Lottie's shoulder with a nod at me.

"You bring her back."

I jerked up. "Of course, I'd love to come back."

"You know any other Elton John songs?" she asked.

"I can learn more."

Bessie nodded as if that prospect was enough.

"We'll be back, sleep now."

Once Lottie was satisfied that everything was left as it should be, she ushered us out of the house and into the truck.

It was a few moments before Lottie started the engine.

"What you did in there . . ." She let her thought trail off.

"I'm sorry. I shouldn't have played such a loud and exciting song. I promise I'll play more mellow songs. I know she is recovering. I feel terrible that I distressed her."

Lottie grabbed my wrist. "No, what you did in there was amazing. Bessie has never let anyone touch that piano in years."

"What happened to her daughter?"

Lottie removed her hand from my wrist and shifted the truck into reverse. "It's a sad story. I'm only telling you so you tread carefully and don't ask her too many questions. Bessie's husband died a long time ago. Marie moved up here to work as a nurse and Bessie sold her old family home in Okmulgee to be closer to her. About fifteen years ago, Marie was working a night shift at the hospital. On her way home, she was in a terrible car accident and died. Bessie has been alone here since, helping the community to stay busy."

I put my hand to my mouth. "That's awful. Poor thing."

"She has been there for everyone. Always with a smile on her face."

I wiped a tear from my eye. Lottie drove in silence for a few minutes. "You gave Bessie a gift. You have a gift." She took her eyes off the road for a moment and looked at me, really looked at me. I could feel her gaze piercing straight through me and to my heart.

"Thank you," I whispered.

Lottie nodded, turning her eyes back on the road. I looked out my window. My heart felt like it grew another size. That was the first true compliment Lottie, my grandmother, had ever given me and I could feel the unspoken message. I was a gift, and so was this time together.

I couldn't squander it.

LOTTIE WENT TO get some equipment from a farm just a couple towns over and took Red and Davey with her. She told me not to worry about preparing lunch, so I had some free time. I wanted to roam the property in broad daylight and get a break from the dust, but something in my gut told me there were more precious treasures hidden in the attic.

I got to work digging through crate after crate. I was no antique expert, but a lot of the stuff up here was junk. Not even fit for a thrift store, with garments so moth-eaten I couldn't even tell what they originally were—they went in the growing dump pile.

Then I found a promising box that was so heavy I had to comb through the contents while kneeling in the corner. There were several leather-bound books and my heart started racing. What if there was a rare first edition book that was worth so much it could save the entire ranch?

I thumbed through tome after tome of the same rich green leather, and I deflated. There were eighteen copies of the same encyclopedia from 1919 sitting on top of old crumpled newspaper. It looked like one of my relatives was a door-to-door encyclopedia salesperson or something. Was it too much to ask for a miracle? I guess there was no secret treasure up here after all. I let myself fall back on my butt to give my knees a break and kicked the box out of my way.

Pain shot through my toe and up my foot. What the hell was that? I breathed through the pain and dug around the wads of old newspaper. Then I felt it, a large metal thing that was wrapped in layers of paper. I reached in to pull it out and was surprised by the weight of it. Peeling back sheet after sheet of delicate faded paper, I discovered a bronze lamp base with flowers on it. It was pretty. If I could find the shade it would probably be worth a little something. Not enough to make a difference though. At least it would be easier to sell than a crap ton of outdated encyclopedias.

I kept searching, sifting through boxes, and organizing, the task so mindless that time passed. A knock sounded on the door, and it made me jump. As far as I was aware, it was just me and Lucas on the property and I'd never once seen him come upstairs. I hunched behind boxes, hiding in case it was an intruder or one of those monsters Lucas feared.

"Avery?" Lucas's voice rolled through the attic. "You up here?"

"Yeah, back here." I popped up like a jack-in-the-box toy on a spring.

He jumped and yelled out.

"Got you!" I laughed. "Serves you right."

"I was just checking on you."

"What? Bored without Davey or Red to boss around?" I cocked my hip.

"Yeah, actually, those lazy bums are still gone and I gotta go find Tilda. She got loose." My stomach made a low rumbling sound. How late was it? I got so wrapped up in the project I forgot to eat.

"Who's Tilda?" I asked.

"She's one of our mares who is a bit of an escape artist. She is expecting a foal and due any day now, so we need to find her before she rolls an ankle or something."

"I didn't know the ranch was expecting a baby!" I clapped excitedly. "You sure you need *my* help?" These creatures hated me.

"Anyone else here in this room?" he asked.

"There is a CPR dummy I found in that corner over there."

Lucas looked over his shoulder and saw the lifeless and limbless dummy leaning against the wall. "The fuck?"

"I don't know." I threw my hands up. My best guess was one of my ancestors was a doctor or something.

"Come on, we don't want her wandering into another property."

"Fine." I sighed as I trudged along behind him.

The sun felt wonderful on my face after being cooped up. The humidity didn't even bother me . . . at first. I started walking down toward the barn.

"I thought you were mad at me," I said to Lucas's back. His black T-shirt clung to his skin with perspiration.

"No."

"Really?" I stopped in my tracks. I wasn't buying that.

"Really," he threw over his shoulder. I let the issue drop. If he didn't want to talk about it, then I wasn't going to make him. I would focus on the task at hand.

"Tilda! Come here, horsey, horsey," I called through my cupped hands around my mouth, throwing in some kisses like people do for cats and dogs.

"What are you doing?"

"Looking for the horse."

"She's long gone and can't hear you. Over here." He motioned for me to follow him to Rakko, who was saddled up and ready to go.

"You're gonna ride Rakko?"

"No. We're gonna ride Rakko."

"I can't get on a horse."

"Sure you can. Now stop dawdling and step into my hands." He squatted at the side of Rakko with laced fingers to boost me up.

I gulped and stepped closer to the massive horse.

"That's it." Lucas's tone was gentle, as one would speak to one of the horses to calm them.

I put my hand on his shoulder and placed my left foot into his hand, and as if I were weightless, Lucas boosted me up in one quick motion. I wrapped my right leg over Rakko's flank and then I was in the saddle. Lucas took a moment to make sure the straps on the saddle were secure, coming around to the right side, and looked down at my right shoe and his black shoelace he had given me. He played with the bow, almost absentmindedly, before snapping himself out of it.

Lucas came back around to the left side of Rakko, vaulted himself up using the stirrup, and settled behind me, snaking his arms around my waist to reach the reins. He clicked his tongue and then we were off trotting out through the pasture and into the woods.

"Tilda!" I called again and Lucas laughed. "What color is she?" I asked.

"She's the pinto." As if that meant anything to me.

"They all look the same to me, Lucas."

"She is mostly white with brown legs and belly."

"Oh, that one." I raised my voice again. "Tilda!"

"Will you stop yelling. You'll scare her further away. You look right and I'll take left. Got it?"

"Got it."

We roamed through the trees and out to a meadow. I did my best to keep my posture straight and limit my physical contact with Lucas, but it was impossible. I looked down at his arm holding the reins; the other was resting on his thigh. He was so sure of himself and his capabilities. He was at home on a horse and in the wide-open spaces of the country. It was hard not to admire him. It was like how I felt sitting in front of a piano. It was part of him and he was part of it. I tried to picture Lucas in Los Angeles and snorted.

"What's so funny?" he asked, his rich voice so close to my ear.

"I was trying to picture you walking down Sunset Boulevard."

He snickered. "That is funny, because it would never happen."

It was an offhand comment and it meant nothing, but it made my empty stomach feel heavy. It was an irrational feeling, because why would Lucas walk down Sunset? Surely not to visit me. Once I left this place, he would never think of me again. Could I blame him? Back home, I'd be hustling trying to get a new brand deal to generate income. Of course, he was entirely oblivious to the ridiculous thoughts running through my head at warp speed. He was focused on the task at hand, and in my internal mind war, I'd forgotten to pay attention and keep an eye out for Tilda. Oops.

He pulled up on the reins and Rakko stopped.

"Did you spot her?" I asked, looking around.

"No, but I think we can take a break here and see if she circles back. You hungry?"

"Very."

He jumped down and dug into the saddlebag and threw an apple at me. I caught it.

"You packed us food?"

"I wasn't sure how long this would take and we gotta eat, don't we?" He reached up to help me down. Was it my imagination, or did his arms suspend me for a moment longer than was necessary, and his hands linger at my waist for an extra couple seconds? I followed him to an old, downed tree trunk and he looked it over. "No fire ants, we can sit here."

So we did. I stole a glance at his profile while he dug into the bag for more food. A thick strand of hair came loose and curled over his forehead. I wanted so desperately to know what his hair felt like. It took all my willpower to keep my hand in my lap. I wasn't his real fake girlfriend. I wasn't even his friend. But it felt like something was there. It couldn't just be me.

"Lucas?"

"Yeah?" He looked up through his thick lashes and if I hadn't already been sitting down, I'd have swooned.

"As your fake girlfriend, I feel like we should know some basic facts about each other."

"You're my fake girlfriend for an evening in a while from now." He lifted his eyebrow.

"I'm a professional, Lucas. I need to know my character. Where did we meet? Where did you take me on our first date? Do you like to be tickled? Are you a boxers or briefs kind of guy?"

"Whoa. What? My parents would never ask about my underwear preferences, and I am not ticklish at all. You're overthinking this."

"What if one of us has a food allergy? We need to know these things if we are going to convincingly pull this off."

He sighed. "Fine. We met at the bus station. Our first date was a PowerBar in the car. I wear boxer briefs, and again I'm *not* ticklish." Oh, this man was so ticklish. Doth protest too much.

"We can't say how we really met! And if that horrendous car ride from the bus station was our first date, then this fake relationship is doomed."

"I thought to sell a lie it has to be based on truth," he said with a shrug.

"Come on, if I were a regular girl you met randomly, where would you take me on our first date?"

"There is nothing regular about you." Lucas looked down into the bag, taking out parchment-wrapped sandwiches and handing me one. "If we were two random and totally normal people, I'd take a theoretical you out for a nice horseback ride to my favorite spot and pack a picnic. We'd talk for hours, and the whole time I'd be working up the courage to give you a goodbye kiss."

Why was I blushing? I cleared my throat and asked, "Where is your favorite spot?"

"That's a secret."

I narrowed my eyes. That defeated the whole exercise, but I pressed forward. "What kind of sandwiches did you pack then?" I asked as I unwrapped the one in my hand.

"Turkey," he said through a big bite of his.

"The most romantic of sandwiches, I approve." I giggled to myself as I took a bite of the turkey sandwich Lucas had prepared. It was perfect from the crispy lettuce to the juicy tomato.

We enjoyed our food for a few moments in silence before I asked, "Did you work up the courage?"

He unscrewed the plastic lid off a water bottle and put it to his lips. He shook his head with a ghost of a smile before he took a sip.

I looked away, blushing.

"What about you?" he asked.

"What about me? Do your parents need to know my underwear preference?"

He spit out his water. "No! You brought that up. I don't need to know and my father sure as hell doesn't need to know."

"Well, that's good since my preference is to not wear any."

Lucas choked on air. It was pure pleasure to watch Lucas's full body flush. He jumped up from the tree stump and spilled the remainder of his water bottle on his pant leg.

"Are you okay?" I asked.

"Fire ant." He cleared his throat not once, not twice, but three more times. "We should probably get moving."

I hid my laughter as we packed up our trash and got ready to go. We didn't get far.

"Lucas! Look! It's Tilda." The pinto horse was staring at us from the tree line. Her stomach was big and round. Lucas got up slowly and whistled. Tilda stayed in place and let him tie a rope around her and lead her to Rakko.

Back up on Rakko with Lucas behind me, I felt a shift in our positions to something more comfortable. His arms fell more snugly around my waist. It wasn't possessive, but the first ride had felt like he was trying his hardest not to touch me more than necessary, and now I felt him everywhere.

We slowly cantered back but I didn't want this moment, this openness, to end. "What is your dream in life?" I asked him.

"I've already told you. Have my own ranch that helps kids."

"Yes, but I mean . . . Do you want to do that alone? Do you want to get married one day? Do you want a family of your own?"

"I do. I'm an only child and I want those big family holidays."

I turned back in my seat. He was smiling.

"What about you?"

"I'm also an only child and always wished I had siblings . . . and a dad. A family in general. This whole experience being here, while not ideal, was always my dream. That I had a big family out there waiting to claim me. I want that big princess wedding and family of my own. I'd let my kids be kids and not force them to work. My mom did what she thought she had to do, but I want a different life for my children if I have them one day."

"I'm sure you will."

I hadn't intended for the conversation to be serious, but it felt good to open up and talk about our values and dreams. It was nice to know we had some common ground. We were more alike than he liked to let on. Before making our way back to the barn, I wanted to lighten the mood, and looking down at his powerful thigh, I did something mischievous. I spread my fingers gently just above his knee and tickled.

Lucas bucked on the seat.

"Devil woman!" he cried through laughter. I could barely hear him over my own.

"I knew it!"

He swatted my hand away. "We will never speak of this again," he growled into my ear, then urged Rakko into a bumpy trot back to the house, where we had to get ready for a night on the town.

14

THE DANCE HALL WAS PACKED. DANCERS LINED THE dance floor in rows as they followed the petite blond caller up on the raised platform, a headset microphone that looked like something Britney Spears used in 2001 hooked around her face. Dozens of dancers stepped in line, their cowboy boots clomping loudly in unison as they all twirled and clapped, following along to the choreography.

"This looks intense," I shouted up to Davey's ear. He was so much taller than me. He leaned down a little. His eyes were scanning the crowd, no doubt looking for his fiancée.

"You'll figure it out. The steps repeat themselves, so you'll get practice and be good at it before the end of the song."

"No one will recognize me here, will they?"

"I doubt it. Why?"

"Oh, no reason. Other than I am public enemy number one and the most canceled pop star since Justin Timberlake got his DUI."

"Justin Timberwho?" Red interjected. Davey laughed.

"Never mind."

"Ain't nobody here who'd lay a finger on Lottie Fox's grand-daughter." Davey patted my shoulder. I felt tiny with his big hand.

"Her reputation extends farther than just the ranch?"

"Her reputation extends through all of eastern Oklahoma."

"Lottie was a hellion back in the day. Barrel racing, shooting contests, the works," Red added. "She can shoot better than anyone here. Her shot is always straight and through."

I nodded. I was safe, that was what I was most concerned about. All the stomping made the floor vibrate, and the music flowed through me. I felt the energy around me and was itching to dance.

"What do we do first?" I asked.

"We drink," Davey said. I could get behind that. "There's my girl. I'll link back with y'all later."

Davey stalked toward a tall, leggy Black woman—Mary Beth. Her eyes were smoldering as she sauntered toward him. Mary Beth was in a cute short floral dress and brown cowgirl boots, her hair was shoulder-length and blown out and styled in big bouncy curls. She launched herself into his arms and wrapped her legs around Davey's torso. She kissed him deeply and with such longing I had to look away to give them privacy.

Never in my life had I ever felt such longing and passion for a partner. Davey had mentioned over dinner that she lived in Tulsa and traveled all around to work on shoeing horses, so they didn't live together yet, because his job was on the ranch. They were saving up for a little house with some land of their own between Lottie's place and where Mary Beth's business was. So, for most of the week, they were apart from each other, carrying on with their jobs. The wedding was still a little ways away, and seeing their reunion now, it was evident that staying apart was difficult.

I wanted that for me one day, where being away from my part-

ner was like losing a part of myself. I'd read enough romances—I
wanted that all-consuming, passionate, forever-and-always kind
of love.

"I see some of my buddies over there." Red jutted his chin at a
high-top table at the back of the place, and around it was a group
of five graying men drinking from longnecks.

"You wanna dance with me?" I asked him.

"Oh no, it's been some years since I could keep up with what
they're doin'. Line dancing ain't what it used to be. If a two-step
comes on, I'll join ya. I don't think you'll be hurtin' for dance partners though." He nodded at some young men who walked by eyeing me and tipping their cowboy hats.

Red nodded his goodbye and headed to the table of his friends.
It was just me and Lucas left, standing in the honky-tonk.

"Want to buy me a drink?" I looked up, batting my eyelashes at
him, hoping he would soften a little toward me and also buy me a
drink, because while it was payday for the men, I wasn't paid and I
hadn't received any money in the mail from my mom. I was flat
broke. And I hoped no one at the bar would card me, because I
didn't even have my ID.

Lucas, with his hands in his denim pockets, looked down at me
with a raised eyebrow. "No."

"I don't mean romantically. I just don't have any money." It was
like our horseback ride never happened.

He shrugged. "There's free water in those dispensers over there.
Have fun." He clapped my back and then walked away into the crowd.

I stared at his retreating form, fighting the urge to give him the
double bird. I tickled the man once and now he was avoiding me.
The drinks couldn't cost more than five dollars here.

Well, I didn't need him. There were several ways to get a free
drink and the easiest was to talk to that group of cowboys who al-

ready showed interest in me. I wasn't proud of it and the inner feminist in me cringed, but a lady's gotta do what a lady's gotta do. It was the oldest hustle known to man. Batting my eyes didn't work on Lucas, but there were a couple hundred people here. It would work on at least one of them.

I'd never been to a country-western dance hall before, nor have I lined danced. So, when Davey said to wear my dancing shoes, those were my regular four-inch stilettos, clear strappy ones. I wore my blue paisley–pattern silk handkerchief dress that tied behind my neck in a halter.

Looking around at all the denim booty shorts and miniskirts, I stuck out like a sore thumb. No woman here was wearing anything higher than a two-and-a-half-inch heel on their boots.

I approached the bar, scooting in next to the tallest member of the cowboy group who leaned against the bar top.

"Hi," I said, and smiled. Flirting in Hollywood was simple. No one was ever actually looking for a connection though. Everyone was out looking to see if the next person they encountered had something that could benefit them. How could you tell the difference? Within the first three questions you would be asked *What do you do?* and if you answered with a regular job, the conversation usually ended there. How did I know? Because I had done it countless times. It was judgy and jaded and I was over it.

"Howdy," the tall cowboy said, using his finger to tilt the front of his hat down.

"Come here often?" I asked. It was corny, but I was a fish out of water here.

"Every Friday. Never seen you before, you new in town?"

"I am. I need some friends. Want to be my friend?"

He smiled, as if he caught me easily. "What do you want to drink?" he asked.

Sucker. I caught *him* easily, but I let him think it was him that caught me. "I'll have whatever you're having." I rested my elbow on the sticky bar. Disgusting. I immediately removed it.

The tall cowboy motioned to the bartender for two beers.

"What's your name, pretty?"

"Avery."

"Avery, I'm Austin."

The bartender popped the tops off and set the beers in front of us. Austin handed me mine and clinked the neck.

"How do you plan on dancing in those?" he asked as he took a swig.

"I've danced in worse conditions." This was true.

His eyes bulged. "So you're a *dancer*? Like an exotic dancer?"

"No, I'm a professional dancer, like I tour." Even if I was a stripper, that work was real work—it wouldn't make me less of a woman or less deserving of respect. I needed to move on to a different cowboy.

"Oh, sorry, I didn't mean to embarrass you. We don't have many types of dancers here . . ." Austin let his sentence trail off, probably knowing full well he put his foot in his mouth.

"Well, thanks for the beer," I said, and stepped away to find someone else to get me another.

Then another.

Then another.

The night was turning into a blur, and I was now on the dance floor trying to keep up with the steps for all the dances.

"All right, everyone, it's the moment y'all have been waiting for. We are gonna do the Caliente!" the caller announced over the speakers.

The crowd went wild.

"What's the Caliente?" I yelled over the commotion to my

dance partner. Was it Dale? Or was that the other guy in the green shirt and Bass Pro Shops trucker hat? This one was in a muscle tank top and the tightest jeans I had ever seen a man wear, and I partied in WeHo.

"It's the fastest dance she's got. It's fun, but you gotta really watch your feet," Maybe Dale yelled over the crowd.

My head was starting to spin but the DJ started playing the song. It was a mix of something familiar but sped up like crazy. I knew I'd heard the song before.

"Jai Ho!"

"Oh my god!" I shouted. "Is this the Pussycat Doll version of the song from *Slumdog Millionaire*?"

Maybe Dale only shrugged. It was! Why the fuck was a country-western dance called Caliente done to a Bollywood song, and not even the original song, but the Pussycat Dolls' version? The track then transitioned into another country song and everyone cheered, while still pivoting and pointing their toes. I couldn't keep up with the turns and steps.

Then there was Lucas resting against a high-top, watching me as a group of men chatted around him. He gave me one of his infamous subtle blink-and-you'll-miss-it smiles and tipped his hat at me before looking away. I flushed crimson. It was time to turn again, and I crashed into a girl in a hot pink crop top and her date.

"Watch it!" they shouted and pushed me away.

I stumbled and rolled my ankle. Wincing, I pushed and squeezed my way off the dance floor with a limp. I needed water.

I got a plastic cup from on top of the cold-water dispenser when another cowboy leaned his elbow on top.

"Hey there." He winked.

I just kept eyeing the water to fill my cup to the brim.

"Been watching you on the dance floor."

"Have you?"

"It was like you were putting on a show just for me."

"Just for you? I have never even met you before. I'm just havin' fun, dude."

"Wanna get out of here and have some real fun with me?"

"No." I started chugging the water; it was gone too soon. I immediately started filling the cup again.

"Ah, come on, gorgeous. Your feet have got to be killin' you in those shoes. I got a big truck in the parking lot with an extra-wide back seat row." He wiggled his eyebrows as he chewed on the end of a toothpick.

Over the rim of the plastic cup, I leveled him my strongest get-the-fuck-away-from-me stare, but he appeared undeterred. Instead, he only leaned closer and took my upper arm.

"Why don't you let me show you a thing or two about cowboys?" he whispered in my ear. I shivered, not from pleasure but revulsion. His cheap cologne was suffocating and all the beers in my belly, now with the gallon of water I just chugged, was threatening to come back up.

I closed my eyes for a moment, taking a few deep breaths to will away the nausea. When I opened them again there were two cowboys. Great.

"Do you have a twin?" I asked.

He laughed. "You could use some air. Come with me and I'll take care of you." He pulled me closer to him and wrapped his free arm around my back, trying to lead me toward the exit.

My ankle screamed in protest as I rooted myself in that spot.

"I'm not going anywhere with you. My friends are coming back."

"I haven't seen you with any friends tonight. Don't play hard to get, I'm just trying to help." His pace was fast, and my ankle throbbed as I struggled to stay upright and not fall on my face.

"Leave me the fuck alone!"

It was loud. My head was spinning, and it sounded like the DJ turned the volume up louder and the crowd was loving it. I frantically turned my head, trying to find a familiar face. It was dark and hazy, and everyone was wearing a damn cowboy hat—it was impossible to find anyone I knew.

The men's and women's bathrooms were right by the exit. I found my new tactic.

"Wait, I really need to pee. Did you see all the water I just drank? It hit bottom, man. I have a bladder the size of a thimble. I need to make a pit stop."

"Don't worry, we're just taking a quick breather, and we'll head back in. Just need some air." The big burly cowboy just kept pulling me toward the exit.

"Do you really want me to pee in your truck? Think of your seats!"

That stopped him. Thank the powers that be that this man cared more about his upholstery than being a decent human. I had been in a few sticky situations in Los Angeles and New York, but never to this extent.

He grunted as he released me.

"Is there a problem here?" Lucas's voice thundered over the loud music, and I'd never felt so relieved. He stepped in between me and the Evil Cowboy.

"Why don't you mind your own damn business? My girl was just going to the bathroom and then we were leaving." The Evil Cowboy stepped closer to me.

"This woman is my business." Lucas didn't so much as raise his voice—no, he lowered it to a menacing growl, and it was so much worse than a shout. The hair on my arms raised and gooseflesh covered my skin. "You his girl?" Lucas turned to look at me; his eyes were charged. It wasn't quite anger that I saw. It couldn't be jealousy over this poor excuse of a cowboy holding me hostage.

"I'm only one person's girl." I cocked my brow and smirked.

Lucas raised his eyebrow.

"Oh yeah, and whose girl is that? This guy?" The Evil Cowboy pointed his thumb at Lucas.

"No, I'm Lottie Fox's girl."

The Evil Cowboy's face blanched.

"Seems you heard of my grandmother."

Evil Cowboy started backing away, arms raised. "Look, there has been a misunderstanding. I don't want no trouble. Lottie and my family go way back. Legend is she shot my uncle in the ass with an arrow. Please don't tell her about this."

"I suggest you leave then." Lucas's voice was pure ice. We watched the man turn back toward the dance floor, looking for some other girl who would give him less trouble no doubt.

"Thank you for stepping in. I think I need to get some air." I took a step on my bad ankle—through the confrontation, I forgot all about my pain. I palmed the wall to steady myself; the floor looked like waves with how it was moving. I drank too much.

"Whoa there." Lucas's voice was in my ear as he swooped down and scooped me into his arms. I clamped my eyes shut, waiting for the dizziness to end. He smelled like sweet tobacco and leather; it calmed me. I took a few more deep breaths.

Lucas started walking while clutching me to his chest. The cool night air hit me, and I felt immediate relief. The cloying hot air of the bar and loud music were too much for me in my current state.

He made to put me down.

"No!" I was like a cat and sank my nails into his shirt. "Don't put me down. I like being up here."

He only chuckled in response, but I thought I felt his arm muscles flex beneath me. That had to have been all the alcohol that went to my head.

I lifted my face from his chest and met his eyes. His storm cloud gray eyes were the most beautiful things I had ever seen. The light of the neon sign behind us reflected in them and it looked like he had a whole galaxy swirling in his eyes. I shook my head to snap myself out of it.

"You can put me down now. It was very heroic of you to step in. Lottie would be happy to know you rescued her granddaughter," I said, my voice small. Did he only do it because of his obligation to Lottie? Or was he starting to feel what I felt?

"I'd do it for any woman, and more if I needed to. Consent matters. Did you want to go off with him?" Lucas's gorgeous eyes were expressionless. "I wouldn't judge you . . ." He looked away from me then. Even in my drunken state, I knew the answer was important; he cared. His answer was a great one—Lucas was a good guy—but I felt a little deflated and it was irrational. I blamed it on the alcohol.

"Of course not. He wouldn't leave me alone at the water dispenser."

Lucas pinched his lips together and nodded once as we stood beneath the overhead lights of the honky-tonk. We could have been in a field standing under stars for all that it mattered, because Lucas was really looking at me.

Soft music from a speaker was playing above us, a slow country ballad I'd never heard before. It was nice. The man's voice was deep, as most male country singers' voices were, but the melody was beautiful and catchy and the harmonies sounded like there were two men singing.

"Who sings this?"

"Brooks & Dunn."

"I like it." I smiled at him. "Did you mean what you said?"

"Yeah, I'd beat the shit out of any man trying to take advantage of a woman."

I laughed. "No, not that. I mean I do believe you about that, but I meant the other thing." I started swaying my head and shoulders to the music. Lucas was stone-still, but after a moment, when I leaned into him a bit, his body seemed to naturally move with mine.

"What other thing?"

"The thing you said about me being your business?"

"Yeah. I meant it."

"Why am I your business, Lucas? You don't even like me."

His arms looped around my lower waist as he looked deep into my eyes, and we swayed together to the song.

"I don't have to like you. Lottie said I had to watch out for you."

It was all the beer making my head and heart do weird things. And my stomach. God, the swaying was a bad idea. I wasn't sure what I expected Lucas to say, or hoped, rather. Of course he cared only that I was in one piece because his employer, my grandmother, ordered him to. From the second I met him, he made it clear he didn't like me and never would. What was wrong with me that I started forming some sort of crush on this man and hoping he did too? It had to be because he was the only handsome, young, unattached man in my vicinity.

Fuck. Maybe I should have found a casual hookup in there, because this was embarrassing. And he was still holding me as we danced to the music.

I pried my hands apart from around his neck and used my palms to push away from his chest.

"Whoa there, careful."

I stepped back and my heel got stuck in a crack and I rolled my bad ankle. The ugliest grunt came out of me.

Lucas used his hands to steady me, but I wobbled away, needing space.

"I'm fine. I just need a minute. I've had a little too much to drink, but the air is helping." I turned away from him. I couldn't bear to look at him right now. I was tired from a stressful week and when I drank too much, I tended to get emotional. If I looked at him right now, after so much irrational disappointment, I'd cry and only embarrass myself more.

I needed to breathe and sober up. I looked at our surroundings. The parking lot was full of mostly trucks. Old trucks, new trucks, lifted trucks, low trucks. Trucks, trucks, trucks, trucks. Oh wait, I spotted one sedan. It looked like an old Camry. But then there were more trucks and SUVs.

Standing in the parking lot were a couple groups of guys smoking and chatting among all the vehicles.

Everyone here belonged. But me? I stuck out like a sore thumb. Of course Lucas wouldn't even start to like me in any romantic way. We had a business arrangement and people weren't supposed to mix business and pleasure. It was absurd that I would conjure up this fantastical crush, as if the cowboy in the middle of nowhere was the only man in the world who would see me, get me, love me. Our little hideaway from the world. That didn't happen for people like me. I was too open to public scrutiny and our lives were too different. Plus, I was canceled. Who wanted to attach themselves to my walking mess of a life?

It was the beer and that was that. In the morning, none of these thoughts and feelings would be there.

"You okay?" Lucas asked.

I did the only thing I could to hide myself and make him see the Avery he hated—the dumb, shallow superstar from California—to get things back to how they were. "No, I'm not okay. I'm drunk and you don't even have In-N-Out here."

I turned around and he had his hands in his pockets, kicking a cigarette butt with the toe of his boot.

"We got other food."

"Yeah, yeah, yeah. I'm going to go find me a nicer cowboy to buy me some." I started walking around Lucas, back to the entrance.

"You aren't going back in there, princess." He was using his nickname for me again. There. I fixed it. It was how it should have always been. Lucas was not my friend, and he most certainly was not my boyfriend.

"Look at all the bumper stickers, Lucas. It's a free country. I can do what I want."

"You can when you're sober. Don't put yourself in danger. C'mon, some ladies are selling meat pies by the gate over there. Let's get some to soak up the alcohol."

I followed his line of vision, and sure enough, there were two women sitting in camping chairs with a cooler on a folding table.

It looked too far away for my ankle, and I whimpered.

"Lean on me." Lucas circled his arm around my waist, and he slowly and gently led me to the food stand.

"Two, please," Lucas said, handing them some cash, and the old women gave us each a foil-wrapped item. It was weighty in my hand.

"Mvto," Lucas said as he unwrapped his and took a big bite. He nodded for me to do the same.

Flavor swirled in my mouth as I bit through the flaky pastry outside and into the ground-meat mixture. It was good.

"Oh my god," I moaned. I finished it in three quick bites.

Lucas's hand tightened around my waist as we walked slowly back across the parking lot. "Let's get you home."

"There you two are!" Davey's loud voice rang through the night air.

"We're gettin' ready to go. You comin'?" Lucas asked Davey.

Davey held the door open and Mary Beth came out.

"No, he ain't. He's comin' home with me," Mary Beth proudly asserted through a giggle.

"Lady's orders." Davey smiled as he shrugged.

"You seen Red?" Lucas asked.

"He said he would see himself home."

"Aight then, we'll see ya Monday." Lucas lifted his chin in farewell. Davey reciprocated. Mary Beth jogged over to me.

"Avery! It's so nice to meet you. I'm sorry I didn't get to talk to you, but Davey says you're great and will sing at our wedding?"

"I'm happy to. Davey is like family." I smiled and really meant it.

"I can't wait to tell everyone. Our wedding is gonna be the talk of the town. You're coming to the tournament in a couple weeks, right?"

"I hadn't even heard of it. Tournament for what?"

"Stickball." She looked at me like it was obvious. "Lucas, you didn't tell her about it? We're all going, you have to go."

"Okay, then I'll go."

"You will?" Mary Beth clapped in excitement.

"Yeah, I mean I don't have much else going on here."

"Great, so I'll see you there and we can chat and hang out more."

"I'm looking forward to it."

"Well, we gotta get goin'. I haven't seen my man in a whole week. See ya." She hugged me. It wasn't one of those fake, uppity hugs with air cheek kissing that everyone in Hollywood does. It was a real, earnest squeeze.

I liked her.

"Guess it's just you and me," I said to Lucas.

He blew out a breath. "C'mon then."

"What's stickball?" I asked on wobbly legs as he led me to the truck.

"It's a really old game we like to play." His tone was patient, even the way he held me up by the arm to get me to the vehicle was careful. We arrived at the truck in no time and he opened the passenger door to usher me in. I lifted my leg to climb in, but got no purchase with these damn heels and I slipped back down.

Warm, steady hands gripped my hips and I was lifted into the truck as if I weighed no more than a feather. I turned to thank Lucas, but his face was too close. My lips brushed his and he reared his head back.

"Oh my god, I'm so sorry. I didn't mean to do that. I just wanted to thank you, oh my god."

"It's fine," he grunted.

"It was an accident." How did that happen? I felt sick.

He pinched his lips together and nodded. He started to close the door.

"Lucas, wait—" That was the only warning I could give before I bent over and threw up the entire contents of my stomach onto the dirt ground—and Lucas's boots.

When I was done, I looked up to Lucas's shocked face.

I used the back of my hand to wipe my mouth. "I'm so sorry."

He closed his eyes, took a step back, and closed the door without a word.

Through the window I yelled, "I'll buy you new boots!"

15

H ANGOVERS WERE THE WORST AND THIS ONE FELT like it lasted the full week since our night at the honky-tonk. I was never drinking again. The image of Lucas's horrified face after I vomited on his boots played on a loop for days. I put everything I had into working and cooking to ignore the under-current of embarrassment in all my interactions with him since the honky-tonk.

The rhythm of the ranch reminded me of a simple eight count of choreography. I could do it with my eyes closed. Every day it was getting easier to wake up at the buck-ass crack of dawn to make breakfast and I was actually getting good at it. The sweet potato pancakes I made were seriously the best; both Red and Davey had seconds. It helped having access to the internet.

Better Homes was good and all, but the recipes felt dated and heavy. If there was one thing I could add my little Avery flair to, it would be adding in lighter and leaner meals. As much as I loved butter, eating pounds of it would do no one any favors.

The attic was looking better, and I started posting things online to sell—mostly the big items first—and raised a couple thousand dollars so far. Lottie was thrilled, and I felt like my contributions were actually making an impact. I was working hard behind the scenes to fulfill my end of the deal with Lucas. It was all administrative and not as exciting or as fast as I thought it would be. I had reached out to my lawyer and financial adviser, but one was on a summer vacation and the other was at a conference, so I would have to wait awhile for their responses.

I kept digging through the attic hoping to discover a gold mine. I didn't find gold, but I did find a box full of vintage leather boots—I had to keep them. I'd add it to the Save the Ranch fund later, because these things were my perfect size. Now I didn't have to go line dancing in my stilettos . . . if I ever bothered to try line dancing out here again. If I did, it would be strictly to dance, sober. No more grab-happy mean cowboys looking for a cheap thrill in the back of their trucks.

Lottie and I visited Bessie again, and I played her piano for her as she rested. I could tell hearing the instrument made her happy and it was no trouble for me to do it. Even if she liked to tell me I was a little pitchy at times. Nothing like the honesty of an unpretentious old woman to keep me humble.

I needed it. The honesty, but also the connection. There was nothing surface level or superficial about my interactions with anyone here and it was refreshing—even if those I encountered were rough around the edges, there was never any malice.

Since finding my mother's girlhood room, I lacked the courage to ask Lottie about it. We had gotten into the groove of life on the ranch together, and I was worried asking any touchy questions would cause her to clam up and shut me out.

Sundays were slow here as I had found out. Lottie went to church every Sunday morning and then had Bible study with her girlfriends. She never pressured me to attend with her and I was grateful. I was already under so much scrutiny that I didn't want to bring God, or Creator, as everyone called Him here, into it.

Of course, we still had to go and care for the horses, but there was a laziness to the cadence of how we completed these tasks. It was like the horses even knew it was supposed to be a day of rest as they took their sweet time to come when called.

I would never get used to these creatures. Peso over there had a twinkle in his eye, like he couldn't wait to eat the rest of my hair. I wove my hair into a braid around the crown of my head to reduce the risk of flyaways being in horse-chomping range. Today, Lottie announced she was going to teach me how to ride on my own.

She intercepted me when I tried to make a run for the landline to call home and beg my mom to get me.

I was stuck and forced to contend with all of my heritage, even the four-legged monsters.

"Do I get to ride Rakko?" I asked, perking up. Lucas made it seem easy to ride him. Rakko. Not Lucas. What was wrong with my brain?

"No."

"He is the only one that likes me."

"Horses can sense if you're scared and will try to assert their dominance. You're gonna ride Peso and show him who's boss and that your hair is off-limits."

"Can't you just tell him for me while I stand safely behind this gate?"

"C'mon, Avery. Time for you to be brave, girl. Peso is one of our friendliest and perfect for beginners. Now step up to him and give him this carrot." She handed me a crooked carrot from her back pocket.

I took the orange offering and walked up to Peso on slow feet.

"Hold your hand out flat and give him the carrot," Lottie instructed.

I did. His lips brushed my palm and his ginormous teeth gobbled it up. I whipped my hand away, lest the creature thought more of me was on the table as a snack.

Peso stood there amused, jaw chewing his treat in small circles.

"G'won and pet his face and tell him how pretty he is." Lottie stood a ways away, petting Rakko.

I stroked Peso's nose. "There, there, cutie. Are we gonna have a good ride?"

I swear the horse's eyes looked delighted. I guess Peso was a cute horse. He was a russet brown and I wondered why he was named after the Mexican currency. Now was as good a time to ask as any.

"That's how much Red paid for him in Mexico," Lottie explained.

"A single peso? That's not even close to a full dollar." I couldn't believe it.

"He was a tiny calf and sick too. Red took him and smuggled him in the back of his car across the border and brought Peso here seventeen years ago. It took a while to get him healed up and strong, but now look at him. You'd never guess the odds were against him surviving a year here."

"That's incredible."

"Yup. You ready to ride now?"

"I'd be honored to ride Peso. You are a cutie, aren't you?" I cooed to him.

Lottie threw me one of the bridles she had over her shoulder. "Lead him to the barn and we will get him ready to ride."

I'd watched everyone saddle horses over the past two weeks, but never with the intention of doing it myself. Lottie walked me through the entire process of getting Peso and Rakko ready for a ride.

The hardest part was making sure the cinch was tight but not too tight. I erred on too tight at first and Peso stomped his back foot in protest. But I finally got it right in the end.

We were still in the barn, but I was on a fully saddled horse all by myself, so I'd count that as real personal growth for me.

"All right, how do I make him go?" I asked.

"Click your tongue a few times and he should follow me."

When Lottie was out of the barn and down past the paddocks with Rakko, Peso still hadn't moved.

"Come on," I urged, holding the reins and waving them back and forth as if I knew what the hell I was doing. I didn't.

"Kick both of your feet to give him a nudge!" Lottie called.

Kick? I didn't want to hurt him. As gently as I could, I brought my heels into his side but still got nothin'.

"You're gonna need to do it harder than that!" Red laughed as he rolled the wheelbarrow back inside the barn.

"I don't want Peso to hate me if I accidentally hurt him."

"You won't hurt him. Just stick your feet out and bring them in real quick—he will know what you mean."

"Okay." I followed Red's instructions a little too well. We blasted out of the barn faster than a shot from a cannon. Peso zoomed past Lottie and Rakko and out into the open pasture.

I screamed as Peso galloped and my butt was bouncing up and down on the saddle.

"Stop!" *Bump.* "Peso!" *Bump.* "Please!" *Bump.* That last bump rattled my head and forced my mouth shut and I bit my tongue. I tasted blood. Great.

"Yank the reins back!" I heard Lottie yell from not that far behind me.

A lesson on how to steer would have been great before sitting on the horse.

"Whoa!" I yelled, pulling the reins as hard as I could, and Peso came to an abrupt stop. I was nearly thrown off him with the momentum. I clutched Peso's neck, my nose up in his brown mane as I hyperventilated.

"I'm sure you realized that kick was too hard."

I turned to face Lottie, Peso's hair in my mouth, and I let out an unhinged burst of laughter. I survived. I was alive. And that was exhilarating.

Lottie laughed too. I looked down to Peso and it looked like he was laughing as well, his big teeth out in a smile.

"I think you need to go real slow and show me the basics, because I'm never doing that again."

"I was thinkin' the same thing." Lottie smiled.

We spent a solid half hour going over how to signal to a horse to get going, stop, slow down, and go faster. We practiced in the open pasture not too far from the barn. Eventually, Lottie said, "Okay, you're ready."

She clicked her tongue twice, and Rakko and Peso started moving. Lottie led us toward the trees where I went with Lucas to find Tilda. I wasn't sure if I should mention that ride with him. It wasn't romantic—we were looking for the horse—but still, that time felt special to me, private.

"Our property continues through here. There is a little horse trail and footpath but be careful comin' out here on your own. It's easy to get turned around if you don't know where you're goin'."

"Don't worry. I don't plan on being out here alone . . . ever." I looked up at the trees overhead and wished I'd worn a sweater or a flannel. I hitched my shoulders up to my ears. "Have there been any reports about ticks carrying Lyme disease out here?"

Lottie turned back to look at me. "Not that I know of. I haven't gotten a tick bite since I was a little girl. My blood has soured in my old age. So I guess I do gotta worry about you."

"Was that a joke, Lottie?"

"I've been known to crack a joke or two." She smirked, then turned around to keep riding.

"Oh yeah? Are those jokes before or after threatening to shoot people?"

"That's usually the joke."

"Most don't find *that* funny . . ." I let my voice trail off because what else could I say? Her relationship with guns was way different from mine.

"Shall our next lesson include some shooting?"

"No. No, thank you. That is . . . I have no interest in holding a gun . . . ever."

"Hah! What about archery?"

"Can't say I have ever had the opportunity to even hold a bow and arrow."

"All right then. I'll ask Red to get the target and old bow out and we can practice shooting one of these days. Arrows."

"Only arrows? You promise?"

"I promise."

I smiled. "Then yes, I'd love that."

"Lucas tells me he is helping you adjust to our culture." I tensed at the mention of Lucas's name. Her tone was casual, almost too casual. Was there a trap in there? We were following her rules explicitly. Since dancing at the honky-tonk, he had kept his distance from me. I busied myself with the work in the attic to see if this little crush I developed would fade away with time and distance.

It didn't.

"He did? Did he say anything else?" Did she know about the

deal with saving the ranch? Was this outing an ambush to put a kibosh on our plan?

"Just that you are too gullible."

Phew.

"Oh well, I'd like to think I am learning to be less gullible. It feels like everyone purposefully baits or misleads me."

"Probably." Lottie pulled up slightly on the reins with her right hand and Rakko turned right and we continued to follow the path.

"I won't always be a fish out of water."

"You stayin' then?" she threw over her shoulder.

"I don't know. Is that an offer?"

She stopped Rakko in front of a small pond and rested her hands on the horn of the saddle and Peso stopped beside her.

"Avery, you are always welcome here. This is your home."

I took a breath and mustered my courage, or stupidity, to finally ask my most burning question. "Then why did my mom leave?"

Lottie's head reared back as if the question were a slap.

"Your mother had her reasons."

"What were they?" I pressed.

"That's not my story to tell. You'll have to ask her."

I threw my arms out wide. "Do you see her here? My whole life she never said anything. Why?"

"Drop it, Avery." Lottie's voice was low and quiet, a warning.

I ignored it.

"No. I have been here slaving away for weeks, desperate for any breadcrumb you will drop for me about this family, this life. Yet when I ask you point-blank, you clam up and get mad. Why? What was so bad? It was over twenty years ago; surely enough time has passed that we can have an honest conversation. Maybe even heal this rift. If that's what you want too." Didn't she want to? This was her only daughter and grandchild.

"You know nothing about time. Some wounds can never be healed. Some betrayals are too hard to forgive." She gathered her reins and urged Rakko to turn around. "Peso knows the way back."

Lottie kicked her heels in and took off, leaving a thick cloud of dust in her wake.

I was left in the hot sun, next to a murky pond, surrounded by flies. Why was everything with this woman so difficult? Why was it so wrong to ask for clear communication? Did she not trust me with it? Did I not deserve to know? I just wanted to fix everything—my career, my family, my self-image. I wanted to be a better version of me. One with a family who loved me and answers about where I came from. It was looking more and more that I couldn't fix shit, except a good batch of biscuits.

Peso knew the way back, but he sure took his lazy time with it. The sun was high and I was soaked through and through. My braided hair crown was now a tangled mess, lying limp against my neck.

Lucas was leaning against the barn, arms folded across his chest. He looked good in clean jeans, a short-sleeved button-down in a light sky blue, with his boots polished to a shine.

"We're late."

Shit. His dad's birthday dinner. The one I invited myself to and confirmed our attendance. What a lousy first impression I'd make. I could smell my pits without even getting close. Gross.

"I'm so sorry. I pissed Lottie off again and she left me out in the middle of nowhere and this lazy bum kept stopping and starting to get back."

Lucas pushed himself off the barn and stalked toward me and Peso. He grabbed the bridle, stroking Peso's snout.

"Go get cleaned up and meet me here in fifteen."

"But I have to brush Peso down and put all the tackle away."

"I got it, just go."

I threw my leg over the saddle and slid myself down Peso and to the ground.

"Thank you."

Lucas nodded in response, so I started to walk to the house, but doubled over in pain after a few steps. "What did that saddle do to me?" I groaned, straightening and walking forward on bowed legs.

Lucas laughed. "You're saddlesore. It will go away. A hot shower will help."

I waved behind me as I kept waddling to the house, then I stopped. Turning around, I asked, "What should I wear?"

He looked up, confused. "Whatever you want."

"So if I showed up in a rainbow clown wig, you'd be cool with that?"

"Do you have one of those in all that luggage?"

"No. I found one in the attic."

Lucas laughed and shook his head. "You now have thirteen minutes." He looked more relaxed already as he led Peso into the barn.

I rolled my eyes and slowly made it inside and up the stairs to take the fastest shower of my life. Tonight, I was pretending to be Lucas's girlfriend. The thought sent a thrill through me.

16

OPTED TO NOT WEAR THE WIG. WE WERE ALREADY LATE, and I didn't want them thinking Lucas's fake girlfriend was ridiculous. Instead, I wore a flowy, floral romper with long bell sleeves, a cinched waist, and shorts that were tastefully short—in my opinion. The flowers were fuchsia against a cream background. I felt like Stevie Nicks whenever I wore this, especially when I twisted my arms around while dancing.

The pain from the saddle made it difficult to move my legs, but I suffered through it wearing the brown leather boots I'd found in the attic. There was no time left to do any makeup, so I slathered a berry-colored stain on my lips, grabbed a hair tie, and went to meet Lucas by the truck.

The stairs were my enemy—forget all the Twitter beef, I forgive all those faceless trolls. The stairs were my sworn nemesis for life. With every step down I had to swallow a whimper, but I managed it.

Lucas was waiting at the truck, resting his arms on top of the truck bed. I could feel my hair instantly start to dry and curl up with the heat and humidity.

"How do I look?" I did a slow circle, making sure I held my arms out so that the sleeves were on full display.

Lucas grunted, tapped the top of the truck, and then got into the driver's seat.

He sure knew how to make a girl feel pretty. I rolled my eyes. I guess it wasn't really his job to compliment me. I did force him into this whole ordeal.

I pushed through the ache and climbed into the passenger seat. I smiled at Lucas, letting him know I was ready to go. He nodded and started the truck.

"Sorry, I got stuck out there and ran out of time to bake your dad a cake."

"It's fine. My mom didn't expect you to really do that."

"Yeah, but I like to think that my word means something."

"It's just a cake. We'll stop at the store and pick one up."

"That's a good idea. When I get access to my money again, I'll pay you back."

He turned onto the dirty road and waved me off.

"So where do they live? Close?" I asked as I started massaging my thighs. It felt so good that I let out a little moan of pleasure.

Lucas cleared his throat and I turned beet red. I knew how it sounded, but it couldn't be helped. Between my thighs and my ass, I wasn't sure which hurt the most.

"You should have a professional do that." His voice was thick.

"You volunteering?" I tried to joke, but the pain made my voice come out sultry and desperate. I needed to get it together.

Was it just me, or did the cab get like twenty degrees hotter? I stared into his gray eyes for a moment, and if it were not for him having to look away to drive us safely across town to the store, I could have stared at them for eternity. Lost happily in the depths of those storm clouds.

Which was dumb, because I promised myself, drunk or not, that I would harbor no delusions when it came to my attraction to Lucas. He was off-limits.

I took my hands off my thighs and focused my attention out the window and repeated to myself over and over again: *Be professional.*

WE STOOD OUTSIDE the huge wooden double doors to Lucas's parents' house. Lucas knocked and waited to be allowed in—a stark contrast to how it was at Lottie's and Bessie's. He tugged at the collar around his neck, then hastily ripped the price tag off the cake box and the big red REDUCED sticker.

There were many cake options, but Lucas opted for the sell-by-date-reduced table to save more money. It was a chocolate Bundt cake with a white frosting drizzle. It looked delicious to me, but there was no way I'd attempt to try to pass this off as if I'd made it, even though Lucas suggested I do it. I was only fifty percent sure he was joking. The plastic lid had the store name stamped on it, for one. And two, it was way nicer than anything I could attempt to make—no matter how much better I was getting at making biscuits and gravy.

The ominous double doors slowly opened. Was opening both doors necessary? I didn't think so, but it did add to the air of drama that coated the place, and the tense way Lucas carried himself.

What exactly did I sign us up for?

A handsome man in his early fifties, if I had to guess, stood there, swirling a fancy glass of amber liquid. He had Lucas's same eyes and nose, and his hair was cropped short and peppered with a lot of gray.

"Come in, come in," Lucas's father said, waving us in. I followed closely behind Lucas.

"Cat! Our guests are here!" he called up the winding staircase.

"Coming!" Cat called from somewhere in the distance.

"Lucas, why don't you introduce me to your friend."

"This is Avery."

His father waited a beat to see if Lucas would tack on anything else, like who I was to him (no one) or where I came from (irrelevant). When Lucas's dead stare continued, his father carried on.

"Welcome, Avery. It's lovely to meet you. Follow me, let's go put that delicious-looking cake down."

"Thank you so much, sir. Er . . . happy birthday!" I tried to muster up enough cheer to cover Lucas's shuttered energy. He followed along, saying nothing. I could feel his tension. It was clear he hated being in this house and near his family.

The home was huge. The floors were made of marble tile, and we passed a sitting room with a big black leather couch and two black leather armchairs. On the far wall was one of those cool, modern gas fireplaces with glass pieces piled on the bottom.

We pressed on down the hallway to the kitchen. It was twice the size of Lottie's and everything was white. The subway tile, the paint, the cabinets, the counters, and even the floor. I placed the chocolate cake onto the counter next to a silver bucket full of ice and a bottle of white wine. On the stove was a roasting pan covered with a lid.

The kitchen was pristine. I could smell the evidence of the cooking, but I couldn't see it. Not a single dirty dish littered the countertop or the sink. Did the Iron Eyeses have secret elves who did the cooking? Or a full staff? I knew I was a beginner and so a little messier than most, but the stainless steel chef's range didn't even have a single splatter of grease.

It was giving major Stepford Wife vibes, and not in a good way. Was there ever a good way?

I could hear heels clacking quickly across the tiled house before Cat rushed in to hug Lucas.

"Lucas! Welcome home, honey!" She tackled him into a big bear hug, wrapping her arms around his arms and torso. It was sweet, if a little awkward.

Lucas's father, whose name I still didn't know, drank his liquor, ambivalent to the emotional display before him.

"Cat, let go of the boy," Mr. Iron Eyes said, his voice bored and cold.

"I hope you brought your appetite." She turned to me. "Oh, Avery, it's so good to see you again. Will, isn't Lucas's girlfriend beautiful like I told you?"

"Yes, a real looker. What're you doing with *my* son?" He laughed at his own joke, and Lucas's shoulders fell forward from his ears, caving in on themselves.

"Lucas is the most handsome man I've ever seen in my life," I answered honestly. Lucas refused to meet my eyes, instead brushing past us all to the upper cabinet by the sink. He pulled out two tall glasses.

"Want something to drink?"

I knew he was asking me.

"Water would be great."

He took the glasses to the fridge and filled them with the water dispenser on the door.

"We have this great pinot grigio from Italy that goes perfect with the baked Brie we have in the dining room. Or of course we have a Cab we took out from the cellar for this special occasion. It's a '95 from our favorite little winery in Napa. It pairs beautifully with Cat's famous roast. Can I pour you a glass?" Will asked. His smile seemed forced, not quite reaching his eyes.

"Oh, no thank you. I'm good with water." I looked away from his face. His eyes were unnervingly like Lucas's, but off somehow, a little harsher. And his teeth were like those of all the actors I've encountered: too big, too square, and too white.

Lucas's parents exchanged a look. "A perfect match for Lucas then," his mother said cheerfully.

"Can we eat now?" Lucas asked, handing me the glass of cool water.

"I'm starved," I added before taking a sip. I hoped the bathroom had Advil in the medicine cabinet. I did my best not to limp as I followed everyone through the door into the formal dining room that was adjacent to the kitchen.

It had more grandiose decor and furnishings. It gave old-money Beverly Hills vibes with the white embroidered fabric, upholstered cushions, and black-lacquered carved wood armrests and legs. The entire room was decorated in black and white, along with a framed Jackson Pollock print. The only reason I knew it was Jackson Pollock was because I briefly dated a tortured screenwriter who had the same print (or similar, it was just black paint on a white canvas—it was difficult to tell) but smaller in his bedroom. He thought it was edgy; I thought it gave serial killer vibes. We didn't make it past six weeks. The man also wore those dumb tiny fisherman beanies that men who have never held a fishing pole wear to look cool, but it just looks pretentious in LA. The relationship was doomed for many reasons.

Being in this house, I was intimidated. Lucas's family was clearly wealthy and was not afraid to flaunt it.

I'd been around a lot of money, and my mother and I were finally in a financially secure place, but I was never this kind of wealthy growing up, and to be honest, most of my Studio City home was furnished by Target and Cost Plus World Market. We love a deal. But Lucas grew up in this *mansion*. How the hell did he end up at Lottie's living in a single-wide? This man was a mystery.

The table was set beautifully with fine china and linen napkins. I was rethinking my outfit choice. I should have gone with a simple long sundress and my denim jacket, because I felt way too flashy and showy in this getup. The bright pink flowers stood out like beacons in this mausoleum of a dining room.

Will sat at the head of the table and Cat sat on the opposite end. There were two seats on either side. We were all spread out pretty far, almost like the end of a chess game when you have a few pieces left scattered on the board. Obviously, I watched *The Queen's Gambit* one time and now I was a chess expert. I hurried to sit in my offered seat and ordered my brain to stop making dumb observations.

I was regretting refusing the wine now, but I was going to stand in solidarity with Lucas, whether he cared or not. He didn't drink, so therefore I wouldn't drink. It wasn't a big deal. I didn't need to drink, but these two people were trying to play hosts in the coldest house with these fake smiles and it had me on edge. If I felt this way as a stranger, there was no telling how awful Lucas was feeling. He just sat in his chair staring at his empty plate.

"So, how have you been, son? Doing any interesting projects for Lottie?" Will asked.

"Will." Cat's voice sounded like a warning.

"What? I can't ask my only son how he's doing? I see him maybe twice a year, how else am I to learn about how he is?"

Cat leveled Will with a look that communicated a lot with those hard brown eyes.

"Same old, same old," Lucas said.

"Wonderful. Avery, can you help me bring the dishes out to be served?" Cat asked.

"Mom, don't make her do that."

"I'd be happy to, Mrs. Iron Eyes." I got up, relieved to have a task, but Lucas looked uncomfortable being alone with his dad. I perhaps miscalculated in judgment with my eagerness to help—Lucas was left to suffer the presence of his father without me or his mother as a buffer. I hurried after Cat through the door to the kitchen to try to get everything as quickly as possible.

Cat Iron Eyes had other ideas.

"What can I take now?" I asked.

"Oh, we need to plate the roast and the veggies under it. So, tell me, how long have you been with my son?"

"Oh . . . it's all pretty new. Time is flying by." I tried to keep my answers as vague as possible, but this woman was a shark.

"When you say 'new,' how new?"

"We don't really want to put labels on it and are taking things one day at a time." I scooped the potatoes and carrots onto the white ceramic dish Cat gave me. I made sure to keep my face down, focused on the task.

"Is he kind to you?" Her tone was light, but I heard a slight hesitation to it. Like my answer really mattered to her.

"Lucas is very kind and caring." I looked up at her.

She nodded to herself. "He was always a sweet boy. I'm glad. We have never met a girl he was seeing before, so this is new territory."

"You don't need to worry about him. He is doing great. I've never seen a harder-working man." I went back to scooping the vegetables.

"I Googled you, you know?"

"What?" I looked up and in doing so, the spoonful missed the bowl. Carrots rolled off the pristine counter onto the sterile floors. "Oh no! I'm so sorry. I'll clean this up."

"Don't worry about the floor. What's your plan when you go back to your real life?"

I was taken aback at her question. "Mrs. Iron Eyes, I don't know if that's something I can answer at this point," I said honestly. Because I really did have no idea.

"Call me Cat. Lucas has had a very troubled life. I don't want him to spiral if you leave and leave him heartbroken. Just promise me you won't upend his life, okay?"

"I would never do anything to harm Lucas."

She gave me a sad smile. "Trust me, in love it doesn't matter your intentions. Inevitably it will get messy. Earlier you said you thought he was the most handsome man you had ever seen. Was that true?"

"Of course. You'd have to be dumb not to think that," I said lightly, crouching on the floor to pick up scattered veggies. It was ridiculous, but I needed to do something while she interrogated me. Not that I could blame her. I wish my mother was as protective of my emotional well-being as Cat was being for Lucas.

"I do believe you're being honest with me." She sighed and set the roast onto the serving platter. She looked up at the wall, her mind clearly elsewhere. "I remember those days, when lust clouded everything we did. It was intense. My Luke is a good man, despite his issues."

"Um," I said, "yes, he is." I mean, what was I to say to all that? I was starting to infer the issues he had gone through had something to do with the fact he didn't drink, but he had never explicitly told me about his complicated history and I wouldn't press him on it.

"Don't break my baby's heart, okay?" Cat picked up the platter and headed into the dining room. I threw the rest of the veggies into the dish and followed her back into the room.

I'd never seen two more sullen men in my life. Will sat with a piss-sour look, staring into his tumbler, and Lucas sat back in his chair, arms crossed with his face directed at the ceiling. The tension was palpable. It was obvious there had been some heated discussion while we were in the other room. The sound of the door broke whatever moment they had. Will shook his head as if clearing his thoughts, then kicked his drink back and sucked down the contents in one gulp.

Lucas's jaw was clenched and his eyes dropped to his empty plate.

"Dinner's here," Cat sang cheerfully. There was no way she was ignorant of what we'd walked into; it was like she was purposefully ignoring it to get the evening back on track.

One by one she served slices of roast onto our plates along with veggies. The cheese, crackers, and grapes were also up for grabs on the table. After my own emotional and unfulfilling confrontation with Lottie and the long journey to get back to the ranch, I hadn't eaten anything since breakfast. My stomach growled. I helped myself to everything.

"Would you like to lead grace, honey?" Cat asked Will.

We all bowed our heads and followed Will's blessing of the meal. Then Will got up and went to the bar and filled his tumbler with more liquor. It was whiskey, the old expensive Scottish stuff.

He took a big swig before he sat back down to skewer his meat with his fork.

"Has Lucas told you about us, Ashley?"

"It's Avery." Lucas was the one to correct him. I had a suspicion that Will was goading him and said the wrong name on purpose.

"Right, Avery. Sorry. Well, has he?"

"No." I cut into my piece of roast.

"He's modest. He comes from a long line of lawyers and doctors."

"That's impressive." That meant nothing to me.

I started chewing my meat hoping if I didn't meet his eyes, then he would move on to a different topic, but no, Cat had to step in and make it even more uncomfortable.

"Will graduated in the top five percent of his graduating class at Dartmouth for undergrad. He received a full-ride scholarship to Yale for law school."

"That's so cool," I said through a mouthful of delicious yet chewy beef.

"Cat was the editor of the *Yale Law Journal*. There hasn't been another like her since she graduated."

Cat giggled. "You're too sweet. I really wasn't all that special. Though the dean of the school did come to the paper's office to compliment me on one particular case review I did on environmental law."

It was like these people were speaking a foreign language and I could barely keep up.

"It's not too late for you, son. People are going to college older now. You would make a fine lawyer," Will said.

"I don't want to be a lawyer," Lucas said, shooting his dad a look. I could tell this was a conversation they'd had more than once.

Will continued as if he didn't hear Lucas's interjection. "What do you do, Amberly?"

"Stop, Dad," Lucas said sharply.

"What? I can't ask your girlfriend what she does for work or where she went to school? Not everyone drops out of high school."

Now it was making sense why Lucas left here at sixteen and never came back. How could they throw it in his face that he dropped out of school—and in front of his girlfriend? *Fake* girlfriend, but they didn't know that. I looked to Cat, but she kept her head down and said nothing. Well, if she didn't tell her husband about me and my very public scandal, then I wasn't going to volunteer that information.

"I'm a musician," I said simply. If he hadn't heard of me before, then I wasn't going to list my achievements. He didn't seem the type to appreciate them anyway.

"A musician. How nice. Can you make a living off music?" Will asked, raising his eyebrows.

The question every single person asks when they hear someone wants to pursue the arts professionally. It was demeaning. The world consumed art and entertainment insatiably and yet those who make it are expected to do it for pennies, all with the threat that they are replaceable. "A living" was a spectrum, but what about passion? Happiness? Creating just for the love of it?

"Yes, I do pretty well for myself," I said, not elaborating.

"Found yourself a rich girlfriend, Luke? Smart. Maybe you could learn something about ambition from her."

"Honey," Cat said, trying to calm Will down, but he was on one.

"We are not talking about this right now, and you need to stop being disrespectful to Avery," Lucas said with steel in his low voice. I really wished I was anywhere else but here.

"I'm being honest, no disrespect intended." Will waved his hand holding the tumbler in my direction as he continued, "There are certain standards we need to keep to uphold the life-styles we want, aren't there? Don't you want to be able to provide for your future family? I'm trying to teach you something here, son. For your future. You can't pay for all her luxuries working on a ranch."

"Will," Cat snapped.

Will ran his free hand through his hair and tipped his head at me with a deep sigh. "Forgive me. It's not like we didn't try with Lucas, but Lucas is . . . well . . . Lucas. We offered him the best schools, tutors, everything. He knows if he wants to come home and go back to school, he can."

"I think we should move on to the cake. We don't want to ruin your birthday with all this talk." Cat made to get up.

"Lucas's cousin, my sister's son, is a doctor—"

"Dentist," Lucas corrected.

Will continued as if he didn't hear Lucas's interruption. "Working at the Indian Clinic, bringing his knowledge and expertise to help our people. While Lucas sits on wasted potential playing with horses all day."

Will looked at Lucas with utter disappointment and it broke my heart.

"I never finished school," I spoke up loudly.

Will's eyes were directed at me now, barely feigning a mixture of surprise and dismay. But I could take it. I spent my entire life sitting in front of casting directors, being judged from my head to my toes, from how I put the wrong inflection on a word to having an unappealing eyebrow shape. Hell, I had millions of people call me trash, and worse, only a few weeks ago. This man was nothing compared to what I've had thrown at me.

"Well, Lucas, it looks as if you've found your perfect match."

"William!" Cat's tone was angry now.

"I didn't even go to real school. I was working so much that I attended classes with random tutors on set. I also took online courses, but when I was sixteen, it was just easier to get my GED and get my mother's approval to work longer hours and make more money. I never even considered college. I don't think that makes me less of a person and less deserving of respect. And my name is Avery. Avery Fox. I believe you know my grandmother, Lottie Fox, who owns the ranch." I stood up to get the hell out of there. But I had to tell these people that Lucas was better than their lousy expectations. He was the best of the best, with so much drive and ambition. "Lucas is one of the hardest-working men I've come to know, and it's clear he's built himself up on his own. He does so much more than 'play with horses,' I'll have you know. He runs the entire business with plans to expand and grow."

"Expand and grow?" Will barked out a laugh. "That business is failing. My buddies at the bank are going to foreclose and I have Realtor friends looking to make low all-cash offers, because Lottie Fox has got to be desperate to get rid of the sinking ship. Expanding and growing nothing is still nothing."

"And being rich and miserable is still being miserable." I gave him a disdainful smile. Lucas deserved better. "This was a lovely meal, Cat, thank you. Let's go, Lucas."

Lucas got up from his seat, his eyes like lightning, so full of electricity that the little hairs on my arms and back of my neck stood on end. He laced his fingers with mine and led me out of that awful dining room, through the unfeeling house, and out the door into the hot, muggy world of Oklahoma.

He said nothing as he opened the passenger door for me to get in the truck. My butt was barely on the seat before he closed me in and jogged around to the driver's side. The cab shook as he jumped in. In seconds, he had the truck started up and backed out of the driveway.

His shoulders were tense as he drove us out of the neighborhood in silence, a silence that stretched on as the scenery changed from track homes to open land. I had no idea what to say and could only imagine what he was thinking. Minutes ticked by and the air within the truck was buzzing with pent-up energy. He put the turn signal on as we drove along a rural stretch of road before pulling over entirely. Lucas threw the truck into park and sat back, rubbing his eyes with a sigh.

"Sorry," he muttered, barely looking at me. "I need some air."

He left the truck, and I watched him walk away. I wanted to give him space but also be there for him. It appeared no one had ever really been there for him his whole life besides Lottie. After a moment of frenzied contemplation, I got out quietly and leaned against the truck, looking at the clear sky that was showing the first signs of sunset, the blue turning indigo.

Lucas turned around and saw me standing there. He took me in, his gaze raking over me until he met my eyes, and started walking to me. His focus was singular, like a predator, as our eye contact never broke. He looked so angry. I couldn't take it anymore. I had to know what he was thinking—what he was feeling.

"I'm so sorry—"

"Don't apologize," he said, now standing in front of me. His voice rumbled like thunder and the gooseflesh on my arms spread down to my toes.

"No, you were right. I never should have agreed to come to this dinner and force you to sit through that. They are awful."

"I don't want to talk about them."

I threw my hands up in frustration. I needed him to give me something more. "Then what do you want to talk about?"

He grabbed my hands, as if the touch was grounding him in the moment. "I don't want to talk at all." And then we were like magnets. Lucas pressed my back against the truck door, threading his fingers into my hair as he kissed me. I let my body weight fall back against the door behind me and I threw my arms around his shoulders, letting my own fingers tangle into the curls around his neck.

His tongue demanded entrance and I let it in, greeting it with my own. They twirled and danced, and heat was starting to swell in my core. I moaned, and Lucas answered by putting his thigh between my legs, pressing me closer to him. I whimpered. It wasn't enough. I jumped up and wrapped my legs around his waist, never breaking the kiss. His hands kneaded my bottom, and it was such beautiful agonizing pain. Having my legs in such an angle after my brutal horse ride hurt like hell, but it was soothed by the ministrations with his deft fingers.

My little romper was riding up and the tastefully short shorts were now more like cheeky underwear. His calloused hands touched the soft, exposed skin of my ass and I was melting. I let my hands wander to discover his toned biceps, then his solid chest, and down the ridges of his incredible abs. Lucas was sculpted from marble. I was getting hot and wet and wanted this to last forever. Lucas held me as he moved us slightly and opened the door before gently setting me in the seat. He peeled my arms from behind his neck and slowly pulled away from our kiss.

"I was really enjoying that," I whined.

"Me too," he said. "But we can't do this here, anyone could drive by."

"Fair point. Where do you want to go?" My stomach gurgled a loud growl. Neither of us had eaten much of anything.

He looked at my stomach pointedly. "Let's go get some food."

While I wished we could continue what we started, my hunger won the battle. "Like a date?" I asked cheekily.

Lucas chuckled and kissed me gently before shutting the door. He got into the truck before I knew it and turned the key. I decided to let that question die. He adjusted himself in his jeans before he pulled back onto the road. Lucas appeared to be a man of action rather than words, but the words he did say meant more. I was on a date with Lucas.

"Where are you taking me?" I asked.

"Sonics."

I laughed.

"What's so funny?"

"I've actually had Sonic before. We have them in California."

"Not like this, and here in Indian Country, it's pronounced *Son-ics*. Consider this lesson five."

HE WAS RIGHT. I'D NEVER HAD *SONICS* LIKE THIS BE-
fore. It tasted a lot better than the sad burger and fries I'd ordered in the middle of central California off the 5 highway during
a road trip.

It felt weird to say *Sonics* like the locals, and Lucas only laughed
when I asked if the *s* was possessive, like Sonic's burgers. I mean, it
made sense in my head. When I asked if this place was related to
that fast blue hedgehog, he ignored my question and kept eating.

I liked the drive-in style of dining. It was retro and just needed a
big projector and a fun movie and it would be the perfect date spot.

We were starving, so we focused only on eating and purposefully didn't mention the intense make-out session that my body
was desperate to continue. This cowboy could *kiss*.

Soon the meal was over and we were in the farthest parking
spot in this big lot, facing an open field. Lucas gathered our trash
and left to toss it, giving me a few moments to gather myself. I
flipped the visor down to check out my reflection.

The berry lip stain was still on my lips and my hair had air-
dried with a little wave to it; I tried flipping it over to the side each

way to see which looked sexier and more voluminous. Neither did and I blew the errant strands away from my face.

At least I picked out the raw onions from my burger. I wanted to be prepared for when the kissing started back up again—which I hoped was really soon.

The truck shook as Lucas got back in. He sat in his seat, looking at the steering wheel.

Oh no. He had that same panicked look he was giving the plate at his parents'. He was stressed and didn't know how to communicate it to me. Who could blame him? He'd just had an awful experience with his terrible parents. They belittled him, judged him, and tried to warn his girlfriend off him—pretend girlfriend, but they didn't know that. All they knew was that I was Lucas's significant other, and instead of highlighting all of his son's many great qualities or keeping things polite and nice for his own birthday, his father had chosen to be nasty.

Lucas must be feeling so humiliated and angry to have experienced that in front of me. Then I, his employer's granddaughter, practically threw myself at him after sticking up for him. He must've just been lost in the moment. Emotions were running high, and he now probably regretted kissing me.

I stole a glance at him again and saw that he was focusing on his breathing. He was no doubt trying to think of a way to let me down easy. I had to save him and myself the embarrassment. I couldn't let this man go through anything else today.

"I'm sorry about the kiss," I said.

He looked up at me. His eyes were hard to read as they discerned me.

"I'm not."

"You're not?" Not what I thought he'd say. I thought he would be relieved I was making this easy for him.

"No. I'd like to do it again." He blew out a breath and looked out to the open field. His demeanor was closed off. I knew what he was going to tell me.

"But you won't?"

"I won't."

"You don't have to explain. I get it." I too looked out at that field. It was easier to have the conversation this way, to hide my emotions. He'd just had a horrible evening with his parents. Kissing should really be the last thing on both of our minds right now.

"Avery." He paused for a long moment. "Thank you for what you did back there. No one has ever defended me like that before in front of my parents."

"Parents should never speak to their kids that way. You are their flesh and blood, and for them to judge you like that—I don't know how you coped growing up with them."

"I didn't cope well. It's why they kicked me out at sixteen." He clenched his jaw, looking down at his hands.

"They just put you on the street?" I turned to look at him, completely in shock.

"No. They paid Lottie to take me. It was supposed to be temporary. Get me straightened out, but I never left."

"You don't have to tell me, if you don't want to. You don't owe me anything."

"After that dinner, I have to explain a few things."

"Like how you come from the richest family ever."

He let out a mirthless chuckle. "Hardly, but they like to pretend as if we are."

I waited, giving him the space to tell me what he wanted to on his own time.

"Growing up with the pressure to be great fucked with my head. I could never be enough for my dad. I never read fast enough.

I couldn't get math right away. I'm dyslexic and when teachers tried to tell him, he refused to accept it. Said I was stubborn and not trying hard enough. I love being outside, so I played a lot of sports, but I was a little shit. I would talk smack to rile up my opponents, and while I was playing basketball, I pushed another kid too far. He shoved me and there was a crack in the asphalt. I fell and landed on my ankle wrong. It completely snapped. I had to have two surgeries to correct it and I have a metal screw keeping my joints together."

I gasped, but Lucas pressed on.

"The healing took forever and the pain was relentless. The doctor gave me Vicodin and my mom couldn't bear to hear me in so much pain, so she let me have more when I asked. I was hooked on painkillers at fourteen. It was all I could think about, chasing the high. The pain was gone, the anxiety with my parents—especially my dad—was gone. At fifteen, I started stealing money from his wallet. Then my mom's jewelry, and by sixteen, they'd had enough. I had one rehab stint, and I was back to getting into trouble."

He stopped, breathing slowly through his nose, eyes closed.

I placed my hand over his, resting on his thigh. He turned his palm over under mine and clasped my hand, as if I was anchoring him to the present.

"I'm so sorry, Lucas."

"It's the past. I've been clean and sober for four years. The longest stretch in my life since I was fourteen. But it's not easy. I think about drinking or pill-seeking every day. I just focus on one thing at a time, one day at a time. Working on the ranch gives me purpose. No matter what self-pity shit I got goin' on in my head, the horses still need to get fed, they still need water, they still need to get brushed down and exercised. Only Lottie knows this, but I got my GED. But I have no desire to go back to school. They can just live with the fact their only son doesn't want to be a lawyer or dentist." Lucas's laughter had a dark edge to it, not that I could blame him.

"So, this is why you want to help kids who have had a hard life? Your dream of having a ranch to help kids like you?"

"This healed me. It won't work for everyone, but no one is a lost cause. Everyone can turn their life around and I wish society understood that. It's so easy to label us as 'troubled' kids and forget about us. We need more tools to help us do what is right. I know I can do it. And I'm grateful you're willing to help save the ranch and make it happen."

He lifted our joined hands and brought mine to his lips. My stomach did a somersault, but it confused me.

"Why can't we kiss again, Lucas?"

He looked at me with raised eyebrows, as if to say, *Are you serious?*

"This isn't your real life, Avery. The internet is already moving on to new things to be mad about. Your life is going to catch up with you and where would that leave us?"

"I hadn't thought about it that way." His thoughts echoed his mother's, and as much as I didn't want to believe anything out of his parents' mouths, that was the most honest thing she had said. I looked at our joined hands. They looked perfect together. His dark, tanned skin, and mine.

"It's all I have been thinking about."

"For how long?"

"Since you called me a dirty cowboy."

With my free hand, I playfully pushed his chest. "Shut up. Liar. You hated me on sight. I'll never forget the car ride from hell hearing you drag me and crap on my music."

"Your song was everywhere, and I judged you based on the image you gave to the public. It didn't take long for me to see the real you and slowly, despite my brain telling me it was stupid, I started to like you. You are also the most beautiful woman I have ever seen in my life."

"And you said you weren't a fan." I laughed.

"Oh, I was being honest. I wasn't a fan."

I couldn't help but smile. "Are you a fan now?" I hedged.

"I still hate that song, but everything else about you is all right."

"Such high praise." I rolled my eyes.

"What do you want to hear? That you drive me crazy traipsing all over the property in little shorts that leave nothing to the imagination? Or that when I see your light on late at night, I just want to talk to you for hours like the night in the barn, but I stop myself so that I don't get too attached, knowing any day now you'll leave and not think twice about this place again."

"How can you think that, knowing I am working with you to save this ranch? I've been trying to get in touch with my financial adviser to see how I can buy this property. How could you think I'd forget about it, about you?"

"Your life is a galaxy of difference from ours. You will be going on tours, starring in movies, and who knows what. There is no way on Creator's green earth that you could ever think about this tiny town once you leave."

I didn't want it to be true, but he was right. Not that I wouldn't think about Broken Arrow again, but that my real life was busy. My days were scheduled for me and it was always go, go, go. This was the first time I'd had a chance to just be me, and while Lottie kept me busy, it was still so much more restful here. But I had to go back. I couldn't hide here forever. There would be a million priorities in front of me, and I'd spread myself thin getting to them all, and any plans to visit Broken Arrow would be the first to be postponed to make room for some "incredible" opportunity. This was why so many of my relationships never lasted. My mother drilled it into me from the beginning—my career came first, always.

Lucas took my silence as confirmation, and he slowly let go of my hand.

"I know myself too well. My last breakup wrecked me. I was an ass and she left me, rightly so. I went on a bender for a week. Davey and Red found me outside the River Spirit Casino, passed out in this truck. My dad was right, I'm a fuckup. But I know my purpose is to help this ranch and help kids like me. I can't do that if I'm heartbroken over a celebrity I didn't deserve anyway."

"You deserve happiness and love too, Lucas." I looked down, feeling a small pit in my stomach start to form. "Maybe at this point in our lives it's not the right time and I'm not the right woman, but don't write yourself off. People make mistakes, and you said it yourself, no one is a lost cause. I really like you, Lucas—I have for a while now. For the sake of the ranch, I can put that aside and focus on keeping our home out of the hands of greedy businesses. We can be . . . friends."

"Business partners. You and me can never be friends." He whispered it with no malice; I could see the fire in his iron eyes. There was too much sexual tension to be "just friends."

"Business partners then." I stuck out my hand to shake on it.

Lucas took mine in his and it was like no business handshake I've ever experienced. Granted, the businessmen I've shaken hands with were all older than Lottie, but feeling Lucas's warm hand in mine gave me butterflies no matter how hard I tried to calm them.

N THE LATE HOURS OF THE NIGHT, A FOAL WAS BORN. IT was all we talked about over breakfast. That and the morning rainstorm that hadn't let up for hours. I'd never seen a baby horse before, and I cleaned the kitchen at supersonic speed to head down to the barn.

Lottie was out at the Realtor's office to discuss a lowball offer on the property. I had to contact my team again to find a solution to save this place. A baby horse needed a stable home after all.

My Golden Goose sneakers sloshed in the red, sticky mud. All the horses were in the paddocks, happily flicking their tails in the break of the rain. Their energy made it seem like they were all aware and excited about the new addition to their ranks.

I was too. I was bigger than a baby horse, so surely it wouldn't try to eat me.

The barn was quiet as I walked toward the stalls where I saw Tilda chewing on some fresh hay and a brown baby horse resting on the ground by her feet.

"Hello, Tilda," I said as I approached the gate of the stall, crouching down to get a better look at the baby.

Tilda snorted at my arrival in what sounded like a friendly snort and not a get-away-from-my-baby snort. She kept chewing her snack in lazy circles.

I kissed the air and stuck my hand in through the gate. "Come here, horsey, horsey."

The baby looked interested as it stretched its neck to sniff my fingers. It uncurled its long, skinny legs and came up to the bars to let me pet it through the gate.

The foal was still sticky from birth, but completely adorable.

"You are such a cutie, you know that? The cutest horse in all the world!"

"Careful, he already has Rakko for a dad. He doesn't need a bigger head." Lucas crouched down next to me, materializing out of nowhere—or more accurately, from the back of the barn—and I was so engrossed in the cuteness that I hadn't noticed his approach.

"He? I didn't know Tilda had a little boy. He is a prince," I cooed as I scratched under his chin.

"All right, you're gonna make all the other horses jealous since you don't pet or talk to them like this." He stood back up, and I straightened, following him.

"It's their own fault since one tried to eat me." I looked around the barn, noticing it was just me and Lucas. "Where's Red and Davey?"

"They went to walk the property to make sure the fences were still intact after the storm. I stayed behind to let the horses out." Lucas rested his arm on the gate, leaning casually.

"Sounds like you got the easier job." I crossed my arms and cocked my hip, getting ready to tease him some more.

"Well, I had to muck the stalls too." His smile caught on his hooked tooth and it did things to me. I was turning to jelly. This was not good, because there was no way I could be friendly with him without it leading into serious flirting . . . which then turned into—horniness. I had to get out of here.

Right after I looked at him some more.

We were standing there like two idiots.

"What are you going to name the baby horse?" I asked to break the lusty spellbound moment.

"We haven't talked about it. You have any ideas?"

"Me? Oh no, I couldn't name a horse. That's so much pressure!"

Lucas laughed. "No, it's not. Look at him. What does the look of him and his personality inspire?" When I didn't say anything, he added, "It's just for fun. Besides, everyone knows I pick the best names."

"You?" I was skeptical. "What ideas do you have?"

"I've always wanted to name a horse Brego after the horse Aragorn rode in *The Lord of the Rings: The Two Towers* movie, extended edition."

"Huh?" It was like he was speaking in another language.

"You've never seen *The Lord of the Rings*?" he asked, completely aghast.

"Nope." I smiled.

Lucas put his hand over his chest in outrage. "How have you worked on movies but have never seen the best franchise ever made?"

"You'd be surprised by how few movies and shows I have had the time to see." I shrugged.

"*Star Wars*?"

"No."

He threw his hands in the air and walked away from me toward the open barn door. I followed him. "*The Matrix*?"

"Nuh-uh."

"*Indiana Jones*?"

"Nope."

"*Back to the Future?*"

"Again no. I am sensing a theme here—"

"*Batman?* The Tim Burton ones? *Superman* with Christopher Reeve? *Terminator, Alien, Spaceballs, Willow, Star Trek, Jurassic Park*—please, I'd take any of them."

"No, no, no, no, no, no, no, and yes," I listed on my fingers.

"Finally! She's redeemed!" He threw his hands in the air and walked outside of the barn, picking up a shovel.

"I only saw *Jurassic Park* because I was approached about auditioning for the reboot with Chris Pratt."

"Now that's cool." Lucas took the shovel and started walking up the path.

"Where are you going?"

"I am going to fill a hole so a horse doesn't walk in it and break a leg, or the cart doesn't get stuck." He used the shovel to point to the deep puddle toward the side of the barn.

"So, you really like movies?" I asked, trailing after him.

"Yeah. Staying in and watching movies has saved me from a lot of trouble. What do you do in your downtime if not watching movies or TV?"

"I like to read or listen to music."

"I've seen the books you read." He turned over his shoulder with a sardonic look, one dark brow raised, and a teasing smile.

"I didn't pick that book out. My friend, Chelsea, gave it to me to read on the bus."

"Sure. You've never mentioned Chelsea before. Sounds made up to cover the fact you read books about Native warriors and white women with heaving bosoms."

"Chelsea is indeed my friend and very real. She is also my hair and makeup stylist who tours with me." I crossed my arms, defending the only real friend I had . . . even though she'd only been able to email me back once since she was working on another artist's tour. I also didn't get many chances to use the laptop, since it was a shared resource. My hands had a mind of their own, and I started picking at a hangnail. I worried me being alone here for the foreseeable future and our sporadic communication would cause us to drift apart. She was the only real friend I had ever had. We told each other everything, and right now, I wished I could tell her about Lucas and get her perspective on, well, everything.

Lucas's mud-covered hand gently stilled my worrying fingers.

"I was only teasing. I never believed she was fake, and you can read whatever you want to read." He caressed my hands. "Though . . . you won't find those kinds of Native men out here."

I snatched my hand back and playfully pushed his shoulder. "I told you, I don't read those books."

"What do you read then?"

"Rom-coms mostly."

"What kinds are your favorite?" he asked, his smile deliciously wolfish.

"Oh, you know, the ones where the girl is a fish out of water and a grumpy handsome man has to show her the ropes." I winked.

"I think I know what you're talking about." Our eyes locked as we smiled at each other. I even wrapped a loose strand of hair around my finger.

"Watch out, lovebirds!" Davey's voice broke our trance.

A dark, cold wave hit both me and Lucas as Davey and Red flew through the puddle in the cart, narrowly avoiding the hole.

"Come on, man!" Lucas yelled.

"I said watch out," Davey laughed over his shoulder as they drove the cart to the other end of the barn.

"This is disgusting." I wiped at the clods of mud on my face. "Did I get it?" I asked Lucas.

"No, you smeared it even more. Let me." He brought his work-rough hand to my cheek, using his thumb to swipe away the muck.

"Better?" I asked.

"No, it's worse." He lifted his hand away from my face and waved his filthy hand at me, laughing.

I laughed too. This was ridiculous. We stood there giggling, covered in mud, and I loved it.

"Come on." He jerked his head toward the side of the barn where there was a hose on a black plastic reel.

I hurried over and reached down for the nozzle, stopping as a huge spider perched comfortably on the nozzle handle. A scream erupted from my throat.

"What is it?" Lucas was next to me in an instant.

"A mutant spider!" I pointed at the tall brown spider with a fat round bottom.

"What? That?" Lucas leaned down and brushed it away with his hand. "It's just a cellar spider."

"Huh?"

"A daddy longlegs. Totally harmless." He walked to the spigot to turn on the water.

"Our daddy longlegs don't look anything like that. Ours are small and keep to ceiling corners. That thing was not a normal daddy longlegs."

"Welcome to the country. Everything is bigger." He gave me a cheeky grin.

With the spider gone, I reached for the hose and pulled to unwind it from the reel. Aiming for Lucas's middle, I pulled the trigger of the nozzle and fired away.

"Hey!" he shouted.

"You sure everything's bigger in the country?" I aimed the stream lower.

"It's cold water!" His voice went an octave higher.

"Still impressive." I bit my lip.

"Yeah, yeah, give me that. Fair's fair." He reached for the hose, which I happily acquiesced.

Lucas twisted the nozzle of the hose to a gentle shower. I didn't know it could do that. Now I felt a little bad for hitting him with a jet stream. Oops.

Lucas stepped closer to me. "Turn around," he said, his voice throaty. I did as he directed. Cool water streamed down my hair; I closed my eyes. I felt his deft fingers comb through my strands, breaking up the mud clots. The spray felt amazing on my skin as the sun rose higher along with the temperature.

He started spraying my shoulders, gently batting the worst of the gunk off my back. It was completely innocent, but with my eyes closed and the memory of what his mouth felt like on mine, it was indecent. His touch left goose bumps in its wake.

My tank top was thin and flimsy, and my bralette was unlined. My breasts felt heavy, and my nipples ached as they pressed against the cold material trying to weigh them down. I brought my hand up to my collarbone to help wipe away the grime, letting my fingers fall down over my breasts as Lucas's hand trailed down my back. I moaned.

Lucas stilled his hand; his face was inches from my neck. I felt his hot mouth on the sensitive skin below my ear. "Make that sound again," he growled.

I gasped, turning around quickly in his arms. He dropped the hose, immediately forgotten. The water was doing nothing to cool down the moment. "Lucas," I said breathlessly. We had talked about this. This couldn't happen. *We* couldn't happen.

But how badly I wanted it to. I looked up into his flint-colored eyes. There was a fire smoldering behind them. I tracked the movement of those beautiful eyes as he narrowed his focus on my lips.

He lowered his head, and it was bliss. I know we said it was wrong, but it felt so right. I had kissed quite a few men professionally and in my dating life and never had it felt like this. Lucas's lips were soft, plush, and so warm. I kissed him back with everything I had.

Then he slipped his tongue inside my mouth and my knees buckled. He gripped me closer to him as he walked me backward and my back felt the wall of the barn. Lucas pinned me there against the wall as I wrapped my arms around his neck, trying to fuse myself as close to him as possible.

What I would have given in that moment to have been in a room with a bed.

"Touch me, Lucas," I whimpered against his lips.

He moaned as he deepened the kiss and brought his right hand to my breast, cupping me and rolling my nipple between his fingers.

"Hey, Luke?" Davey's voice sounded close.

I gasped against Lucas's mouth and pushed him away from me. I frantically wiped my face and hair.

Lucas adjusted himself in his pants and picked the hose back up.

"Yeah?" Lucas sounded annoyed. They did purposefully spray us with mud, so the tone was justified.

"My bad," Davey said, appearing from around the corner. "Was just checking on you."

"Just rinsing all this crap off. Will be done in a minute, and we can get the stockroom ready for the feed shipment."

"Cool." Davey stood there looking from me to Lucas. I crossed my arms to cover my chest. "I didn't interrupt anything, did I?" he asked in a teasing way.

"Nope!" I mustered all my cheer and marched back to the house, not sparing Davey or Lucas another look.

That was too close.

STAYED AWAY FROM THE BARN AND LUCAS AS MUCH AS
I could for a day. We could not afford to slip up and get caught
by Lottie or the guys. I had to focus on my part of the bargain and
save the ranch.

Getting access to the phone lately had been impossible. Lottie
was on the phone with her Realtor and what seemed like every
bank in the country. She would hide away in her room or the study
with the door closed so I couldn't eavesdrop and see how bad it
was getting.

With the ranch's laptop, it was easy to get business done, all
without cc'ing my mother—a first. Luckily, we did not have a joint
bank account. She took a ten percent manager commission off all
my checks, but what was left over after paying my agent and entertainment lawyer was mine. My lawyer and financial adviser returned my emails, and their news was a devastating blow.

I wasn't filthy rich. I had a hit song right now and was nowhere
in the ballpark of rich. They had to explain to me that most of my
"wealth" was on paper. I could liquefy my stock investments and
sell my Studio City house, but it would take time, and I'd have to

pay major penalties and taxes. It wouldn't be enough to buy the land, equipment, and horses for the listed price of $1.5 million. I was going to have to tell Lucas that I couldn't deliver on my promise.

To add insult to injury, Niles left my messages unanswered, so the state of my album and music video was still up in the air. The song I was working on had potential to be something big, I could feel it in every fiber of my being. If only I could record it and release it, I just knew it would take off. If I could work on getting a licensing deal for it or something, that could help us fund Lucas's ranch plans. But without word from my label, I was stuck. These plans could never come to fruition unless I found capital, and fast.

We all had finished breakfast a while ago and Lottie was going to visit Bessie with her friends. I had to tell Lucas the truth, and maybe we could come up with a plan together. I tucked the laptop under my arm and headed for Lucas's trailer. The heat always surprised me every time I walked outside from an air-conditioned place. I didn't think I'd ever get used to it. I was panting by the time I reached Lucas's door. I had to calm my breathing for many reasons. It was just a few days since we'd decided to be "business partners" only, but my body still craved Lucas's touch, especially after our slipup with the hose. I had been trying to keep my distance. When I was satisfied that my breathing was normal enough, I knocked.

Immediately, the breath was knocked from my lungs again as Lucas pushed open his door and poked his head out. He must have just finished his chores and showered, as his hair was wet and curling. He lifted his chin in greeting then opened the door wider to let me in.

He was shirtless. Fantastic.

He closed the door behind me and motioned for me to sit at the table. I was nervous. I was a woman of her word, and now after he had given me so much lately by showing me the ropes around here, I wasn't going to be able to deliver.

I started worrying my hands until I found a hangnail and started picking, looking at the spot on the table in front of Lucas. I needed a moment to gather my courage.

"Are you okay?" he asked, bending his head so it was in my line of vision.

"Yes and no . . ."

He sat, blinking, waiting for me to continue.

"I can't buy the ranch."

"What do you mean?"

I let it all out in a whoosh. After I finished explaining, my heart started rapidly beating, waiting for his reaction. He straightened back up.

"So let me get this straight. You're rich but not *really* rich?"

"Basically."

"What about all the royalties from the song?"

"I get practically nothing. I didn't write it. With how the contract is structured, I owe Grand Records the money they advanced me before I see any other money. What I have is from my acting residuals and a few investments."

"It's not enough," he agreed.

"I know and I'm so sorry. I really thought things were a lot cheaper out here."

"Hey, don't apologize. You tried your best." He gave me a reassuring smile. "Property is cheaper out here than California, but this is a lot of land with mature lumber and the business as well."

"My best isn't good enough. Maybe your dad is right, and Lottie would accept a much lower all-cash offer to rid herself of the headache."

"Never say that again." Lucas's tone was sharp. "My father is never right. I would never shortchange a woman who has helped me."

"She's my grandmother, I'd never want to do that either. But what if we just approached her with this idea. Maybe she would accept it?"

He shook his head. "Lottie's too proud."

"So, you think she'd rather sell to a complete stranger than let us help her? We don't even know how much she owes the bank. It could be so much less than the list price."

"Did your lawyer finish setting up the foundation?"

"Well, the good news is the paperwork was filed for the Fox Equine-Assisted Therapy Ranch Foundation."

"What's the bad news?"

"It can take thirty days or more to hear back on the approval."

"Shit," he muttered.

"I am nothing if not a problem solver, so I have a work-around." I beamed, turning the laptop around to show Lucas the screen. "Ta-da!"

Lucas peered at it before his eyes widened. "A crowdsource campaign. This is great."

"And a handy QR code we can share with anyone and everyone."

"You put the goal as one hundred and fifty thousand dollars. Why?"

"Because I can get a loan with that down payment."

"There is already an anonymous donation of twenty-five grand." He looked at me over the laptop screen.

"It was all I could move myself online."

"This is brilliant. You're brilliant." He closed the laptop, pushing it to the side. "Thank you for doing all of this."

Lucas folded his arms on the table, and I had to look away, but there was so much of him. He needed a shirt or something. The way his muscles rippled with power from such a casual motion was indecent. How was I supposed to keep up a professional pretense when he did things like that subconsciously?

"My eyes are up here."

I ripped my vision from his pecs and blushed as he chuckled.

"It's time for your biggest lesson on being Indian."

"And what is that?" I gulped, because even though he was talking casually, the sexual power this man exuded was too much for little ol' me. I was going to have to get out of here quick.

"Community. We can't do this ourselves, even Lottie has tried it and failed. We need to ask for help and really publicize the hell out of the crowdsourcing through word of mouth. We need all of Broken Arrow behind us."

"What, like a fundraising event?"

"That's exactly what I'm thinking."

"Do we have enough time to do it? We are already close to the thirty-day deadline the bank gave Lottie." Knowing everything that went into planning my shows, I was a bit skeptical.

"Oh, we have time. We just need to get the word out. Keep it casual. Lottie has done so much for everyone. I haven't been the only person she has taken in over the years. They will all come out and support. Especially if we can get it online and crowdsource hard. This town has over a hundred thousand people in it. Even if we only had a couple thousand people contribute and come to the event, we can get the bank off of her back."

"You have a lot of faith in this little town. No one I've ever known has shown up for people in this way."

"We're in rural America. Community is all we have here."

His optimism was infectious. I wish I could have been the savior and swoop in with my credit card and make it all better, but I couldn't. What I did have was a network of people I had accumulated for years. Even if it was likely that no one would take my calls, for Lottie and this ranch, I would reach out and keep trying. "I can't promise anything, but I could try to make some calls and get more publicity for it, see if I can cash in on a few favors to get more talent here."

"We have so many local bands too. We can host it here on the property, set up a dance floor, include food and drinks." Lucas sounded excited, and as he talked, I could see the event unfold in my mind, almost like a fair with booths of food, activities, music, and lots of dancing.

"We need a big headliner, someone people couldn't resist. Someone who would take a very small fee for a good cause," I mused.

"That's a big ask."

I deflated, only a little. "Yeah, it is a big ask and with next to no notice. I don't know anyone who would do it."

"I do," Lucas said, his voice quiet, but his eyes were intense as they bored into mine.

"Who?" I asked excitedly.

"You."

I blinked. "No. I've never headlined anything. I've always been an opener. With the way people hate me right now, they would be more inclined to pay to watch me fail . . ." My voice trailed off and our eyes locked. That was it. I could cash in on the expectation of failure and humiliation. If it will fill seats and get the money we needed, who cared why they attended so long as they did?

"Not everyone hates you, Avery. All they have to do is hear you sing to know you're the real deal. We are more than the sum of our mistakes."

"They might come and expect me to fail, but that doesn't mean

I will. I just don't know how good a performance it will be without my costumers and dancers."

"You forgot about your band?" Lucas asked with a smirk.

I rolled my eyes—of course he had to get his digs in where he could. "I perform to a track, anyone can play it, but I don't have access to any of it. My phone was stolen, remember? I've been using this brick." I motioned to the heavy laptop that rested between us on Lucas's dining table. Maybe I could find a karaoke track on YouTube or ask Chelsea to work her magic with My$teriou$ Money to get me some tracks.

"You don't need dancers or flashy costumes or any other theatrics. You just need to be you. Why don't you perform your songs acoustically? We can bill it as an unplugged performance, and you can sing that song you've been singing all over here."

Those theatrics were what made performing the songs I do possible. It was a mask to hide behind, or else I'd feel how close to naked I was, performing songs with suggestive lyrics. I couldn't do that barefaced and in jeans—then I'd be truly naked. The world thinks they have seen Avery Fox, but the real me was something I didn't let everyone have access to . . . because I'd only just found her. In my isolation, I had finally realized who I was in my core. I discovered that I was a songwriter first and a performer second. I was capable of more than just being a pretty face that could memorize lines and hit my mark. I was able to make food from scratch and work this land—I wasn't any good at it, but I did it and I'd keep trying to get better.

"'Heartbeats'? That song isn't ready to perform live. Even you said it needed work."

"It's not ready yet, but we could get it there."

"We?" I lifted my eyebrow.

"The hook is there. I haven't been able to get it out of my damn head. But you need a better bridge to get you there."

"I know what you mean. I've been working on it a bit as I work in the house. I still don't know if it's exactly right, but I feel like it's closer." I sighed.

"Show me." Lucas nudged the guitar in my direction. Piano was my instrument of choice, but I could strum a few chords on guitar. I was nervous to touch his guitar. I felt naked with Lucas's attention on me and my music. I didn't keep a traditional diary. I laid myself bare in my music, and he'd been less than complimentary the first time I'd sung this song.

"This thing in tune?" I asked to buy me more time.

"Impeccably." He raised an eyebrow and leaned back in his seat in wait.

"I'm not much of a guitarist."

"Stop stalling and let me hear it."

I gave a nervous giggle. "At least it's in the key of E and those chords are easy on a guitar." I practiced strumming chords A, B, and E to get a feel for the instrument. Then I turned to face the wall of books and music, because I couldn't sing looking directly into his eyes. It was just too intimate.

I played the first chord and began, my voice low and timid as I warmed up to performing a song so close to my heart with an unfamiliar instrument.

> *Moving fast*
> *Enough to make you spin*
> *Always chasing fame*
> *And the will of what some man says*

I let the song take over me as I sang the next verse and chorus. Finally, it was time for the revised bridge. It was similar to what I had before, but I tweaked some words here and there and rearranged the order of a few lines. What it was now was better, sharper.

> *And I let it all go*
> *The crown and the robe*
> *As I walk through the door*
> *One million heartbeats sound*
> *One people's heart in this ground*
> *One woman lost*
> *Is now found*

I finally met Lucas's face; his eyes were glassy. I had never had anyone listen to one of my songs and take it so seriously and connect so deeply with it. This was my dream all along.

I closed my eyes for the final chorus, my voice an octave higher. I gave everything I had within me, belting the words out. I stopped playing the guitar and let my voice carry me through the end of the song.

> *I'll never let this go*
> *Take your hand and I'm home*
> *I'll never let go*
> *Oh no*
> *Take your hand and I'm home*

With the last notes of the song I was breathless, trying to suck air down my nose, but the energy within the small trailer had drastically changed. We were charged. Even Lucas's bare chest was heaving, and he looked at me with such intense heat, I melted on the felt seat.

"You're singing this song," he said, his gravelly voice throatier than I'd ever heard it before.

"You liked it?" If I were anywhere else, with anyone else, I'd be embarrassed by how breathy my voice was.

"Like it? No, I love it. You flew through that bridge, each line building on top of the other. Your voice soared. It's incredible—you're incredible."

My fingers buzzed with unspent adrenaline, itching to get back to the piano to play the song the way it was meant to be played. I was feeling inspired in a way I hadn't in a long time, like my soul was bubbling and wanted to float along the air with my melody.

For the first time since coming here, I felt . . . hope.

Here on this ranch, I was allowed to be me and I was given the space to figure out who that was. I went through some tough things and came out the other side . . . sort of. Thinking about getting onstage again made me feel a little light-headed. Announcing to the world that I was back as if nothing had happened and leading strangers here, right to me, felt like I was asking for trouble.

I needed to do it, but I wasn't doing it alone. I was returning to the stage for my family. I believed in Lucas's dream for the ranch. I could picture all the kids he was going to help pushing wheelbarrows around, exercising the horses, and mucking the pasture.

This plan would come together, and it would be a triumph.

"What is the fastest way to spread the word and make sure people show up?" I asked.

"We hand out flyers at the stickball tournament."

"The stickball tournament?" I asked dubiously.

Lucas responded with only the cheekiest grin that definitely did *not* make my heart flutter.

WHO'S READY FOR SOME STICKBALL?! YEE-OW!"
Davey shouted as he stuck his head out of the truck window like a dog. I laughed, squished in the middle back row between Red and Lottie. Since Lucas and Davey were playing, we all let them get the legroom, so they wouldn't cramp before the "bloodbath," as Lottie called it.

A group of people outside—men, women, and children—screamed back in excitement, lifting brown wooden sticks with small leather baskets at the end.

Lucas parked the truck next to all the other vehicles on one side of a large, open field. So many people were setting up what looked to be a tailgate with food and drinks, camping chairs, and blankets. Canopies were being erected while players gathered to warm up.

Lucas and Davey had all their gear in the bed of the truck along with our picnic supplies to watch the game all day.

A horn behind us started honking rapidly. I twisted as much as I could in the cramped quarters and saw Mary Beth waving from her bright yellow Jeep.

"That's my baby!" Davey yelled as he hopped out of the truck, folding the passenger seat forward to let us crawl out.

"That's my man!" Mary Beth yelled back as she parked next to us. She got out and shared a passionate greeting with Davey. We all had to look away—way too much tongue was involved.

"Avery, come over here and give me a hand with the food and chairs," Lottie called over her shoulder. I'd never been more grateful for a task in my life. Davey and MB's love was palpable, and a seed of envy rooted in my stomach. I had to force myself not to glance at Lucas and to forget those feelings from our last kiss.

I hopped into the truck bed and scooted the cooler to the edge, and Red wordlessly lifted it and carried it over to the field. There were two duffel bags, one containing both Lucas's and Davey's gear for the tournament, and the second, two thousand mini flyers we had printed for the fundraiser. Lottie at first said she wasn't planning on coming to the tournament, but since there had been a slew of showings on the property today, she opted to come with us. So, we had to get the word out stealthily. I hated the deceit, but it felt like begging for forgiveness when it was too close to the date to cancel was better than asking for permission—especially knowing how stubborn she was in general.

I looped the handles of both duffels around each of my shoulders and moved to hop off the truck. But before I could dismount, a strong, sturdy, and work-rough hand clasped mine, steadying me.

My Golden Goose–clad feet landed on the dusty ground and that simple touch left me feeling off-kilter as Lucas took his duffel from me and headed to the field. I shouldn't have watched him go. His hand flexed as if it were in pain. The hand that had helped me.

Mine throbbed too.

"Earth to Avery." Lottie snapped her fingers in front of my face.

I shook the thoughts and feelings from my mind and smiled at Lottie. "Sorry about that, guess I need more sleep."

She harrumphed and proceeded to follow the guys toward the field and other groups setting up to spend a day watching stickball.

Men and women in athletic wear jogged to the center of the field carrying their sticks. Everyone had two, whereas Davey, with his one arm, had one. The men eyed him and his single stick warily, as if the players with two sticks were really the ones with the disadvantage. Davey flipped his stick in the air, winking at Mary Beth, who was sitting in her camping chair blowing him kisses.

Lucas and Davey wore blue shirts while their opposing team wore red ones. Some even had red headbands and sweatbands. Lucas and Davey kept it simple. Davey's hair was shorn with no worry of it getting in his way. I watched as Lucas swept his chin-length hair off his face with a headband. Listen, I'd seen my fair share of hipsters walking around greater Los Angeles in beanies, man buns, and bandannas, but none pulled off an elastic headband the way Lucas Motherfucking Iron Eyes did.

Two shorter pieces fell out around his face and the sweat on his temple from the heat was already making those hairs curl.

"Avery, would you stop gawking and help me set up?" Lottie barked.

Dammit. Not again.

"Sorry, Lottie." I hurried to set up our stuff next to where Mary Beth planted herself for the best view of the game. I grabbed the other end of the big blue sheet Lottie was trying to spread out on the ground. It was worn through on the left corner I held and there were a few bleach stains, but it was soft from the decades of washing it must have endured. I set the duffel with the flyers on one corner, not that there was any breeze to lift the edges like you'd experience at the beach in Malibu.

"I hope this wraps up before the weather turns. I don't like the look of those clouds," Lottie muttered to herself. I looked up to the sky. It was just gray, but didn't look too scary to me.

Red came back from his second trip to the truck and dropped our two camping chairs on the ground. I worked to take them out of their travel sleeves and set them up so that Lottie had a more comfortable place to sit while I sat on the ground.

All of our attention was ripped from what we were doing when a huge, lifted army green truck with the top off like those Jeeps in *Jurassic Park* screeched from the road and into the dirt parking lot.

"Ah shit," Red mumbled.

We watched as a person jumped out of the monstrosity of a truck: a woman of short stature wearing a bright red cut-off tank, showing off rippling muscles, tight black bicycle shorts, and a fauxhawk.

"Who is that?" I asked as the woman's friends hopped out of the truck and people started cheering.

"Bad news," Lottie answered as she opened the cooler, unpacking the sandwiches.

"Damn co-ed teams."

"Whoa, that's some ass-backward thinking, Red. I didn't expect that from you," I said, shocked by the blatant sexism.

"Ain't that. Molly Burright needs to stay on the all-women teams. Our guys stand no chance. It's gonna be a brutal and humiliating loss. Her elbows are sharper than a brand-new bowie knife. She just jabs left and right. Gloats too and it's relentless. Calls all the men babies. This is a hobbyist team trying to have fun and she takes it too far. Terrible attitude, because she knows she is the best," Mary Beth explained, disappointment coating her voice.

"She's that good?" I asked.

"Mm hm. Molly is lethal. She is faster and stronger than any of the men out there. Even Davey. He got one tackle on her last year, and she said next time she would get revenge. Don't worry, baby!" Mary Beth yelled to Davey.

Both Davey and Lucas broke off from the rest of the Blue Team huddled in the middle of the field and met Molly halfway, close enough for us to hear her taunting words.

"Y'all looked surprised to see me," Molly called as she walked straight up to them, surrounded by her friends and admirers, then hocked a loogie onto the grass, barely missing Davey's tennis shoe.

I turned to look at the rest of the players milling about and stretching on the field. The Red Team looked smug, while our Blue Team looked like the life had drained from every player's eyes.

Davey and Lucas stood feet apart at attention, their backs ramrod straight to appear at their tallest.

"Heard you were recruited to play in the stickball World Series out in Mississippi." Lucas crossed his arms over his puffed-up chest. This athletic posturing was a tad off-putting, but the stakes appeared to be great, given the tension that filled the field in only a few moments.

"The player I was subbing in for had a miraculous recovery, so now I'm here." Molly turned to wink to the still-growing group of onlookers waiting for the game to begin.

"Aight. We gotta warm up. See you out there." Lucas jutted his chin. Davey followed suit. Molly jutted her chin back.

"They won't get hurt, will they?" I asked Red, Lottie, and Mary Beth.

"Not too bad. No one is allowed to whack sticks in faces and tackling isn't really allowed unless it's the person with the ball," Red answered as he cracked open a beer from the cooler. "It's gonna be an even more interesting game now."

I nodded, taking a look at the field and the two tall poles that marked either end. It was maybe the length of a football field, not that I was all that familiar with sporting fields or arenas. There were no baskets or anything.

"How do you score points?" I asked.

"Stickball can be played many ways depending on the tribe. Usually you see a casual, fun social version with just one pole to score points on, boys versus girls. But this is tournament-style based on the Mississippi Band of Choctaw Indians. It's more competitive with two poles. They'll toss a coin to see which goalpost is theirs, then they have to catch the ball or scoop it off the ground with their sticks—no hands are allowed. Then they have to hit the post with the ball to score. The first team to reach twelve wins."

"That doesn't seem so bad. Sounds like a quick game."

"Ha!" Red choked on his sip of beer and started coughing.

"Oh honey, this game can last hours. It used to last for days, historically. These players take it very seriously and will do whatever it takes to keep the opponents' ball from touching their post. We will be here for a while." Mary Beth patted my head like I was a child.

Okay, so we were going to be here for the long haul. That explained all the food and drinks we'd brought.

"Avery, I want you to come with me to meet a few people." Lottie stood from her chair and reached her hand out to me to help me up. I wore my denim shorts, which gave me a wedgie unlike any I had ever experienced in my life. I tried to innocuously pull down the ends to get myself comfortable as I followed Lottie to a canopy a few yards away from our setup.

Inside the shade was a group of six older people, four women and two men. The women lazily waved fans at their faces.

"Hensci, Lottie. Is this who we think it is?" The woman in a folding chair at the right end of the group greeted us. She was wearing a purple tie-dyed dress, sandals, and thick glasses with dark lenses clipped on.

"Hensci, Shauna, yes, this here is Hattie's daughter, Avery."

"Good to meet you, Avery." Shauna inclined her head in greeting.

"Shauna works in our citizenship office. She can help us get you *enrolled* as everyone in the country is obsessed with."

Shauna and her group laughed. "You made a mistake on that magazine cover, honey."

My shoulders immediately drooped. I was tired of the Southern patronizing *honey* everyone used, even if well-intentioned.

She continued, "But we don't believe a person is defined by their mistakes. Bessie says you've been visiting with her."

"Yes, ma'am. I do what I can, even though it's limited."

"That's all we can do. So many people have come and stolen our knowledge to use for personal gain."

"I wouldn't dream of doing that. I am Muscogee and I am trying to figure out what that means for me. We don't have many successful female musicians in the popular genres who are Native."

"Carrie Underwood is popular. She's Muscogee, and her extended family comes out to events every now and then," the older man sitting next to Shauna said matter-of-factly. He wore a black baseball cap with an embroidered marijuana leaf on it.

"I had no idea she was Native," I said.

"It's not exactly something she leads with, but she's ours. We know. Now we got you," one of the other women in the group said. She sat in the middle, wearing an oversized T-shirt from the 2013 Muscogee Festival and a pair of black basketball shorts.

"I want to introduce her to everyone else before the game starts. We'll drop off the application soon to get the ball rolling on citizenship," Lottie said as she started leading me away to the next group.

"See ya soon, Avery," Shauna said. They all waved their fans at me in farewell.

Lottie stopped at several blankets and canopies to introduce me to people she had known her whole life. Many asked after my mother and I saw firsthand how Lottie fielded those questions, brushing them off with vague generalities like, "Oh, you know Hattie. Busy doing who knows what in Hollywood." It was obvious everyone had heard these answers so much they smiled it off and nodded and quickly changed the subject.

As we went from group to group, this event felt like a big party with everyone waiting to watch this game, and it was full of fun and community. I loved it.

Lottie and I started heading back to our spot when the opening notes to my song started blasting on a stereo. I would recognize the hand drum beat anywhere. I looked around in a panic, trying to see who was playing it and if it was a friend or a foe.

My voice singing the "oh oh ohs" echoed around us and even Lottie knew it was me.

Across the field was the Red Team, led by Molly, doing a terrible version of the choreography from my music video. Molly saw she had my attention and started pointing at me and laughing.

Then a couple of the men ripped their shirts off and screamed across the distance, "You need a warrior tonight? Ow ow!"

I shuddered in embarrassment.

"I'm sorry, Lottie. I didn't think this would happen." Maybe I could make a run for it to the truck and hide out there, or drive down the road and wait out the game there, away from prying eyes. I couldn't blow my cover here before our fundraiser was announced. It had to happen right.

"Just ignore it. They'll get bored soon and then the game will start," she said, trying to reassure me as we met back up with Red and Mary Beth.

Mary Beth stood from her seat and was flipping off the group with both her hands.

"Mary Beth!" Lottie snapped. "There are children here."

"What? They are humping the air right now. How is the bird worse?" Mary Beth cried with her hands out.

"We don't stoop to their level, and we can't be distracting Davey when he is going to be the sole target of Molly's wrath," Lottie gently scolded.

Mary Beth dropped down into her chair, arms crossed. "You're right."

Both teams started heading for us, and I wasn't proud of it, but I sat and hid behind Mary Beth's and Lottie's chairs.

"Red, we need your help. Travis pulled his hamstring and can't play. We need you to cover. Can you do it?" Lucas asked with the rest of the players standing behind him.

"Ah shit, I'm already three beers in. I won't be much help."

"Aw too bad, Luke. Looks like y'all will have to play down a player or forfeit. Unless that scrawny little fake Indian princess wants to get her hands dirty and play with us," Molly taunted, coming up to stand by Lucas. "What say you, little songbird? Up for a friendly game?"

Nothing about Molly sounded friendly. "She isn't a fake and she's never played before. Go see if Derek's here. He could do it," Mary Beth said.

"Derek had to work. Everyone else is too young or too old."

"But inexperience is okay? You'll eat her alive. I'll do it." Mary Beth stood up.

"Oh no you won't," Davey said as he stepped forward and used the basket end of his stick to gently push Mary Beth back down into her seat. "Not in your condition."

The group of thirty men and women yipped, yelled, clapped, and shook Davey by the shoulders.

"Dammit, Davey, we were going to wait to say anything until after the wedding." Mary Beth was fuming.

"That was before you were going to volunteer to play this game." Davey was smiling proudly.

"I'll do it," I said as I stood up from the ground. What was the worst they could do? It wasn't like I could catch the ball anyway. I would just be there for numbers.

"I don't know about this—" Lucas said but was cut off.

"Great, let's play!" Molly yelled, jumping with her team to the chant "Red hot we on top!" over and over again.

The Blue Team started following the Red Team, less excited and cheerful. In the core of my essence, I knew I had made a terrible mistake agreeing to volunteer. I started to follow them, leaving Davey to kiss Mary Beth into forgiveness.

And then that familiar, warm, rough hand grasped my wrist. "Wait here a minute," Lucas said.

I gulped.

He pulled out two backup sticks from his duffel and handed them to me. "Hold each in your hand like this." He demonstrated, showing his hands at the end, about six inches up from the bottom.

Thank god I didn't have those stiletto nails anymore, because they would snap from the grip I was using to hold on to these sticks. Lucas put a spare ball on the ground and showed me how to use the sticks to pick it up and the best way to use both to cradle the ball to run.

"I'll just stand on the outskirts and stay out of everyone's way, so you don't have to worry about me. I want you to play and have fun. You won't even know I'm there."

"I'll know." His voice was low, only for me.

I hitched a breath. The feeling was mutual. No matter where Lucas was in my vicinity, my body was aware. He was like a magnet, and I was drawn to him.

"Keep your guard up. The Red Team is riled up and will want to haze you. Stay out of their way and you should survive."

"Survive?" I shrieked.

"You wanted a crash course on being Indian. Well, here it is. Just . . . be careful. If you see someone charging at you, just run away, got it?"

I nodded, nerves stealing my voice. Lucas's lips pressed together in a grim line, and he led us to our team. Once we joined them, everyone started banging their sticks together in unison. The sound thrummed around me like a thunderous heartbeat.

"We are gonna go out there and we are gonna give it our all!" Lucas said. "We have a green player who is the size of my pinky. We need to protect her. Davey, you and Avery are both on goal with Gill and Perry."

Gill and Perry nodded and walked over to stand next to Davey. Davey's height towered over everyone. Gill was only slightly taller than me and Perry was more in between, but very stout and wide.

"Jon Deerwood is reffing today and you know he accepts no nonsense. No hitting below the knees, no sticks in the face, and no horse wrangling."

At my confused expression, Lucas leaned down to explain. "No grabbing necks or hooking arms around necks. This isn't wrestling."

I nodded my understanding again and wished I could hightail

it off the field and hide somewhere far away. I gripped the smooth wooden sticks with my sweaty hands.

Every single player gathered around the center of the field. The referee was distinguishable by the bright orange shirt he wore with a whistle around his neck. He held a red ball, the texture of the leather weaving hardly visible from where I stood behind everyone else. I stayed close to Davey, Gill, and Perry so that I could follow them quickly to our goalpost.

The ref blew his whistle once and everyone lifted their sticks into the air. He threw the tiny red ball up and whistled again.

Then chaos broke out.

The sound of sticks slapping together mixed with a cacophony of grunts and screams. I tried to look for Lucas in the chaotic dog-pile and couldn't make him out in the midst of red and blue shirts, bare arms, and sticks.

"Avery!" Davey yelled and nodded for me to follow him to our position.

The goalpost looked like a simple piece of wood painted white and stuck into the ground. It had to be at least twenty feet tall, and Gill and Perry were already standing up against it with their sticks straight up in the air.

"Use your sticks to whack the ball away from the post if it comes anywhere near you. Like this." Davey demonstrated with his stick, the basket side facing out and down.

I practiced.

"That's good. Make sure you keep both baskets as close together as possible so that it's wider to really knock the ball away."

I practiced a few more times before Davey was satisfied, and soon I had it down. He made me stand on the far back side of the goal while he, Gill, and Perry would block the front to protect me.

It was a long wait before the Red Team had the ball in their possession to make it to our end of the field. I finally spotted Lucas; he dove and stole the ball from the Red Team. He had the ball clasped between his two sticks and was seamlessly running and dodging the Red players, running to the opposite side of the field toward their goalpost.

"Go, go, go!" Everyone was screaming as he made it with a clear shot to the goal.

"Shoot it!" Davey screamed with all his might.

I watched in awe as Lucas stepped forward on his left leg, launched his sticks, and released the ball. From this far back, I couldn't see the ball at all, but the entire Red Team converged on Lucas and the goalpost when we heard a loud WHACK!

The ball connected with the post.

The crowd erupted as the first point in the game went to our team.

Molly ran by him, chucking him with her shoulder as she did so, before the ref threw the ball back into play. It looked like a bloodbath down there with elbows flying and players being tackled down left and right. This was not my idea of fun. There were contact sports and then there was stickball. I couldn't believe no one was wearing any protective gear. Some people were straight up running around the field barefoot.

The Red Team was in possession of the ball again, and a bull of a man was sprinting our way with the ball nestled between his two sticks. Gill and Perry blocked his path to the post, but it was high, and the player took his chances, shooting the ball in an arc, and it missed.

Players were running toward our goal and Davey was running toward me, pointing to the ground. "Get the ball!" he yelled.

I felt like those hungry hippos in that game, trying to clasp the ball in my sticks. I got it and felt a millisecond of satisfaction before

I was looking around to give it to someone else—anyone else. Davey was next to me, blocking a Red Team player from clasping on to me.

"Run now! Find a blue shirt to pass it to!" Davey barked his order.

I started running, praying the ball stayed put like an egg-and-spoon race with much higher stakes.

Then I saw him. Lucas waving at me to chuck the ball to him. I tried to mimic his throwing stance, stepping forward with my left leg and letting the momentum propel the ball forward, but before I could release the ball, I felt a sudden impact like I was hit by a train at full speed, and then everything went black.

21

HEARD MURMURING AROUND ME. IT WAS STILL DARK while my body caught up with the fact that I was awake, and it needed to open my eyelids.

"She's stirring!" A female voice sounded excited and relieved. Where the hell was I? My hands felt around. I was lying on soft grass. It felt like I'd thrown my back out.

"Avery, can you open your eyes?" Lucas's deep voice was quiet against my ear. I still couldn't open my eyes, but I commanded my body to lift my hand and reach for where his face must be. My fingers brushed across his usually smooth face, but there was a little bit of prickly scruff that tickled the pads of my fingers.

Finally, I forced my eyelids open, and I winced. It was still daylight, but the number of red- and blue-clad bodies around me cast a shadow over me.

"What happened?" I groaned as I slowly tried to sit up. Lucas's hand was on my back to help ease me into a sitting position.

"You had the ball. I told you to stay away from the ball." Lucas's voice was lethal.

I tensed at his anger, unsure if it was directed at me.

He rubbed my back in slow, comforting circles.

"Molly full-on decked ya! She came right around you and knocked you out with her elbow," one of the players in red explained, a little too enthusiastically, in my opinion. "Whack!" He brought his elbow up to demonstrate.

"Thanks, Brian." Lucas's sarcasm made me laugh. Then the crowd gasped in unison, taking a step back as they all stared at me in horror.

"What is it?"

"Aw shit! She knocked out your tooth," Red said as he came to kneel at my other side while Lottie stood hovering behind him.

"Why is there a tiny sharp tooth there? It's terrifying!" someone yelled.

"What? Does it look bad?" I looked at Red and when he didn't say anything, I turned to Lucas.

"I'm gonna be sick. She has two layers of teeth." Someone else started gagging.

"They're veneers," I cried, urging Lucas to reassure me I looked fine.

"No, it doesn't look bad." He refused to meet my eyes.

"This is just great." My eyes watered and my tongue felt around to see if anything else had been knocked loose. On the bright side, no other teeth were loose or even cracked, but on the very not-so-bright side it was my front left tooth.

"We can get it fixed," Lucas said softly in my ear.

"I found it!" A woman's voice yelled from behind everyone. It was Molly. She pushed her way through, and it was clear Lucas didn't want her anywhere near me, and I felt the same.

"Hey, gap tooth," she said, and nodded in greeting as she kneeled next to Lucas, whose lip was hooked over his tooth as if he would growl if she came any closer. "It's the whole tooth—if you put it under your tongue and get to a dentist quick they should be able to pop it back in."

"Is that a thing?" I asked, completely bewildered.

"Hell yeah." She handed my tooth to Lucas, who then gave it to me. "Welcome to the team," she said as she popped out her bridge with three teeth attached, showing a big gappy smile. "Now you fit in."

"Great." I popped the tooth under my tongue like I was told and Red and Lucas each took a hand and helped me stand.

"We gotta get her to the clinic," Lottie said.

"It's Saturday, the clinics are closed," Red countered.

"I know where to take her." Lucas clasped my hand in his and started leading me away, but I was still dizzy from being knocked unconscious and stumbled into him. He dropped my hand and scooped me up into his arms before continuing his long strides across the field.

"What about the game?" I asked with a lisp as my tongue held my tooth under it.

"Forget about it."

"But the flyers!" My urging made me drool a bit, and I had to do a gross slurp to suck down all my built-up saliva.

That made Lucas stop. He turned his head over his shoulder and whistled. "Hey, Davey!"

"Yeah, man?"

"Make sure you handle all our stuff, especially the equipment bags."

"You got it! Avery, don't feel too bad about getting your tooth knocked out if the doctor can't fix it right away. We would never make fun of you." Though his tone suggested otherwise.

"Where are we going? I don't even have money or my insurance card. Do they even take SAG-AFTRA Health here?"

"Don't worry about it. It'll get sorted." We made it to the truck and Lucas tenderly placed me in the passenger seat, then leaned down to look me in the eye. "Follow my finger with your eyes."

I tracked his movement easily and he nodded, relieved. He closed the door, and through the side mirror, I saw him at the back of the truck on his cell phone, talking to someone while kicking a rock with the toe of his tennis shoe.

I couldn't make out any of what he was saying except for his curt "thanks" before he hung up. I straightened and looked ahead as he settled into the driver's seat and backed us out of the big dirt parking lot and out onto the road.

"So where are you taking me?" I asked, using my hand to cover my mouth and the *terrifying* tiny tooth.

"It's a Saturday afternoon, so I had to call in a favor."

We were silent for several moments. "I'm sorry I volunteered to play in the game." I sounded absolutely ridiculous with this tooth under my tongue, but Lucas didn't seem to care. He looked like his mind was a million miles away as he focused on driving us.

"You're never doing that again," he said, surprising me by breaking the silence.

"Well, duh, look at me. I'm a mess."

"I think you earned everyone's respect though." Lucas finally cracked a small smile.

"You mean if I ever see them again, they won't mockingly sing my song and make sexual innuendos at me?"

"They might still do that, but in a camaraderie kind of way and not a hostile one . . . ?" Lucas shrugged and we both laughed.

He directed the truck out of Broken Arrow and down past rural country. The miles passed quickly, and soon we pulled off the road and into the parking lot of a large medical center. The lot was empty apart from our truck and a security van.

"Could this favor you called in be from your very successful dentist cousin your dad mentioned?" I asked.

Lucas cut the engine and took a deep breath through his nose before slowly letting it out. "Yeah."

"Are you afraid I'm going to find him devastatingly handsome?"

With a wry grin, Lucas looked over at me and said, "No. I'm sure you will, but you're missing your front tooth. He ain't gonna look twice at you."

I smacked his arm in mock outrage. The booming sound of a loud, souped-up engine stole our attention. A matte black BMW sedan came to a screeching halt and parked along the curb, directly in front of the entrance.

"Shitass," Lucas mumbled under his breath.

"What was that? Did you just say 'shitass'?"

Lucas only rolled his eyes and got out of the car. I moved to open the door, but Lucas motioned for me to wait for him. Then it was me rolling my eyes. I didn't need him carrying me in to get my tooth put back in my mouth. But with our keeping-things-professional promise, maybe having his arms around me wasn't such a bad thing. Certainly something that felt this good couldn't be so bad?

He opened the door and took my hand to help me step down. I may have feigned my lack of balance so that I'd fall into his chest. Maybe. I wouldn't cop up to it in an interrogation. His strong arm came around me and boy did I love the smell of this man. I took a deep breath and let him lead me to his cousin.

"All right, so what's the emergency?" The tall, dark, and exceedingly handsome man stepped out of the BMW. He was wearing a button-down shirt, black jeans, and shiny shoes.

"What, were you on your way to some Holiday Inn dentist convention?" Lucas asked.

"It was the Hilton Garden Inn," his cousin said in a dramatic sigh.

They were silently eyeing each other up before his cousin smiled and offered his open hand. Lucas clasped his and then he was pulled away from me and embraced in a big bear hug.

"It's been too long, man. How ya been?"

"Busy," Lucas said gruffly.

"Man of few words. So, who is this?" He turned his hawkish gaze fully on me.

"Avery."

"Hi, Avery. I'm Dr. Wyatt Cole, Lucas's cousin. Wanna show me what I'm working with?"

I made sure to swallow all the accumulated saliva before smiling my most winning smile at Wyatt.

"Oh shit! How did that happen?"

"Stickball accident," I said with an exasperated lisp.

"What's going on with your tongue?" he asked.

I spit my tooth out into my waiting palm. "Some people on the field said if I kept it under my tongue then it would be easier to put back in."

The man only laughed. He laughed and he laughed until tears sprang from his eyes. I was certain my face was as red as the shirts the opposing team had been wearing.

Lucas hit Wyatt on the back of the head. "Shut the fuck up, man, and put her tooth back in. What's so funny?"

"Sorry, sorry." Wyatt wiped his eyes with his thumb. "I haven't laughed like that in so long. Avery, those tricks like soaking the tooth in milk or keeping it under your tongue only work for live teeth, often with the root still attached. What you have is a veneer. Your real tooth was shaved down into that tiny nub of a fang. Freaky-looking, but effective for creating a whole new smile."

"Can you glue it back?" I asked.

"I can do better than that. I'll cement it back into place, but you'll probably need to get this replaced with a new one soon. An intense blow like that could have compromised it, and it's likely it will chip easily with another hit like the one that took it out in the first place."

"She isn't playing stickball again," Lucas said firmly.

"And here I thought I was pretty good and found a new hobby." I exaggerated a pout, letting my bottom lip balloon out.

"Take up knitting if you need a hobby," Lucas grumbled. "Can we speed this up?"

Wyatt looked between me and Lucas with obvious giddy delight. "Of course, follow me this way."

He led us through a side entrance for employees. It was eerily dark and quiet, but Wyatt knew where to go, turning on a few lights to illuminate our path. Quickly, he ushered us into his office, going past the waiting room and into an examination room. He motioned for me to sit in the chair and turned the overhead light on.

Wyatt grabbed a pair of purple gloves from a box attached to the wall. "Luke, you might want to look away from this."

"Why? What are you going to do?" I asked. I couldn't help the panic that grew in my voice. Lucas's hand found mine. He used his thumb to lightly brush the back of my hand. It was steadying me.

"Nothing bad, but the veneer mouth is not for the faint of heart."

Lucas rolled his eyes as he stood next to me. "I can handle it."

"If you say so. Avery, can you tilt your head up and open your mouth wide?"

I did.

"Mm hmm." Wyatt used his finger and thumb on my chin to

direct my face more toward the light. "Mm hmm." He moved my head again. "Mm hmm."

"Got any words besides mm hmm, *doctor*?" Lucas said "doctor" like one would say *idiot*. Wyatt only smiled.

"I'll be right back with some supplies and have us all out of here in less than forty-five minutes."

Wyatt left me and Lucas in the examination room. Lucas still had not dropped my hand. My nerves were shooting off as the adrenaline was waning and I could feel a splitting headache form. The pain made me wince.

"Hey, are you okay?" Lucas stepped in front of me, as much as he could given the awkward way the examination chair had my legs sticking out. His right hand rested beneath my jaw as his left brushed my hair behind my ear. The glide of his fingers sent shivers through me.

"I'm fine, I just need some Advil or something." When he went to pull his hand away, I brought mine up to keep him there. I leaned my cheek into the most beautiful and hardworking hands I had ever felt. They were so gentle with me.

"I'll make Wyatt get you some when he comes back."

I nodded, feeling the black cloud of self-pity starting to form in my stomach. Every time it was starting to feel like I was gaining my footing here and fitting in, I screwed something up. Now I was in a random dentist's office, missing my front tooth, had the worst headache of my life, holding Lucas's hand to my face, and I just really wanted to kiss him.

Lucas took a step back, ripping his hand out of mine. "You want to kiss Wyatt?"

"What? Where would you get that idea?"

"You just mumbled that you want to kiss him."

"I did?"

"Yes." He frowned.

"I don't want to kiss him. I don't know him. I want to kiss you. My brain's all scrambled."

"You want to kiss me?" His smug smile set off an inferno in the dentistry. He stepped closer to me, leaning down to brush his lips against my ear. "I want to kiss you too."

I slurped at my saliva and gulped.

"But we won't," I said.

"We won't?"

"I'm missing a tooth, remember? And we are stupid business partners."

"Valid point there, but you could be missing all of your teeth and I would still want to kiss you."

The sexual tension was mounting, and I was dizzy from his words and proximity. And while it was sweet of him to say that, I couldn't help picturing us making out, me all gummy and thrusting my tongue into his mouth. It was ridiculous, and I hid my laughter behind my hand.

He pushed my hand away. "Don't hide from me. Missing a tooth doesn't define you and we are getting it fixed."

Wyatt knocked on the door before poking his head back in. "Okay to come in?"

"Yeah, let's get on with this." Lucas pushed himself off the armrest of my examination chair, going to the spare rolling stool in the corner to give Dr. Cole space to fix me up.

"I'm going to inject some local anesthesia to numb the area and then will bond this back in with the light resin cement."

I hated needles. I gripped the armrests and shut my eyes so I wouldn't see as Dr. Cole brought the needle close to my face. I could feel Lucas's presence return in an instant, his hand in mine, anchoring me as I felt the first pinch of the injection before losing all feeling.

Once the procedure was over and Dr. Cole assured me the resin was set, I moved my tongue around my mouth. The top section of my gums on my left side was still numb, but my mouth felt normal again. He handed me a small paper cup full of blue mouthwash. I gratefully swished it around before spitting it out.

"Thank you, Dr. Cole." I beamed my winning, fresh smile up at him.

"It was my pleasure, and please call me Wyatt. We're practically family." He winked. Lucas groaned.

"Well, thank you, Wyatt. I appreciate your kindness and help." I paused and glanced at Lucas before continuing. "How much do I owe you?"

"I can cover it," Lucas interjected.

"What? No, you can bill me."

"It's fine. I don't charge family. Just be more careful."

"Thank you for fixing me up." I thought about the horrible stickball game and the reason why we were there in the first place. We needed to get the word out about the fundraiser. Wyatt looked like he knew some friends who could help support the effort. "Are you going to be around next weekend?"

"I'm pretty sure. You wanna hang out?" Wyatt leaned down, all swagger and flirtatious charm.

"We're hosting a fundraiser for Lottie's ranch." Lucas stepped in, placing a hand on my shoulder.

Wyatt straightened, smugly smiling as he pointedly looked at where Lucas rested his hand.

"We all love Lottie. Count me in."

"Thank you!" I clapped. "Invite everyone you know."

"Will do. See you then, Avery."

I jumped and hugged him. I was a hugger, and he saved my smile. I moved back to stand next to Lucas, and he took my hand, lacing his fingers with mine.

"Wyatt."

"Lucas."

They nodded their farewells, and Lucas and I left the medical center hand in hand.

"How's your headache?" he asked me as we made it to the passenger side of the truck.

"It's doing better actually." I smiled.

"Great." He gently reached his hands under my jaw and pressed our lips together in a kiss that was all-consuming hunger.

The sky was fading into dusk above us, and the summer heat grew a few degrees hotter as I gripped his shoulders. Lucas stole his mouth away to trail his lips down my neck, the tip of his tongue leaving a scorched wake.

His growing arousal pressed against my stomach, and I brought my hand down to grip his girth with my hand. It was substantial and I wanted more than just a fondle above his pants.

He let out a strangled groan. "What do you do to me to make me lose control like this?" he panted into my ear.

"The same thing you do to me." I gazed up at him. "I'd invite you back to my place, but it's basically the same place as yours and I'm currently roommates with my grandmother."

"She would have my hide for this." He groaned.

I nodded. "We should stop."

"We should."

I melted as I looked into his soft, gray eyes, mirrors to the clouds darkening the sky overhead. I'd never seen anyone look at me with such tenderness underneath the heat of desire. His look set me on fire.

We fused together again, our hands going everywhere. I jumped up and wrapped my legs around his torso, his fingers so dangerously close to the edge of my shorts and the growing heat there.

He took one hand away and opened the truck door, then set me gently into the seat. I grabbed his face for another kiss that was slow and lazy. It was our last kiss and we both knew it. When we separated, I caressed his cheek for a moment, memorizing the feel of his skin, the look of his gray eyes, clear of worry or stress. We were in this tiny bubble the size of the cab of the truck and as soon as we left it, nothing would be the same.

My heart constricted. I wanted to live in a world where I could have it all: a successful music career; an affectionate boyfriend with his dream job caring for horses and kids who needed it; a functional relationship with my mother and my grandmother. But at this moment I had to choose, and I worked too hard on my career and music to give it all up and stay in Broken Arrow with Lucas.

I had to sacrifice something, and I wished it wasn't always my heart.

22

I T WAS A SOMBER DRIVE BACK TO THE RANCH, FULL OF
lost potential and heartache. In another world, we could have
been great and had it all, but we were stuck in this one. It was fully
dark by the time we pulled up to the house, and a sleek black Mer-
cedes car was parked in front of the porch steps.

It mirrored how I'd arrived here that first day.

Lucas and I exchanged a glance.

We walked together into Lottie's house, not touching, and the
inches of distance already felt like too much. It was quiet, but the
tension made the air thick as if we were walking through slime.
Something had happened.

"Avery, that you?" Lottie called.

"Yeah, it's me. Lucas brought me back."

"Is your tooth all fixed up?"

"Oh yeah. I'm good as new." We turned left toward the sound
of her voice, and I came up short.

Sitting at completely opposite ends of the dining table were
Lottie and my mother.

"Hello, Avery." Her eyes narrowed at Lucas and me standing next to each other.

"Hi, Mom."

"What happened to your tooth?"

"It popped out, but it's all fine now."

"I should call Dr. Agassi. That smile cost a fortune. They shouldn't be popping out like that."

Just like my mother to focus on the money spent.

"I got a dentist to put it back in. It's fine."

"A dentist from here? No, we should really get it checked out by someone who knows what they're doing."

"Dr. Wyatt Cole went to OU College of Dentistry. It's the best in the state." Lucas stepped in, defending his cousin.

"And you are?" My mother sat back in her chair, crossing her arms and looking down her nose.

"I'm Lucas, ma'am. I help Lottie with running the ranch."

My mother let out a sarcastic laugh and picked up a piece of paper off the table. Our flyer. Shit. That flyer was the complete opposite of lying low. We hadn't brought it up to Lottie yet, so I'm sure she was pissed too.

"Good job running it into the ground."

"Harriett!" Lottie snapped.

"What? This man is making a desperate attempt to grab cash, banking on Avery's name and stardom too, and I'm quoting, 'save Muscogee's own Red Fox Ranch.'"

"We can talk about this later, Lucas. Thank you for taking Avery to get fixed up," Lottie said through bottled emotions. It looked like at any moment, she would blow.

"It's my pleasure, ma'am." Lucas stepped back to head out.

"No, he should stay." I grabbed his arm, unwilling to let him go.

My mother eyed my hand clutching Lucas's arm. "So, this is what you've been doing? Making moon eyes at some ranch hand while I've been working around the clock doing damage control?"

"I've been doing what you asked me to do. Getting to know our heritage. The only reason I'm even in this mess is because I listened to you. I've always listened to you, followed as you led my career this way and that. Commercials since I was a baby, and when those dried up, it was acting and auditioning for anything and everything. Music is mine and I've listened to you and all the people we have hired who have only led me astray. I'm not here making moon eyes. I've been working and getting to know all these lovely people who *you* kept me from." My voice hitched. I'd never spoken to my mother that harshly, ever. Years of pent-up emotions were threatening to explode out of me. I just wanted her to care about me for once, not my brand.

"If you knew the truth, you wouldn't be quite so forgiving."

"That's enough, Hattie." Lottie's voice cracked like a whip, and it made me jump. "Avery, you should go up and rest. We can discuss everything in the morning. Lucas, go, please."

I turned around, giving him a silent plea to stay. I didn't want to be in this house full of ghosts, scorn, and lies. I saw his family at its worst and stood by him. Lucas was the only one who really knew me or cared. I needed someone on my team right now.

His stormy eyes held so much in them, and I knew he was telling me to be strong, that he couldn't stay. We both knew it. He was the first to break eye contact and leave, the thud of the front door casting an echo in the silence.

I had to get out of this room. I needed more space, more time before confronting my mother. I thought I had more time with Lottie too. I thought I could fix everything and instead it was all just as broken as it ever was.

"Good night." My voice was quiet, but I knew they both heard me.

I slowly made my way toward the stairs, but my mother's angry voice carried.

"History tends to repeat itself, doesn't it?" she said. I hardly recognized her, her voice so ugly with malice.

"When you don't teach the lessons learned from mistakes, those mistakes will be made again," Lottie said, her tone forlorn. I paused at the bottom of the steps, eavesdropping when I knew I shouldn't be.

"The only mistake was letting her come here alone."

"You've always been welcome. You never even had to leave."

"You and I both know that's not true. You refused to let me stay here pregnant and unmarried, 'like a common harlot' was what you said."

"I never should have said that."

"Then had your creepy pastor talk to me about sin, as if my getting pregnant out of wedlock made me dirty."

"I haven't been to that church in two decades."

"You and everyone were so obsessed with who the father was. So determined to keep our Indian line from being diluted, as if that matters at all."

"Hattie, I made so many mistakes."

"Don't call me Hattie. You lost that privilege."

There was tense silence, and I was starting to piece together the story of my existence. I sat down on the bottom step, absorbing the implication of the terse exchange, but before I could empathize for her situation, my mother said, "You want to know who her father is?"

I was gripping the edge of the stair, leaning forward. I had asked so many times as a little girl, and she kept saying it wasn't important so eventually I stopped asking.

"He was a no-name nobody. Some white guy with a pretty smile I met in a bar when I snuck in with friends from school. I hooked up with him in that filthy bathroom. I never even caught his name. So that Fox lineage you found so important is meaningless."

A loud sob cracked out of me. Never had I ever heard my mother speak with such resentment, pure vitriol. No wonder she worked me to the bone all these years. I wasn't born of love. I was born of spite.

"Avery?" Lottie called out.

I couldn't go back in that room; I couldn't even stay in this house. I did the only thing I could—I ran out into the night. I needed the open air, to be as far away from my mother as possible. I sprinted, my heartbreak fueling me as I sped faster and faster down the hill toward the barn.

Rakko was standing by the paddock, a bridle still in his mouth. He must have just had his evening brush-down. I slowed my approach, coming at him from his front and letting him sniff my hand. He was looking for a treat. I had none, but maybe an evening ride and some freedom would be good enough. No one was around. Red must have gone to get something from his trailer, so I had little time before he came asking questions.

I led Rakko inside the barn and saddled him up. It wasn't the best, but I made it work. Rakko stood patiently, waiting for me to finish. He was a little bigger than Peso, and I had to try twice before I was able to swing my leg around and seat myself up on the saddle.

I tsked my tongue, and he started moving out of the barn. "You want to fly, Rakko?" I kicked my heels in, and we shot off toward the pasture.

Voices sounded behind me, growing distant with every gallop. "Avery!"

"Come back!"

"Where's she going?"

I ignored them all. I needed space. Rakko was used to the land, but there wasn't much moonlight; thick clouds hung heavy in the sky. Still, I pressed us on. Let them worry I had Lottie's precious horse. I was dirty, a spite-child born to sully the blood and the name of this family. I didn't belong to the fake world of Hollywood I was forced out of, and I didn't belong here. I was in limbo.

Staying here with Lucas was out of the question, especially after learning the truth about how I came to be and why my mother left.

Rakko slowed his steps and meandered through the dense wood. He tried to stop at the pond, but I urged him with the reins to keep going. I wanted to be as physically lost as I felt, floating along with no tethers anywhere. Lottie said the horses knew the way back, so I wasn't in any danger of becoming truly lost.

The night grew darker, and I let Rakko stop to nibble on some grass. The air was suffocatingly hot when I left, but the temperature had dropped at least twenty degrees. Gooseflesh pebbled my exposed arms and legs, a few water drops landed on my legs.

I wasn't too concerned. What was a little rain? I was on a horse, not the 405 in Los Angeles.

Thunder boomed above me. That felt ominous. I was still angry, but going on this ride helped cool me down a bit. The heat that felt inescapable was gone. In seconds, the temperature dropped what felt like twenty degrees. The hairs on my arms were standing up.

"Okay, Rakko, boy. Let's turn back. I don't want to be stuck in the rain." The giant slowly turned around toward the direction we'd come, when sheets of rain started slamming down. It was a freak storm that came out of nowhere. The deluge was so intense, I couldn't see through it. Rakko was rearing his head in fear.

A loud rumble of thunder sounded overhead, and the wind, which had been nonexistent for days, started howling against me. I cupped my hands over my eyes to see if there was a place among the trees that would provide some shelter until the worst of it was over.

A siren from somewhere far off was wailing and Rakko froze, raising his head with his ears pointing straight up. I leaned down to pet his neck, trying to calm him down, but he was breathing hard. I squinted in the rain and noticed his nostrils flaring wildly in fast succession. I had made a huge mistake taking him with me. It was selfish and now he was stuck with me, terrified, in this awful weather.

I had no idea what the siren meant but it was gone now, and I tried to kick Rakko's sides to get him going, but he refused to budge. Sheets of rain came down and I tried to remember what Lucas had taught me about the directions. It was impossible to see anything, and I was so turned around, I couldn't remember the way I'd come and where the house was to determine south. If I could find south, then I could figure out the rest. But it was all gray and windy. I never should have come out here. It was impulsive and childish and now I placed Rakko in danger. Why couldn't I do anything right? My tears mixed with the rain that pelted my face.

"Avery!"

I looked up, searching around for the source of the voice.

"Avery!" It was Lucas. Relief flooded within me, and I frantically looked around to find him.

"Lucas! I'm here!"

"Stay put, I'll find you!" He already sounded closer.

Thunder rumbled again, and finally Lucas reached me.

"I'm here!"

He pulled the reins up on Peso and quickly jumped off his back, slapping his flank, and Peso took off running.

Lucas jogged to me, reaching up and grabbing my waist. He pulled me off Rakko's back and set me on the ground; it all happened in a blur.

"What are you doing?" I shouted over the rain.

Lucas slapped Rakko's rump and set him off galloping.

"It's tornado weather," Lucas yelled back. "Didn't you hear the siren?"

"I didn't know it meant there was a tornado."

"You have to set horses free to run or else they panic, and you could get thrown or worse."

"Will they be okay?"

"They'll be fine, it's us that we need to worry about. Come on!" He clasped my hand and started running, and I did my best to keep pace. The wind started picking up, leaves whipping me as we ran past the trees.

"Are we going to make it back to the house in time?" I didn't even try to hide the panic in my voice.

"No, but there's a safe place not too far. We can make it."

He veered left through the trees, and all I could do was follow. I had no idea how Lucas knew his way up from down in the chaos, but I trusted him. The trees opened up to a small farmhouse. We sprinted to the side, and Lucas threw open the old, creaky cellar door.

"Feel your way down, but there are a few steps," he instructed. "Be careful."

"When was the last time anyone was down here?" I knew we were in the middle of a tornado threat, but the spiders or whatever else was in the creepy dark almost felt scarier.

"Yesterday. This is my house and property."

I paused midstep. *What?* He was a property owner? What the hell was he still doing in Lottie's trailer?

He must have sensed where my mind was. "I bought this last year with every penny I had saved since I was sixteen. It shares a border with the ranch. It's bare bones, but clean—it'll be okay, don't worry."

With his reassurance, I slowly made my way down the stairs, missing the last one and slipping, but Lucas jumped down, forgoing the five steps, and caught me.

"You okay?"

"Yes."

It was pitch-black and rainwater was getting in. Lucas let go of me and climbed up to close the cellar door. Once it was secure, he came back down. The underground cellar muffled the sound of the storm. Our scared breathing was louder by far.

"There's a lantern around here somewhere."

I heard him shuffle around for a while and mumble swear words as he groped every surface, looking for the light.

"Aha!" he exclaimed in victory. The small light illuminated the space. There was not much by way of furniture or anything, really. In the corner was a simple futon sofa that looked clean.

Lucas handed me the lantern and opened a cupboard and took out a folded quilt. He brought it to me, draping my shoulders with it like a cape. He began rubbing his thumbs over my arms in circles. It was comforting, and I didn't think he knew he was doing it. He dropped his hands and went to the futon, moving it out from against the wall and flattening it out to a full-size bed. "Why did you run off like that?" he asked gently. I could trace no judgment in his tone. He stood in front of the futon.

"It was stupid. I'm sorry."

"Something must have really upset you to do that. What happened?"

"Just some stuff my mom said. I don't really want to get into it."

He spread his arms out open. "Well, if you do want to talk, I'm here. We don't really have anything else to do, as you can see."

I set the lantern down on the ground between us; our shadows were contorted and exaggerated against the walls. Caricatures of who we really were—how befitting, considering my life was an absolute circus.

"How come you never mentioned you owned a house before?" I asked, delaying the inevitable of telling Lucas the truth around the circumstances of my entire existence.

"I've only had it a year and it needs so much. It needs all new plumbing and electric, so I can't even live here until that's fixed. But the fifty acres shares a property line with Red Fox Ranch."

"It looks really cute from what I can see."

"It has a lot of charm."

We sat in silence for a few moments.

"You ready to tell me what happened?" he asked in the quiet.

"My mom told Lottie I was conceived by some random white guy in a dirty bar. She gloated that I tarnished the family's bloodline and good name."

Lucas frowned as he took this in. "You can't believe that bullshit. The women here have hearts of gold but are catty and petty when they want to be. Has your mom ever told you about your dad before?"

"No. Never."

His hands were on my cheeks in an instant, wiping away the tears mixed with the water dripping down into my hair.

"If there is anything I've learned since cutting off most of my family, it's that where you come from is only a tiny portion of who you are. Who do you want to be, Avery?" he murmured, his face so close to mine.

"I don't really know anymore." I whispered the truth. If he had asked me two weeks ago, I would have said the most successful singer-songwriter pop act out there. But now that dream rang hollow. I didn't want insincerity in my interactions, and I didn't want to be viewed as a commodity. I wanted my dreams to have meaning; the people in my life to be meaningful. I wanted to fall headfirst into love and not be scared because I didn't know what tomorrow brought.

I wanted so many things and they all felt destined for someone else.

"Can I tell you what I see when I look at you?" he asked, wrapping his arms around my waist, pulling me into a caress.

I nodded into his chest as he stroked my wet hair.

"I see a woman with kindness in her heart who sees the good in everyone around her. A woman who, when faced with skepticism, mockery, or even getting her tooth knocked out, has stared down every challenge without cowering. You are brave, talented, and the most beautiful woman I have ever laid eyes on. Your father could have been the boogeyman and it wouldn't make a lick of difference, because you are you and you are incredible."

"Sure, I'm *so* talented except for my music and styling choices." I rolled my eyes, trying to step away, because it was too good to be true. But he held me there, against his beating heart.

"Just as you are. Loincloth and all." He squeezed me tighter and held me as the tears that poured out of my eyes rivaled the storm above us that felt a light-year away now. Inside this old cellar was the whole world.

"I have never worn a loincloth," I giggled into his chest.

"There's my girl."

"Why couldn't we have met before all this?" I asked.

"I think we met exactly when we were supposed to."

I sniffed. "Even though we can't be together."

"I don't know what will happen tomorrow, Avery. I told you I can only work on taking my life one day at a time. I know that tonight, I'm with you and I'm not going anywhere."

"But you said you didn't want me leaving here—leaving you—and going back to my real life, to leave us both devastated." I looked up. A single drop of water beaded on the tip of his nose. We were shivering and still wet. I wrapped my arms around his waist, engulfing him in the quilt for warmth.

"Maybe you do leave here and forget all about me," he said slowly, voice rugged and low, "but I know I'll regret it until I am lying on my deathbed, kicking myself for never having you. Tasting you." He slowly moved us toward the makeshift bed.

"What do you taste like, Avery?" He kissed just under my ear. "Are you sweet like honey?"

"Lucas," I moaned.

"I'm here, baby." He cupped my face, kissing me, moving his lips over mine in lazy, luxurious movements, as if he was savoring every moment.

I refused to hold back when this man had given me so much. I kissed him with everything I had. All the feelings I had been harboring away inside, afraid of spilling over and getting too attached.

The back of my calves hit the low mattress of the futon, and instead of letting me fall down onto it, Lucas swooped me up into his arms and he laid me down gently onto the bed. It was a simple full-size mattress, but with how reverently he placed me, it was as if it were a bed of roses. He lay down next to me, perching on his hand in a fist as he looked down at me, the other hand moving a wet strand of hair off my face.

"You're sure about this? Us?" I asked, because he was so honest about his past, how he didn't want to chance a broken heart and picking up the pieces of himself again. I couldn't make any promises about staying, at least not yet . . . or ever, with how poorly the reunion with my mom and Lottie had gone. I needed to make sure we both wouldn't regret this.

"I will always want you. We can go as fast or as slow as you want, or if you want me to stop then I will hold you through the night."

"I've wanted you for quite some time, Lucas." The sound of the storm was gone, or I was too far gone to notice it anymore.

"Then have me." He descended onto my mouth again, devouring me. I was matching him in kind. The stickball disaster was only hours ago, and yet it felt like a lifetime ago. I was still in the clothes I'd been knocked out in. Lucas smelled like he had showered before coming after me. His new T-shirt and jeans were soaked through with the rain.

He was already rock hard, his length pushing into my stomach, and this time I didn't bother cupping him over his pants. I reached inside his waistband, breaching his boxer briefs, and took his firm, smooth length in my hand. He continued to kiss me as I discovered how to touch him, to see what would elicit a response.

I squeezed his girth firmly and he groaned against my lips, deep like a bear's roar. I rubbed him up and down and he started grinding into my hand, so I pumped him faster.

"Stop," he hissed.

"Sorry, too much?"

"I'm not busting a nut into your hand before I've had any fun with you."

He sat up and peeled my wet tank top up. It was a bit awkward to maneuver to get it off my head with the tight space of the bed. He flung my shirt onto the ground and started showing sweet devotion to my breasts, kneading and cupping their heavy fullness in each hand, humming appreciatively.

"They're real," I panted.

He looked up through his eyebrows. "Of course they're real." His voice was heavy and hoarse.

"There has just been a lot of talk online about people saying they're fake. My teeth might be, but not my boobs."

"There isn't an atom about you that is fake. I see you." Enough of the talk. He bent his head down and peppered my breasts with kisses, trailing his tongue along my skin in between each one. My nipples had been hard since the temperature dropped and the rain started. He put his hot mouth on my right one, and I cried out. It was so cold that the contrast to the warmth of his mouth nearly seared me, and the way he ran his tongue over its hardness sent lightning bolts straight to my core.

"Good girl," he murmured as he moved on to my neglected left breast and the sweet torture began anew. He had me panting and begging for release. When he was finished with my breasts for now, he lifted himself off me, and I immediately missed his warmth. The cellar was so cold, and we were still sopping wet from the storm. "This okay?" he asked as he played with the waistband of my drenched, and not only from the rain, shorts.

"Mm hmm." I nodded.

"I need to hear a clear yes, baby." The way he said "baby" melted me. His wet hair curled over his brows and his eyes were black in the tiny light of the lantern.

"Yes, Lucas. Please take off my pants."

He caressed my hair as if I had done a good job and it made me want to please him in so many other ways. He slowly lowered the zipper, then pulled at the ends of my cutoffs. I lifted my ass off the bed to help him get them off. He hissed.

"You played stickball in those?" He eyed my tiny, navy blue silk lace G-string.

"I hadn't expected to play at all when I was getting dressed this morning."

He slid the shorts down to my ankles and I flung them off somewhere, knowing my toned leg was giving him a show. He patted the inside of my knee, and I got the message; I spread open for him, and he settled himself between my legs, resting on his knees as he played with the edge of my panties.

"I have lots of pretty panties, Lucas."

He groaned and slowly peeled them down my legs. "You're going to have one less pair." I watched, captivated, as he bunched the tiny, lacy thing into a ball and shoved them into the pocket of his jeans.

I felt it then, the realization that this was probably our one and only time to be together. This was never supposed to happen and yet here we were, and my mother and contractual obligations would sweep me away from here soon enough. I could see it in the set of his mouth, he was mourning what could have been.

"I'm cold," I whispered. I needed him close to me, not just for heat, but to know he was mine in this moment.

He ripped his soaking shirt off and it landed somewhere in the room with a heavy *whack*. He settled himself on top of me, but his pants were still on, wet and very cold.

"Why aren't you taking your pants off?" I asked, my voice husky with need.

"There is no protection in here." He brushed my hair back off my face. "Tonight is all about you, baby. Let me take care of you."

"Then who will take care of you?" I cupped his cheek.

"I'll be okay." He brushed a kiss on my palm. "I'm not taking a chance and giving you no choice but to stay."

"I've been on birth control since I was fifteen. I don't think we need to worry about that."

"And you would trust me to enter your tight little body bare?"

I raised my head up, biting his lip. "I'd insist on it. I haven't had a partner in almost six months and my last checkup came back clear."

"Mine too." He took my mouth again as he took off his pants and briefs in one quick movement, never taking his lips from mine. He was eager and I couldn't blame him. We were both pebbled with gooseflesh from the cold, but Lucas gave off so much delicious heat, I pressed myself to his chest.

"What am I working with down there?" he growled against my mouth as his hand parted my folds, exploring my arousal. "Perfection." He rubbed my already swollen center, taking his time. Of their own volition, my legs fell open wider, giving him better access to me.

Lucas brought his mouth down, taking my left nipple into his mouth as he continued to work my core with his hand. It should be illegal for anything to feel this good. He touched me right, as if his hands were created to know exactly how to caress and stroke me, as if his lips were made for kissing me.

He inserted a finger, stretching me as he increased his pace.

My toes curled as my release was building. I tipped my head back and let the orgasm wash over me, my body shaking.

"That's my good girl," Lucas murmured as he kissed my lips, still rubbing lazy circles. I opened my hazy eyes and was captivated as he removed his finger, brought it to his mouth, and sucked it clean.

"Honey," he growled in confirmation.

"More," I moaned.

He settled himself between my legs, positioning himself at my entrance. With one thrust he entered me, and I felt full and complete.

Lucas kissed my lips as he kept his pace slow and lazy, discovering me. I lifted my legs and wrapped them around his waist, urging him to go faster.

"Slow down, we're in no rush." He continued his unhurried pace, driving me crazy. He bowed his head into my neck. "Imagine if this was our real life. That you were mine. I come home at the end of the day, welcomed by these long, gorgeous legs." Lucas stroked my leg, thigh to ankle and back up again, pushing my leg back as he ground into me deeper.

"I'd wake up with these legs around me. A lifetime of making you come and come again."

He painted the picture, and it made me whimper as he started picking up the pace, bringing his hand back to my core, working it, bringing me close to the precipice.

"I would work to give you the world. Building this house into a home with my bare hands. You'd want for nothing. You'd be my princess, and no one would love you as hard as me. We'd make the most beautiful babies, and we would be so happy. Then we would grow old together, our hair turning white, lines on our faces, and all I would see would be the most beautiful woman to grace this earth."

I was crying again, because it was a beautiful fantasy. He would have this dream, but it wouldn't be with me. I'd be alone somewhere, trying to carve my place in this world, writing and performing songs, and Lucas would be here in Broken Arrow, changing kids' lives for the better. Because there was no doubt in my mind that he would take over the horse ranch and make all of his dreams come true. And one day, a woman would turn his head, and he would live that picket fence life with her. He deserved a happily ever after, and I so desperately wished it could be with me.

His pace was fast now, and I held on to him, feeling that release rising within me. I clung to him as I hung on to that beautiful dream he painted, trying my hardest not to let it slip through my fingers. We reached that apex together, me shaking around him in ecstasy, his name on my lips. He finished with his head buried in my neck.

"I could love you forever too," I whispered through my watery smile, feeling so complete and heartbroken at once.

It wasn't long before sleep claimed us both. I had my best night of sleep since coming to the ranch, wrapped in Lucas's warm arms.

LUCAS NUDGED ME AWAKE WITH HIS NOSE ON MY cheek, sprinkling kisses across my face. I didn't want to wake up. I wanted to stay in the dream Lucas had woven for us last night. I wanted to keep pretending that this cellar was our beautiful home, and the old futon was *our* bed. I wasn't ready to go back to reality.

"I'm not ready," I whispered. Tears started falling from my eyes.

"Baby, everyone will be worried sick about us. I'm sure they are gathering in groups to come look for us. We haven't had a storm that bad hit our area in years."

"I'm not ready to say goodbye to you and there is no way my mother will leave here without me."

"It doesn't have to be a forever goodbye," he whispered in my ear, pressing a kiss below my ear.

"The woman you do end up with will be so lucky. I want you to know that. You are worthy of the world too." Whoever she was, I was insanely jealous of her. I wanted her life, and she was imaginary right now. I was angry at a pretend future woman.

"You think I'm not sick with jealousy at whatever model yahoo you end up with? There is no way on Creator's green earth that it wouldn't kill me to see you on TV on the arm of some pretty boy while I am here, craving you."

"Lucas, what are we going to do?" I turned over, tangling myself with his limbs, needing to be closer.

"We do the next right thing," he said as his morning wood throbbed against my belly.

"And what's that?" I asked, voice low and sultry as I caressed his hardness.

"I take what small part you can give me before we go back to the house."

And he did. I laid myself bare, giving him all of the promises of the future we couldn't have. He took and he gave generously, and when we were finished, we were glistening, our sweat like drops of morning dew.

We walked hand in hand back to the house, keeping our pace slow to remain in our fantasy a little while longer.

It all shattered when we got to the main house and heard the shouting between my mother and Lottie.

"This is all your fault!" my mother shrieked.

"Mine? If you had been honest with her, this wouldn't have happened," Lottie fired back.

Lucas squeezed my hand in support as we walked up the steps together.

"We're back," Lucas called into the house.

"Avery!" Mom came flying out, throwing the screen door open and letting it slam shut on Lottie's concerned face. She flung herself into my arms, forcing my and Lucas's hands apart. "You had us worried sick. How could you do such a thing?" She peeled herself off me to grab my face.

The porch door slammed shut again as Lottie came out.

I pushed her off. "I'm sorry you were worried, but I needed space."

"Thank you for finding Avery, but you can go now. We need to talk privately." She dismissed Lucas without even looking at him.

"No, Lucas can stay."

"Oh?" My mom crossed her arms and finally gave her full attention to Lucas. "So, you're gonna throw your whole career away for a ranch hand? Some future, Avery."

"Mom, stop," I warned. Lucas had heard enough lies from his parents about how he didn't measure up. I wouldn't let mine add to the chorus.

"No, I want to hear from him. How does he think he can possibly provide the life you want? Don't you live in one of those trailers behind the barn?"

"Yes, ma'am." Lucas stood there, his hands clasped behind his back, his face an emotionless mask.

"What future do you have? What do you aspire to be? When Avery's being booked for tours, are you going to guilt her into turning down opportunities we have worked years for just because you'll miss her? Or would you tag along and ride her coattails?"

"Stop." I threaded my arm through his, anchoring him to the present and what we just shared.

"She's right," Lucas said, taking his arm out of mine. "We knew this couldn't work and I'd never let you sacrifice your dreams."

"She isn't right. What about this morning and what you said?"

"I said we had to do the next right thing and that is you talking to your mom and grandmother. I have to give you the space to do that."

"But we'll talk after, right? What about the fundraiser and saving the ranch?"

"Avery, you don't need to worry yourself about the ranch," Lottie said as she stepped in.

"But Lucas has plans, amazing plans."

"And I can talk to him about that, but your mother is right. He should go and the three of us can talk as we were always supposed to do."

"But Lucas." My voice cracked. Anxiety bubbled up within me as everything was coming to a close, the pressure of it all signifying there was no hope for me and Lucas. Even though I had felt our time with each other was ending last night, I refused to accept it now in the light of day. I was willing to try anything to make it work. The fantasy he'd painted was so beautiful I didn't want to let the illusion go.

"We can catch up later," he said gently. He gave me a long, sad look before jogging down the steps and walking away. I stood there watching as his figure retreated down the hill.

"Come on, it's for the best," my mother said, ushering me through the door.

"Why were you so mean to him?" I snapped.

"You can't be serious, Avery. It was a fling, and he said you'll talk later." She rolled her eyes.

I marched to the living room with my mother and Lottie on my heels.

"You dismissed him, told him he was basically worthless. Why did you have to do that?"

"It's the truth. He isn't good enough for you, honey—your lives are too different. You are destined for bigger things and some cowboy ranch hand in Broken Arrow, Oklahoma, would only hold you back. You have opportunities."

"What opportunities? I thought the label was dropping me after the *Rolling Stone* cover backlash." I threw myself down on the couch.

"That's water under the bridge. I booked a flight straight here when I heard the news. Your single is number one on the Official Charts Top Forty in the UK!"

"What?!" I screeched as I jumped up from my seat, momentarily dazed. Number fucking one!

"BBC Radio 1 is begging for you to come perform live. *The Graham Norton Show* has booked you to perform on next Friday's show. That's why I'm here. We have to get you ready. You need to pack up, because I have tickets to fly to London tonight. It's all over now, honey. No one hates you in England, they don't care about the cover at all. They all love you. When your performance over there goes viral, everyone in America will turn around too."

My brain processed everything one at a time. BBC Radio 1 show? A performance at *The Graham Norton Show*? That all sounded fine, great even, except—"Next Friday?" I stopped jumping. "I can't do it."

"What do you mean you can't? Of course you can. You have absolutely nothing else going on. Now come on and get ready."

"No, I really can't go. The fundraiser is next weekend."

My mother waved off the thought. "We already said you don't need to be troubling yourself about the state of affairs here."

"Your mother is right, Avery. We have it all taken care of here."

"How can you say that? Without the fundraiser, you have to sell."

"That's not the worst thing, honey," Lottie said with pity, as if I were a child who couldn't understand adult things.

"Letting the past go isn't a bad thing," my mother added unhelpfully.

"Oh yeah? Are you going to come back and help her let go of

the past? Your bedroom is exactly as you left it. The attic is full of generations of memories. Who is going to help Lottie go through it all?"

"Your grandmother has employees, Avery."

"But she also has family. Us."

"I appreciate you wanting to help, but I've survived just fine these last twenty-odd years, and I can keep on going." Lottie put on a brave face, but I could see how tired she was, shouldering this huge property all on her own.

"But that was before I knew you. I don't want you surviving. I want you thriving. I don't want you alone here emptying this huge house full of memories. It's a tomb. Can we help you pay the bank?"

"I've already told you that I don't need or want your money." Lottie started tidying the space, stacking old magazines on the coffee table.

"What about Lucas's business idea? Converting this place into a ranch to help kids who have gone through trauma. Horse therapy."

"It's a fancy dream, but I don't know the first thing about doing that."

"But Lucas does. He has a whole business plan figured out and has grant applications ready to go. He can do this. You can do this."

"Just drop it, Avery." Mom slumped onto the couch, rubbing her temples with her forefingers, drilling into the sides of her head.

I ignored her and continued, "Think of every person you have helped. Think of a ranch full of kids like Lucas."

"Pfft. That man looks like he can barely read or write," my mother mumbled.

"Shut up, Mother," I snapped, her rude comment hitting too close to the mark with his dyslexia. She had no right criticizing him; she didn't even know him. I did, and I knew Lucas could do anything. I'd bet my entire career on it that Lucas could turn this business into something that helped so many and make it flourish.

"All right, Avery, we have entertained this long enough. We really don't have time for this. You need to pack and get ready to go or we'll miss our flight. Niles is going to meet us there and I hired Chelsea to do your hair and makeup. You just need to leave all the baggage this place carries here. You have a bright future, and I won't let you squander it. I sacrificed so much to get you to where you are."

And there it was. The story she had told me over and over again. She sacrificed everything, went through so many hardships to bring me into this world and provide for us. But what about all of my sacrifices? Why must I always continue to sacrifice? When would it ever be enough?

"What if I want to stay?"

Lottie gasped.

"Four words, Avery. *The. Graham. Norton. Show*," Mom snapped. "I won't let you throw it all away. I'm doing what's best for you like I've always done."

"As my manager or my mother?" I asked, glaring into her eyes.

"Why can't it be both?"

"Harriett, she's an adult. She can decide what she wants to do. She has been working so hard all her life."

"And why is that, Mother?"

"I made mistakes and I am trying to atone for it. You sent back every check I mailed to you when she was a baby and then never gave me your new address. I couldn't even reach you when my parents died."

My mother's eyes watered.

Lottie sat down on the armchair adjacent to the couch, sighing heavily.

"I never wanted you to repeat my mistakes. I took us to church. I was just trying to give you a better life and do better."

"What does she mean?" I asked my mother.

"She hasn't told you our sordid history the whole time you've been here?"

"I was never married to Harriett's father. We had a whirlwind romance one summer. He was the star of the rodeo, could tie down a calf faster than anyone I'd ever seen, to this day. He wasn't local. He said he loved me and went to compete in a rodeo in Texas. He died. Had gotten drunk one night and his buddies urged him to try bull riding. I was four months pregnant when the news of what happened reached me."

"What was his name?" I asked, sitting on the couch, reaching my hand out to her.

"Melvin."

"You never learned his last name?"

"Oh, I know it, but you'll laugh and this is a serious conversation."

"What is it?" I looked to my mother.

"Duck," she answered.

I blinked. "Melvin Duck. That doesn't sound real."

"It is. There are a lot of Ducks all around Oklahoma." This tragedy couldn't get worse. We were really Ducks and not Foxes? Avery Duck was a horrible stage name.

"So, when my mom got pregnant at eighteen, that scared you?"

"Of course. I wanted more for her. People were more forgiving of my situation because Melvin died, but there were whispers, judgment. She was so talented. The lead in all the school plays and musicals. I didn't want that for her."

"Who is my father, really?" I asked. I couldn't believe she hooked up with some random person in a bar bathroom.

"Question of the century. She refused to answer before she left."

"Because it doesn't matter. He left. I told him I was pregnant, and he left."

"Who was it?" Lottie and I both asked.

My mom bit her lip, before sighing in defeat. "Tanner Berry."

"I knew it!" Lottie threw her hands up. "I would have pulled him by the ear back here. Why didn't you say anything?"

"Because I didn't want to be forced to marry a man who wanted nothing to do with me or a baby."

"Who was Tanner Berry?" I was so lost.

"He worked for me one summer. Came from Montana. He was nineteen. Had no business chasing your skirt."

"It's of no consequence now. You satisfied with your answers? Because we have to go. I still have to return the rental before we check into our flight. Niles sprung for first class for us, since we weren't sure what would happen if you were recognized."

Satisfied? Hardly. I was a Fox, a Duck, and a Berry. It didn't seem real. Avery Berry was an even worse stage name.

"Is this why you don't want me pursuing a relationship with Lucas?"

"Honey, what relationship could there be? You'll forget about him in a month. We have you booked to make appearances. You'll be so busy, you'll eventually forget to call him, and then he will get resentful. It's doomed before it could begin, even if you wanted to try. Just trust me."

It was exactly what Lucas and I had been saying. The reality of the logistics. But I hated it. I didn't want any of it to be right.

"Your mother is right. You both are still so young. Handling your commitments won't take long. If you both can't wait a month, then it would never work out anyway." Lottie leaned back in her chair, drilling the side of her forehead with her pointer finger just like my mother. They were twins.

"When do we have to leave?" I asked, shoulders stooped in defeat.

"We need to hit the road in an hour."

I nodded, getting up to go to my room. I wasn't ready for my life to go back to how it was, but I had no choice. My label took a gamble signing me and this was a chance to prove to them that my song and my album were worth it.

The first thing I did was shower off the stickball game grime. I went through the motions of everything else—toweling off, putting some clothes on, and throwing everything into the Rimowa luggage that I had once valued so much. I zipped up the biggest trunk, smiling at the scuffs from when Lucas hurled them into the truck.

One by one, I carried them down the stairs. My mother helped me load them into the trunk of the town car and the back seats. When we were loaded, I had one last thing to do. I couldn't leave without saying goodbye to everyone. I borrowed the golf cart and booked it down the hill, barely shifting it into park when I came to the barn entrance.

"Lucas!" I yelled, running into the barn. "Lucas!"

"What's the emergency?" Red came out holding a heavy bucket of carrots.

"I need to see Lucas. Is he here?"

"Nah, you just missed him. Didn't you notice the truck was gone? He went to town."

"Everything okay in here?" Davey walked into the barn. "The shouting is spooking the horses."

"No, everything is not okay. I'm leaving. I came to say goodbye. I have to try to find him." Tears streamed down my face.

"What about the fundraiser?" Davey asked. He sounded like a disappointed toddler.

"Lottie said she was selling. It was all wasted effort," I said.

"Oh," Red said. He set the bucket of carrots down.

"I'm sorry. I really wanted to help save this place. You are like family to me."

"We aren't like family, Miss Avery. We *are* family."

I cried again and wrapped each of them in a hug.

"I'm gonna miss you guys."

"You'll still come to our wedding, right? Mary Beth is really looking forward to it. She's told everyone you're gonna perform there."

"I wouldn't miss it for the world."

I gave them each a kiss on the cheek in farewell. I walked out of the barn and stopped at the eastern paddock. Peso was standing at the gate, head hanging over it.

"Hey, pal." I stroked his snout. "I'm gonna make sure Lottie keeps you and Rakko. Even if she sells the ranch, I'll find stalls for you both. You've had a tough start, but this is your home and family."

He chuffed and I kissed his nose. How far I had come from running scared of this creature after he tried to eat me bald. Now I was kissing his nose? I had really changed.

I hoped it was for the better.

I met my mother back at the car. "I'm driving," I said as I brushed past her and settled into the driver's seat.

"You never volunteer to drive." She sounded confused as she belted herself into the passenger seat.

"I need to find Lucas."

"Avery. How many times do I have to repeat myself? We don't have time for this."

"We can make time. I can't leave without saying goodbye. I won't do it." I gave her my full attention, letting her see the seriousness in my eyes, my resolve.

She threw her hands in the air. "Fine. You have thirty minutes to drive around to try to find him and if we can't, then we are heading straight for the airport."

I nodded, shifted the car into drive, and peeled out of the gravel driveway.

Where would Lucas go? I hardly knew the town or where anything was. I went the only way I remembered, and that was to the grocery store.

"Keep your eyes peeled for a white truck," I instructed my mother.

"This is Oklahoma. Nearly all the trucks are white."

She had a fair point.

I drove on, scanning the roads and parking lots with no success. The clock was running out and I was stuck in this car with my mother.

"I know you think I was too harsh, but I have only ever done what I thought was best," she said.

"For you or for me?" I asked.

"For us both. We are a team, you and me. It has only ever been us two against the world."

"No, Mom. It hasn't been that way for a while. I've just worked and done what you told me to do because it was easier. It's too hard confiding in you or talking to you."

"You have had one minor setback in your entire life, but look at you. You have a number one single in the UK. There is no way Grand Records will can your record now."

"God, Mom. Listen to yourself." Tears started welling in my eyes. "Even now when I am trying to find the man I care deeply about to say goodbye, you are only talking about my career. You haven't even stopped to ask me once if I was okay after meeting my family you hid from me. Or if I was okay after hearing you lie to Lottie about my birth father and then hearing the truth. You stopped being a mother years ago and have only been a manager." I slammed my hands on the wheel when we came to a stoplight. I couldn't find Lucas's truck anywhere, and the thirty minutes was almost up.

"I'm sorry that me wanting to make sure you are provided for with a roof over your head and food in your belly made me harsher than you would have wanted. Sometimes we just don't get what we want. You had what you needed."

"What I need is a mom."

She floundered, searching for words, then gave up. "We have to get to the airport now. I'm saying that as your mother and your manager. You can't afford to lose this opportunity."

The view in the side mirror was clear. I flicked the turn signal on and headed for the highway. The oppressive weight of failure pressed against my heart as I ended my search.

I had this one chance to fix my career and the victory felt hollow.

LEAVING BROKEN ARROW WAS A BLUR—RETURNING THE rental car and checking in for our first leg of our journey with a layover at the Dallas Fort Worth International Airport. The city where all this started. Only a couple short weeks ago, where I was sent away by bus to hide out. My mother was on her phone checking her messages, and it was like how it always was. I had no energy to continue the conversation from the car.

We walked through the terminal, making our way to the flight that would take us to London, where I could get my career back on track. We passed four bookstores to get to our international flight. All four had my magazine cover prominently placed.

Unlike the last time I was in public, I wasn't recognized. Perhaps it was the deep tan I'd acquired after spending so much time in the sun with the horses. Or the haircut, no makeup, and filthy shoes I was sporting. No one had their cameras up filming me. I was just a regular person.

We boarded first, and I settled into my usual window seat, picking at the hangnails that never ceased to appear at times of high stress.

"Stop picking at your fingers. You're going to look all scabby in close-ups of you holding the microphone. Here." My mom dug through her tote bag, pulling out a new black iPhone. "I got you a new phone. It has your old number, but you'll need to sign in to everything again. At least it will give you something to do instead of picking at your fingers."

"Thanks," I mumbled.

It was tedious signing in to a new phone, but at least I was able to get logged in to my Apple ID and connected to the plane's Wi-Fi before takeoff. When I logged on to Instagram, I was scared to see what the notifications would look like.

Three hundred thousand notifications. My DMs were unmanageable. I looked at my most recent post on my grid and was shocked to find a debate had unfolded among my fans. Many people were commenting that I should be ashamed of myself, but so many more recent comments were defending me. I went to the Explore page and there was a viral reel of Molly being interviewed on the stickball field surrounded by her Red Team. It must have been filmed after the game yesterday. How could that have been only yesterday?

"Is it true Avery Fox was here today playing stickball?" the male journalist asked.

"Yeah, man. She was here. Her first time playing, and she got the ball. Not bad. She didn't have it for long, but the girl has guts."

"Is it really true that she's Indigenous then?"

Molly grabbed the microphone and stepped toward the camera. "Avery Fox is Muscogee, no doubt about it. She's ours, we claim her."

The journalist pulled Molly back by the arm, grabbing the microphone back. "So what do you say to the critics that claim she isn't *Native enough*, and are you personally offended by her cover spread on *Rolling Stone*?"

"The *BLEEP*? Who can define what it is to be Native enough? C'mon, team, what do you think? Are y'all Native enough?"

The team started yelling and chanting, "Yee-ow!"

Molly turned back to the camera. "Are we Native enough for your viewers?"

"Oh, don't put words in my mouth. I was just asking about the vocal critics online. Surely her song is offensive as well as the cover?" he prodded.

One of the men who had ripped his shirt off before the game and danced to my song jumped in, pulling the microphone to his mouth. "We love the song. Anyone out there looking for a warrior tonight knows where they can find me." He winked before Molly pushed him away, taking the microphone again, and nearly the journalist's arm with it.

"That photo was stupid, but why do we allow Cher to still wear it? Why is no one asking the photographer or the magazine why they put her in the warbonnet? We get so few opportunities and visibility. I think you should be reporting on that. Molly out." She dropped the microphone, and the video ended.

It had been viewed six million times since yesterday.

They accepted me? Molly, the team, the town? I didn't know who any of these random people were online. I didn't care to know what they said or thought of me. The only people who mattered were in Broken Arrow, and they loved me. A weight that had been on my chest since this whole thing started lifted. I felt like I could breathe for the first time. Lucas was right, it was all about community.

I quickly signed on to my old Twitter and then TikTok to see how the conversation was turning. I scrolled through videos, clips, and sound bites.

One of the most popular videos with a million views was from an account with the handle @DeerLadyIsReal responding to a comment on TikTok: **she isn't native if she's not enrolled #pretendian.**

The account holder, @DeerLadyIsReal, said in their response video, "I am not the enrollment police, but her tribe enrolls based on descendancy. So, if her mother and grandmother are citizens of the tribe, then it's just a matter of paperwork to be enrolled." She put up her finger quotes around the word "enrolled." Many comments agreed, and many others devolved into blood-quantum propaganda. I exited out of it.

On Twitter, Molly's interview was trending along with my name. The discourse was divided. One tweet had six thousand retweets and read: **She's fake AF but still hot.**

I put my phone down and threw my head back against the seat. The chorus and the discourse didn't matter to me anymore. For the first time, ever, I knew who I was and where I came from.

I was Avery Fox, Lottie's granddaughter, and Muscogee.

Now if only I could find Lucas's profile somewhere. There were so many Iron Eyes Cody fan accounts but zero Lucas Iron Eyes accounts. Either he never had his real name attached to a profile or I found the only man in the world without any social media presence. He really was perfect for me.

I tried to ignore my tag notifications on Instagram, but one stood out against the rest.

@saveredfoxranch tagged me in a post with the flyer Lucas and I had made for the fundraiser. The song they used on the post was my song "I Need a Warrior Tonight"—the one Lucas hated—and it had hundreds of likes and comments.

My record label's PR team told me not to post anything unless they read over the statement first. Fuck that. I shared it onto my story with the crowdsource link and a caption that read: **If you could find it in your hearts, please help me save this horse ranch and read about their mission and how they are helping youth who have experienced trauma and addiction.**

I turned off responses to my stories and put my phone away. Even if I couldn't be there for them in person, I wanted to keep my promise and help save the ranch.

25

SLEPT FITFULLY ON THE RED-EYE, MISSING LUCAS THE
entire time. Worried that I had failed them all and Lottie would
lose our entire family legacy. Since my outburst in the car, my
mother had kept unusually quiet. It was hard for me to understand
how she could feel such apathy for her family home—*our* family
home.

Grand Records released my music video while I was on the
flight, fast sleep. The response I had seen online was still divided. I
had not seen the fully edited and polished cut prior to my exile. It
looked phenomenal. The choreography, the makeup. I hardly recognized myself. The dancers in loincloths were ridiculous, but it
worked for the song. Thinking of Lucas watching it made me smile,
knowing the rant he would go off on about it. Somehow, I knew
deep down that he would be proud of me and the work I put into
it. He just wouldn't admit it out loud.

Niles was on damage control, and everyone was all-hands-on-
deck to make the launch of my song and album in the UK a success. We had three days of rehearsals lined up in a dance studio to
prepare for my *Graham Norton* performance. Line dancing didn't

count as staying on top of my dance-and-exercise regimen. Two male dancers would be joining me. We were doing a simplified version of the choreography from my video.

In addition to the rehearsals, I was expected to make the PR rounds to promote the video and my album. Niles scheduled a full day of press with podcasters, journalists from papers and magazines, radio DJs, and strategically chosen influencers from TikTok. The first set of interviews were happening in my hotel suite later this morning.

"Knock knock," Chelsea said as she poked her head into the bathroom where I was sitting in the chair in front of the vanity.

"Hey." I motioned for her to come in. My energy was low from all the traveling.

"Isn't this so exciting! It's like old times. We told you it would all blow over. Number one in the UK! Don't tell your mom, but I snuck some champagne in my bag so we can toast to your success."

"We can save the champagne for another time. I have so many things to catch you up on."

"Oh, that makes sense. Yeah, of course, we can do a toast another time. So, how was Oklahoma? I hate that we only got to email a couple times." She set her bag down and took out her makeup palettes and brushes to set up.

How did I answer that question? What had at first felt like a jail sentence ultimately changed my life. I left my heart there and I wasn't sure if I'd ever get it back. So as Chelsea pinned my hair back to start priming my face, I gave her an abbreviated version of events. By the end of it, she dropped her brushes and gave me a huge hug. I almost started crying then and there.

"Have you tried calling Lottie and getting Lucas's phone number? Surely the cowboy has a cell phone." She leaned against the counter, my makeup and hair forgotten.

"I'm scared to call Lottie and tell her that I fell for Lucas."

"He needs to know you drove all over town looking for him to say goodbye. You can't end it like this."

"I know." I groaned and hid my face in my hands.

"Have you ever been in love before?" she asked quietly.

"No. Have you?"

"Once." She gave a small smile.

"What should I do?"

"I think you finish up everything you have to do here in London, and then get on the first flight back to the States and get your man back."

"Niles said I could be here for six weeks if everything goes to plan. He wants to kick off a tour here and extend to Europe."

"They can plan all those logistics without you. You can easily go to Oklahoma and talk to Lucas. You *have* to."

I looked at my friend with tears in my eyes.

"I was so worried you'd dump me as a friend the longer I stayed in Broken Arrow," I confessed. I missed her so much. I needed someone to talk to about my Lucas feelings, to be validated and encouraged. It would have been a lot easier if I had been able to talk to her more while on the ranch.

"It will take a lot more than sporadic emails for me to dump you. Shoot, I stood by you as you wore a loincloth and feather headdress."

"I never wore a loincloth! What is it with everyone thinking I was in a loincloth!" I threw my hands in the air.

She laughed. "I've been seeing these TikTok videos about the Mandela Effect. It's when everyone is having the same false memory. That must be it."

"The dancers wore the loincloths," I grumbled, crossing my arms.

"So do you have a plan? Are you going back?" she asked.

"He said it could never work for people as different as we are to be together."

"Oh, that's nonsense."

"Why haven't you started? The first journalist is going to be here in an hour, let's go." My mother swooped in, snapping her fingers. She had on a pencil skirt and cropped blazer with her hair pulled into a sleek low bun. She was back to being all business. Her presence immediately broke the moment Chelsea and I were having.

"Sorry. What are you wearing today? What's the vibe you want to go for?" Chelsea asked me.

"Can we shoot for Cindy Crawford from the Pepsi commercial?"

"Oooo, big, bouncy, sexy hair. Let's do it."

And she did as I filled her in on more tidbits of my life at the ranch and Lucas. I didn't share the specific details of the night in the storm cellar, but based on her smug look, she was convinced it was the book she'd given me that had planted sexy-Native-man attraction.

I got used to roughing it at the ranch, but I had to admit that I missed glam. My hair and makeup were perfection. They had to be, because this was my armor to gather courage to face the press that had so easily turned against me.

My mother and Niles hovered about the suite; these interviews could not go wrong. So much was riding on them. Chelsea left after my hair and makeup were done. I'd see her again later, but she didn't have to sit and listen to the hours of interviews.

I sat in front of the windows looking out over Grosvenor Square park, waiting for the next journalist to enter the room. So far, it had all been iterations of the same question: *How does it feel to have the first number one single in the UK as a Native American woman?*

There was only one thought that went through my mind: When will I have done enough to earn that place? I knew my family and some of my culture now, but there was a part of me that never thought I would be worthy of such an accomplishment. That surely there were better artists out there who were "more" Native, grew up in their communities, spoke their languages, who had never been nor would ever get the opportunities that had led me to this fancy hotel in London talking to reporters.

Lucas was right. I gained this platform and the most important thing I could do with it would be help the community I had grown to love.

I was antsy during the next fifteen-minute interview. I couldn't remember the name of the man in front of me. I answered his questions as if on autopilot while my knee bounced up and down. Finally, it was over, and he left. I was supposed to get a lunch break before the stylist Niles booked came for my fitting, but I knew what I had to do.

"Niles," I called after him as he was about to step out.

"Yes, darling?" I had to take a breath and force myself not to roll my eyes. I had most certainly not been his darling while I was in Oklahoma convinced my career was over.

"I have to play you my song 'Heartbeats.' I have to record it. I think if we release it as an exclusive song with the digital album, we won't have to worry about CDs and vinyls that were already printed."

"Avery, baby, we've talked about this. You're simply not ready to write and have your own song on your album. I'm not saying it's never going to happen. Just trust us. We know your sound. Look at you, you're number one right now."

"Listen to Niles, Avery." My mother's voice sounded from the couch on the other end of the room. I was sick and tired of being treated like a child.

"I am listening to Niles, and I am asking Niles to listen to me. I worked on the song while in Oklahoma. The problem was the bridge, and no one here was honest about it, they just said it wasn't good enough. But I fixed it, and the song is too good to let you brush it off again. I've never felt this way about a song before."

His cell started ringing in his hands.

"Please don't take that," I said. I needed to be taken seriously, and it had to start now.

"I have to take this, but that does not mean I'm closing the door to this conversation, just tabling it for now." He pressed his phone to his ear and walked out of the suite.

I started pacing. I couldn't fire my label, so I had to convince them to believe in the song like they believed in my ability to make this record.

"Relax, Avery. Just have patience. You'll get to record your songs. It's all about strategy," my mother said, getting up from the couch.

"How can you say that to me? It's always 'Wait, Avery; pay your dues, Avery; just listen to them, Avery.' I'm sick of it. You're my manager. You need to be fighting as hard for me on the things I genuinely care about as much as all the other mainstream stuff. This song . . . I don't even know how to explain it, but it's magic. It's real and raw, and you'd feel it too if you all just took a chance and listened to it."

"I do fight for you. Every single day. Just because I choose not to get in a screaming match with your A&R rep over a song doesn't mean I have not gone to bat for you. This month I was a nervous wreck making every call I could fighting for you." She raised her voice. "I sent you to my mother for Chrissake, Avery. Your safety was my priority while I worked to keep your team from dropping you as a client, so you could even have a chance to keep doing what you love. I love you and only want what's best for you." The wind left her sails, and she suddenly looked so small.

"Mom, I—"

The door to the suite opened, interrupting me. Niles popped his head in, phone still pressed to his ear.

"Pom Pom is here. This call is going to be a while but have fun and find the best look for *The Graham Norton Show*." He stepped aside, holding the door open for what looked like Naomi Campbell's twin. Pom Pom the stylist was over six feet tall in her four-inch stiletto heels. She was dressed in head-to-toe black patent leather—a full catsuit and calf-length trench coat. A glossy, bold red color on her full lips.

She rolled in a rack full of hangers. When she settled into the suite, she stood next to the rack casually with her hands in her trench coat pockets. She looked like she belonged on the cover of *Vogue*.

"I have three words for you. Assless. Leather. Chaps." She blew a bubble with her bubble gum.

None of those words were what I thought she would open with. "I am always open to bold fashion risks," I said diplomatically, so as not to offend her style.

"Love that you said that. Pairing it with a hot pink bikini top and pink rhinestone cowboy hat would be *the* look."

Despite what I just told her, I couldn't wear it. I was tired of the costumes and the whole charade. I looked through the options on the rack. There wasn't a whole lot of material to most of them.

"Do you have anything simpler? Like maybe a dress without as many cutouts?"

"Niles asked for hot, babes. I brought the hottest stuff in my wardrobe," Pom Pom said, her cockney accent becoming more pronounced as she smacked her bubble gum. "Western is in right now. I saw your music video. This would be so cohesive. Beyoncé is doing it. Chappell Roan is doing it. Dolly Parton has always done it."

She brought up valid points, but after the warbonnet incident, I was taking no chances. I would ask many questions and push back if I needed to.

"You'll look great, honey." It was almost like my mother was trying to smooth things over. Now I didn't want to wear them just because she liked them. "These Brits love the American culture right now and they love you."

"It's true. Your song is bringing it down in every club. Your fans here are going to eat you up in these."

"See? These people want a show, give them a show," my mother encouraged.

I sighed in resignation. I wasn't going to win this one. I had to pick my battles. "Okay, if I must wear the chaps, can you get something with a lot more coverage to wear on top and under? Like what if we did a black mock-neck long-sleeved crop top, and some colored leggings to wear under the chaps?"

"A crop top would look hot, yeah, especially with how high-waisted these chaps are. Babes, I know just the thing. I'll bring it all to the studio. Don't you worry one bit." Pom Pom air-kissed my cheeks before she left.

"Things are really turning around. I need to arrange your car for rehearsal this evening." My mom walked away, muttering her to-do list to herself.

I stood there, exhausted, and felt depressed knowing that all I had to look forward to was Pom Pom and her bubble gum in my face and a pair of assless leather chaps.

26

BRITISH STUDIOS WERE NEARLY IDENTICAL TO AMERI-
can ones, except sometimes it was hard to understand the
crew when they were talking fast in all their various accents. The
green room was not green and Lance, the makeup artist my team
hired to assist Chelsea, had hot pink bushy eyebrows that rested on
top of his round wire-framed glasses.

Lance dusted my face with highlighter as Chelsea gelled the top
of my hair in a tight half pony that put Ariana Grande's to shame.
My stomach was a ball of nerves as she worked to get me ready for
the show, and I hadn't been able to get our conversation out of my
mind for the past day, her telling me to go to Broken Arrow, to Lucas. But I couldn't, could I? There was so much riding on this
performance—my entire career essentially. While the show was
not broadcast live, it was taped in front of a live studio audience.
The memory of the death threats still stung. To distract myself
from thinking about everything that could go wrong, I scrolled
through my DMs on Instagram.

One stood out from @blacksmithMB. I clicked the message
open and there was a photo of Red Fox Ranch and a stage being

built in the middle of the pasture. The accompanying message read: **sad u had to leave. The setup for the fundraiser is coming together. Lucas misses you, but don't tell him I told you that**. Mary Beth! I felt a jolt through my body at the mention of the fundraiser and Lucas. The fundraiser was still on?

"Mom!" I called, startling Lance as he was dusting my cheekbones with highlighter.

"What is it?" She ran in from the hallway.

"The fundraiser is still happening."

"So?"

"*So* you and Lottie made it seem like she had given up on the ranch."

"I haven't kept up with her or the ranch since we left. She probably didn't want us in her business."

"It's too late for that. I helped Lucas set up the crowdfunding website and we have almost reached our goal." I flashed my mother my phone screen. The red bar was almost at the $150,000 goal line. "I donated the first twenty-five thousand dollars."

"Avery!" My mother clutched her chest in shock. "That was nearly all the money you had in your checking account."

"I know. I wanted to buy the whole thing. We're going to reach our goal though. The ranch is going to be saved." I smiled and felt lighter. We really did it. I needed to talk to Lucas. My body was buzzing with energy.

I shot up from my seat.

"Hey!" Chelsea protested, her fine-tooth comb stuck in my hair.

"I can't do this. I need to be there." I went to gather my bag, digging through to make sure my passport was in there with my new wallet and credit cards.

"Are you hearing yourself? You can't leave now! You're expected on set in thirty minutes." My mom blocked the door.

"You're my manager, manage the situation."

"What are you doing, Avery?" Chelsea asked nervously.

I turned to her, trying to appeal to someone here. I needed an ally. Lance just stood silently, his pink eyebrows up to his hairline as he looked from me to my mother.

"I love him. I can't stay here when he needs my help, and I gave my word. I should have never left Oklahoma."

Chelsea held her hand over her heart. "Then go."

"You are not throwing your opportunity away for some Okie who lives in a trailer. I'll not stand for it. If you leave, we will never be invited back. No one will want you. Do you hear me? You're throwing it away!" my mother said.

"The only thing I'm throwing away is letting you decide my life for me. I'm not a little girl anymore."

"You don't understand what you're doing. This is your life, Avery. I'm just trying to protect it." My mother's voice cracked.

"I'm sorry, Mom. But I'm leaving. If I go now, I can make it back for the fundraiser. I have to." I rushed to the door, and at the top of my lungs, I shouted, "We need more toilet paper! Oh my god! I've become violently ill. It's coming out both ends! Someone get another trash can!"

"Avery!" My mother seethed as silver lined her eyes.

"Tell them I caught a terrible stomach bug, and we have to reschedule my appearance. I'm sorry, but I have to go. I have to do this."

I stood at the door, fighting for the handle while my mother looked like she was on the verge of tears.

"Please, Mom. My story isn't your story or even Lottie's. It's mine and this is what I want. He is what I want." I looked at her imploringly. "I promise you this isn't some impulsive decision I'm making—a mistake or silly crush. Please, trust me."

"Do you know what this could do to your career? You have only just gotten this reprieve from public scrutiny."

"I know I'll have to work even harder to please my fans and I am prepared to do that. I want to be happy. My best music comes from my happiest place. I have you to thank for all of this. All my life I dreamed of a big, supportive family. You sending me to Broken Arrow finally gave me that. I can't turn my back on them. I know this performance is a commitment, but I made a commitment to them too. I have to do this. Mom, *please*."

My mom looked at me for a moment, a war going on internally, and I held my breath until finally, she released the knob, stepping away in resignation. I hugged her and whispered into her ear, "I love you, Mom. Thank you for helping me achieve my dreams. This is my new one and I have to go. I'd regret it for the rest of my life if I don't."

She was sobbing now. "Just go. Hell, you're number one here, so clearly they want you. I'll cover."

Tears were running down my cheeks and I nodded at her and looked to Chelsea and then Lance.

"Go, girl!" he said, clapping.

I ran past a PA in a headset juggling eight rolls of toilet paper. I sprinted in my crop top and assless chaps with neon pink spandex underneath. I made it to the street and hailed a cab.

"To Heathrow, and step on it!" I demanded, always having wanted to say that.

"Step on it? Are you mad? It's half past five. There'll be no gettin' to Heathrow in less than ninety minutes," the old cabbie said, looking bewilderedly at me through the rearview mirror.

"Oh well, I didn't know it was rush hour. To Heathrow as safely as possible then, please."

We finally made it to the airport, and I rushed to the United

Airlines kiosk. I managed to get on the next flight with a connection to Tulsa. It was in coach right in front of the bathroom at the very back of the plane, but I didn't care. It was another hour before I made it through the security line. All the rivets on the chaps set off the metal detector and I had to get patted down.

After that humiliating ordeal, I waited in the long line to board and opened the DM thread from Mary Beth and shot off a quick message and a prayer.

This had to work.

EXHAUSTED, I EXITED the Tulsa International Airport, searching for Mary Beth's bright yellow Jeep, and she was right there at the curb, waiting for me.

"What the hell are you wearing?" she asked as I let myself in through the passenger door.

Assless fucking chaps. I'd been in these for over fifteen hours of travel. I needed a shower, a toothbrush, and some clean clothes.

"It's a long story. Did you get in touch with Bessie?" I asked.

"Yes. She gave me this to give to you." She reached behind the passenger seat, keeping one hand on the wheel, and pulled out a plastic bag.

"What's this? I just wanted to make sure we could get her to the fundraiser so she wasn't home alone."

"Oh, I know. She's coming. I'm borrowing a wheelchair from the medical center, but she insisted you wear this."

Intrigued, I unknotted the plastic bag handles. Inside was a gorgeous green ribbon skirt with red, purple, and blue ribbons sewn around the bottom and a cranberry-red finger-woven belt. A note was on top in scratchy handwriting.

Marie would have loved you. This is
one of her skirts. I made the belt with
the yarn you brought over. Wear them
with pride.

I wiped a tear from my eye. "You sure you can trust Davey? He kind of has a big mouth."

"He wants Lucas to get his surprise, so he won't say anything. He knows he'll be castrated if he tells another secret after announcing our pregnancy to the entire stickball league before I could tell my mother. That was a drama." She huffed.

I laughed, and it felt so refreshing. I needed a good laugh after the last few days I'd had. It was hard to believe I was just in London yesterday. Looking at my haggard reflection, however, it was undeniable. My eyeliner was smudged around my eyes, but my hair looked the same. Chelsea was the best in the game. I was going to have to call her after all this to thank her.

But first I had to make sure I could pull off my plan.

27

LOTTIE'S PLACE WAS PACKED. CARS AND TRUCKS LINED the road. It was like a mini fair, just as Lucas had envisioned. He pulled it off with the help of everyone. I'd never been prouder of anyone. Mary Beth led me through the crowds to get to the stage where Davey was reading off auction winners into the microphone. I stood on my tiptoes trying to get a glance at Lucas. It was to no avail. I spotted Red by a keg laughing with other older cowboys, and dozens of kids ran around looking at the horses.

"Come on, this way. We're getting some looks. I think you're being recognized," Mary Beth said hurriedly.

I put my hand up to shield my face and started walking faster and came up short. There he was. Lucas. Standing in front of the stage talking to a musician carrying a guitar case, surrounded by the crowd clapping at the auction winners. With Lucas distracted, we sprinted to the side of the stage without him noticing just as Davey was getting down.

"Avery! Welcome back! Where ya been, loca?"

I laughed as Davey wrapped me in a big bear hug.

"Around the world and back. You have everything ready?"

"Keyboard is all set and you're right on time. Don't make a habit of that. We run on Indian time here, got it?" He jabbed a finger toward me in mock seriousness.

"Babe, we're supposed to be breaking stereotypes not enforcing them. 'Sides, you better be on time for our wedding," Mary Beth said in all seriousness.

"Scout's honor, I'll be days early for the wedding. Wouldn't miss it for the world." I smiled. "Davey, it's showtime. Do your thing."

"Okay, buckle up." He ran back up the steps and spoke into the microphone. "Attention, everyone. We have a huge surprise for y'all here today. Can I ask that everyone make their way to the stage? This next performer has toured the world, graced the cover of *Rolling Stone*—but we forgive her for that—and just flew back from across the pond to be here today and support her grandmother, Lottie Fox. So please give me a nice, loud welcome for our very own Avery Fox!"

The crowd cheered. I dusted off the ribbon skirt and took a deep breath.

"You got this—we all believe in you." Mary Beth squeezed my hand in reassurance. I squeezed back.

I walked onto the stage, taking the microphone from Davey. "Thank you so much. Give it up for Davey, everyone. I can't tell you how good it is to be back in Oklahoma. It's cold and gray in London, where I just came from."

The crowd was silent. Waiting for me to do something, entertain them. I walked to the keyboard and the folding chair in front of it. "As some of you may know, a photo shoot I did came out at the beginning of the month, and it was . . . not great." There were a few laughs and boos.

"I deserved that. It was culturally insensitive and instead of uniting our people, the decision to pose in a warbonnet incited more division. Instead of fostering conversations around positive representation in media, I caused a media frenzy. I came here to learn about where I come from. I thought it would be easy to learn what it means to be Indian. Surely, I could learn how to be like the movies depict us—stoic, wise, and mystical."

More laughs. My eyes found Lucas in the crowd, right in front. Silver lined his eyes, and I smiled at him. He was there, beautiful and encouraging in his turquoise ribbon shirt and black cowboy hat. He blinked slowly as if I were a mirage and his eyes were deceiving him. I looked into his eyes, letting him know that I was really there—this was real.

"But we aren't that way. We are kind, tenacious, loud, hardworking, and a million other things. The people I've come to know and love are amazing in so many ways, and this culture isn't a costume I can take on and off as it suits me. Someone really wise but not so mystical once asked me what I would do to help this community. I know he is here today, and I finally have an answer for him. The first step in helping this community is loving it. This home I've come to know, I'll protect it. Which is why I'm matching all donations at one hundred percent until we reach our goal to keep this ranch away from developers. We are so close to reaching one hundred and fifty thousand dollars. If Lottie has helped you at all throughout the years, please consider donating." I would drain the last of my bank account to save the ranch, the Fox legacy, and invest in Lucas's dream.

Cheers erupted, and I had to wait a few moments before I could continue. So many phones were directed at me, and I had to get this right. I drew in a breath as I sat down behind the keyboard, placing the microphone in the stand. I kept my eyes on Lucas and only him. This part was for him and him alone. He needed to know where I stood. The money was for them all to save the ranch and make his dreams come true, but I came back for him. I had to be here in person for my message to ring true, for Lucas to believe that he was worthy of this dream and that so many people believed in it. That I believed in him, and in us.

"I learned so many things while working here, but the most important thing I learned was how to love. There is a man here who put all this together—Lucas Iron Eyes. I'm only good at delivering lines written for me, so the best way to say what I need to say is with a song. This is a new one, and I want you all to hear it first. It's called 'Heartbeats.'"

I played the beginning notes on the piano and let the music take over me. My voice shook from nerves as I sang one of my songs for a crowd of thousands for the first time. I had no costume to hide behind, no backup vocals—it was all me. The song soared, with every note building on top of the next. As I came to the bridge, I put all the love I felt for him behind my voice, urging him to feel the truth as I sang looking into his eyes. I loved him. We were people who came from two completely different worlds with the odds stacked against us, but I didn't care. I could face anything so long as I could face it with him. Love is not a perfect melody that only happens when all the right notes and rhythms present themselves. Love is a war song, a battle cry. Something to fight for. And I would fight for us.

His gray eyes smoldered like coals.

My last belt trailed off and my chest was heaving as I tried to catch my breath. The crowd of thousands of people cheered. A cacophony of whistles, claps, whooping, and hollering.

"Thank you." I bowed, and when I raised my head, Lucas's eyes bored into mine as he worked his way through the throng of people around the stage. When they realized his intention, they parted like Moses with the sea, clearing a path straight to the stage. I kneeled as he stood, head barely reaching over it.

"You came back." His eyes were bewildered.

"This is my home."

Lucas reached up and took my face in his hands and kissed me. The audience's screams were thunderous. Lucas pulled away laughing, waving them off.

"Come with me," he said as he reached up. I flung my legs over the edge, bracing my hands on his shoulders as I let myself fall. Lucas caught me and set me gently on the ground. He took my hand in his and led me around behind the stage.

There he kissed me again. I let my arms snake around his neck and my foot popped. It was a kiss so beautiful, so pure it blocked out the world. I kissed him with everything I had, and his thumbs softly caressed my cheeks. I could feel his smile beneath our kisses.

Too soon, he pulled away. "You saved the ranch."

"*We* saved the ranch."

"You sharing it in your stories set it all off."

"My follower count had to do something for me. How did you get Lottie to agree to all this?"

"I put my property for sale, and I made her a contingent offer to buy the ranch. She first refused, but then the donations kept coming in. She agreed to let me sell my property and buy half the ranch and business. I'll be a co-owner of Red Fox Ranch."

"But that was your first real home!" I was shocked.

"No, Red Fox Ranch was my first real home. That property was just a house. I can get another one someday."

I kissed him again.

Through the kiss he asked, "What happened to London? You were supposed to perform. You're number one over there. I'm so proud of you." He peppered me with more kisses.

"I had to be here for you."

"Sweetheart, you can't miss big moments like that for me."

"I can do what I want. I don't have to live in Los Angeles. I can live anywhere and travel where I need to go for shows, but my home base can be Oklahoma. Just like it is for Garth Brooks, Blake Shelton, and even Reba—yes, I Googled. Also, it kind of has to be since I have to sell my Los Angeles home to ensure I have enough funds to cover the promise I made to match all donations." Lucas's hard exterior cracked. His gray eyes were full of hope and awe, as if he still couldn't believe this was real. I caressed his cheek, and he leaned his face into my palm.

"I love you." He pressed his forehead to mine.

"I love you too."

"Get a room!" Davey shouted.

We turned to look at the small gathering of our friends and family who were watching with smiles and happy tears. Mary Beth, Davey, Red, Lottie, and Bessie.

Lucas wrapped his arm around my waist, and we walked to greet them.

"Welcome home," Lottie said.

"Thank you." I paused. "Lottie."

"That's Grandma to you." She smiled at me.

"What? Really?"

"I was spiteful for suggesting otherwise. It would be my honor if you called me Grandma." She wiped a loose tear away from her cheek. "Now g'won an' git outta here. That display was embarrassingly romantic. No one will ever let Lucas live it down."

"I hope they don't. Avery Fox is *my* girl!" he shouted, and those nearby cheered him on.

Lucas squeezed my hand, and I squeezed his back. I was finally home.

EPILOGUE

One month later . . .

DAVEY AND MARY BETH'S WEDDING CEREMONY WAS beautiful. It was full of so much love and laughter and the newlywed couple swayed in the middle of the dance floor as I sang for them.

I meshed the last trickling notes into the next song, requested by the bride. "All right, everyone, let's party! Debuting for the first time, 'I Need a Warrior Tonight (Tvstenvke Remix)'!" Everyone rushed the couple on the dance floor to sing and dance to my song—Lottie helped translate the hook in Mvskoke—a huge pop anthem with the traditional Muscogee language.

I ate it up and so did the wedding guests.

When my performance was over and the DJ started his set, Lucas waited for me on the edge of the dance floor, watching as the first four teenagers who were living and working on the ranch were passing out hors d'oeuvres.

"May I have this dance?" he asked, offering me his hand.

"You may." I placed my hand in his, and he pulled me into his chest and swayed with me. "Suits look good on you, mister."

"Don't get used to it," he said. But I wasn't teasing. The slate gray suit became him, as well as his long hair slicked back in the most debonair way. Lucas Iron Eyes was hot and he was mine.

"I can't since I have to go on tour for six months." I pouted.

"I'm going to be seeing you on tour. We promised, we won't go more than two weeks without seeing each other."

"You get so focused on your work. I don't want you forgetting about me." I swept a nonexistent piece of lint off his shoulder.

"I could never. I was surviving before I met you. Now I'm living."

"You always say the right thing." I looked up into his beautiful eyes reflecting the twinkle lights that were strewn about the property. "In the time I'm away, you can make sure the cottage construction doesn't get delayed."

"Don't worry."

I wasn't comfortable shacking up with my boyfriend under the same roof as my grandmother, and the trailer was too cramped and couldn't fit my carry-on let alone my closet. Lucas and Lottie agreed it was time Lucas had his own space, and since he owned half the property, he was building a house for himself. It was all going to take time, and I was going to enjoy every second of it.

Once the song was over, he led me off the dance floor and back to our table, where Bessie and Lottie waited. I needed a break from my heels.

Lucas pulled my seat out for me, and I blissfully sank down into it.

"Can I get you ladies refills?"

"Oh, could you please?" Lottie asked.

He gave a slight bow before kissing my head and heading to the refreshment table.

"You seem happy," Lottie said.

"I told you she just needed a boyfriend," Bessie joked.

I refrained from rolling my eyes. She was half-right. I didn't need a boyfriend, I needed Lucas as my boyfriend.

"I have some mail for you. It arrived at the house yesterday," Lottie said with a smile.

"I got mail at your house?" I asked, surprised.

"It's something you've been waiting for." She slid a white enve-lope across the table to me.

On the sender line it read BUREAU OF INDIAN AFFAIRS.

"Is this what I think it is?" I asked.

"Part of it, at least," Lottie answered.

I ripped open the envelope and peeled the thin plastic card off the letter.

CERTIFICATE OF DEGREE
OF INDIAN BLOOD

"I'm confused. Is this my citizenship card?"

"No, that's coming. This is how you get the citizenship card."

"I was never really good at math, but can this fraction be right? I've never seen anything like this."

Bessie and Lottie shrugged.

"The horses have percentages closer to one hundred."

"Welcome to the tribe." Bessie laughed.

My journey getting to this moment was far from smooth, and in my hand I held the proof so many faceless critics demanded I show after my cover shoot and music video. Yet I felt the same as I did five minutes ago when I didn't have it. I was still Avery Fox, daughter of Harriett Fox, granddaughter of Lottie Fox. Muscogee Creek. I never needed this laminated card to belong.

I was right where I needed to be, with the people who claimed me, and I claimed them back.

Dear Reader,

Thank you for reading my version of a cowboy / pop star rom-com. I loved movies like *Flicka, Hannah Montana: The Movie, Country Strong,* and a million others growing up and wanted so badly for there to be Native American representation. The fish-out-of-water trope mixed with the grumpy/sunshine one makes for a rich environment to have so much fun on the page. Throw in the topical conversations that are always present online of who can and cannot say they are Native and "cancel culture" (what even is that really?), and I had the perfect ingredients for a fun and humorous romantic comedy. Taking this popular genre and making it Indigenous is my way of reclaiming the "western genre" in romance that has perpetuated harmful Native stereotypes for decades.

I chose the setting of Broken Arrow, Oklahoma, because the town is so charming and looks like it came straight out of a Hallmark movie. Walking through downtown was incredibly inspiring, and I just had to set my story there. I conversed with locals, toured the museum and art galleries, and visited a horse ranch dedicated to helping youth heal. Tulsa Hills Youth Ranch has an incredible vision and dedicated staff to help kids and young adults work through trauma by taking care of horses and providing one-on-one mentorship to those in the program. Kyle and Patricia Livingston, the directors of the program, welcomed me and my rambunctious toddler to their ranch and answered so many of my questions, from as basic as "How do you feed a horse?" all the way to "What do you do with the horses in tornado weather?" After our visit, they offered to hop on FaceTime if I had any questions while drafting the story and were just all-around amazing, supportive people. This story and Lucas's dream would not be as rich and well-rounded without Tulsa Hills Youth Ranch.

I love the state of Oklahoma and how rich in culture it is from the thirty-nine federally recognized tribes within its borders. While I am not Muscogee—I am Chickasaw—I chose to make Avery and her family Muscogee, because logistically it just made sense for the story. It is important to remember that not all tribes are alike in language, culture, and custom; however, because the Muscogee Nation is part of the Five Tribes displaced to Oklahoma during the removal (the Trail of Tears), I chose to focus on the similarities the Muscogee Nation has with the Chickasaw Nation. I intentionally did not put any sacred or spiritual teaching within the text as I did not feel it was my place to do so. I want to emphasize that this story and these characters are in no way claiming to be how all Muscogee citizens think or feel. Identity is a complex topic and should always be handled with care. The hook of this novel is Lucas teaching Avery how to be "Indian," but as you read, that is not as straightforward as it may seem.

What I hope you can take away from this novel, like Avery, is the support of community. We are all humans looking for connection and belonging.

With love,
Danica Nava

ACKNOWLEDGMENTS

Thank you so much to my incredible publishing community, who championed this story from the very beginning. Thank you to my brilliant editor, Angela Kim, who pushed me hard to get the best version of this story out of me that I could give. Thank you for encouraging every joke and letting me indulge in all my favorite tropes that the genre offers. Thank you to the rest of my Berkley team: the queen, the icon, Cindy Hwang; my publicists, Tara O'Connor and Dache' Rogers; my marketers, Jessica Mangicaro and Kim-Salina I; copy editor Randie Lipkin; and proofreader Shana Jones. Thank you to the talented art department, who has gifted me with another stunning cover: art director Colleen Reinhart, book designer Jenni Surasky, and star illustrator Britt Newton. Thank you to the entire team at Penguin Audio.

To my firecracker agent, Laura Bradford, thank you for your advocacy and for listening to all my story ideas with such patience. The entire Bradford Lit team has been incredible to work with. Thank you to my foreign rights agent, Taryn Fagerness, for your continued enthusiasm for my stories and for working hard to get them out into the world at large.

To my incredible UK team at Headline Eternal and my supportive editor Sophie Keefe, thank you so much for believing in my Indigenous stories and working hard to get them in stores across the pond.

To my beautiful and supportive writing friends, who I have leaned on when I thought I wasn't good enough to be writing: Ellie Palmer, Myah Ariel, Naina Kumar, Heather McBreen, LE Todd, Jessica Joyce, Sarah Hawley, Marcella Bell, Annaleigh Sbrana, Elizabeth Schultz, AJ Eversole, Mallory Marlowe, and Alexis Richoux. There are so many writing friends I have made, and to list every name could fill the pages of a novel. You are all awe-inspiring—keep writing. To the incredible Berkletes, who have all kept me sane: thank you. I aspire to be as talented as you.

A special thanks to Kyle and Patricia Livingston at Tulsa Hills Youth Ranch. Thank you to Sterlin Harjo for creating amazing works that inspire and all your amazing food recommendations in Tulsa. To the wonderful people who keep Museum Broken Arrow running and generously gave their time answering my questions while I viewed the exhibits.

Chokma'shki' to the Muscogee Nation of Oklahoma for the beautiful lands that inspired this story. To the people of Broken Arrow and Tulsa who welcomed me and my family as I researched the area, thank you.

Lastly, I thank my family. I dedicated this book to my mother, who raised me on country music, introduced me to romantic comedies, and always encouraged me and my sisters to laugh through the hard times. To my brilliant husband, Chris, who took my silly voice memos with the initial idea for "I Need a Warrior Tonight" and made it the incredible pop anthem dance jam of my dreams. I love you and how you still get excited to show me new songs you know I'll love all these years later. I'm your biggest fan. And to Isme, my darling girl, keep singing at the top of your lungs. You are the soundtrack to my life.

GLOSSARY

Mvskoke (mus-koh-gee)—Muscogee

rakko (thlock-go)—Mvskoke for horse

púse (poo-zeh)—Mvskoke for grandmother

hensci (hins-chay)—Mvskoke for hello

estonko? (es-ton-go)—Mvskoke for how are you?

mvto (muh-do)—Mvskoke for thank you

tvstenvke (tuh-stuh-nuh-gee)—Mvskoke for warrior

Danica Nava is an enrolled citizen of the Chickasaw Nation and works as a chief of staff in the tech industry. She has an MBA from USC Marshall School of Business. She currently lives in Southern California with her husband and daughter.

VISIT DANICA NAVA ONLINE

DanicaNavaBooks.com
Danica_Nava

Ready to find
your next great read?

Let us help.

Visit prh.com/nextread

Penguin
Random
House